FLAT 407

KINGSLEY PEARSON

FLAT 401

ORION

First published in Great Britain in 2025 by Orion Fiction,
an imprint of The Orion Publishing Group Ltd
Carmelite House, 50 Victoria Embankment
London EC4Y 0DZ

An Hachette UK Company

The authorised representative in the EEA is Hachette Ireland,
8 Castlecourt Centre, Dublin 15, D15 XTP3,
Ireland (email: info@hbgi.ie)

1 3 5 7 9 10 8 6 4 2

A CIP catalogue record for this book
is available from the British Library.

ISBN (Mass Market Paperback) 9781 3987 2299 6
ISBN (eBook) 9781 3987 2300 9
ISBN (Audio) 9781 3987 2301 6

Typeset by Deltatype Ltd, Birkenhead, Merseyside

Printed in Great Britain by Clays Ltd, Elcograf S.p.A.

www.orionbooks.co.uk

To my family: both my parents, for having worked to provide me with the privilege that enabled me to write; my mother, additionally, for her love of reading, and all those trips to the library; and my siblings, with whom I first started making up stories.

Prologue

Then

As I look into his eyes, made dark by what he is doing to me, I realise: some men are not to be trusted.

I can't move, I can't speak. But I can see – I'm in my bedroom in flat 401.

I can't focus, I can't escape the dizziness. But I can remember – I'd felt proud of myself for taking the risk of letting him in.

I can't be certain, I can't scream. But I can smile as I look up at him – he's going to take care of me.

What *is* this look on his face? Shame? Despair?

Triumph.

I can't breathe. Constricting pain seizes my lungs, burning away my vision. Spit flecks my face, blood pounds in my ears, sickness threatens my throat.

I can't breathe. Trying to choke out my plea. 'You're the one I want to be with.'

I can't breathe …

As clammy darkness creeps in, as the pain ends and the world fades away, my mind leaves me with memories. A voicemail. *'Hey Steffan, hope you have a nice time with him today.'* A text. **Not every man will be as bad for you as your ex.** An email. Don't blame me if you die in that flat.

I'd locked myself away, to keep myself safe. I'd deserved to reclaim and rebuild my life.

I'd been so sure that I would.

My lover leaves my flat as my life leaves me.

I

Now

Jay

As Jay waited behind the till, the smell of leather and keys grounded him. Sighing in the stuffy heat, he moved a square white notepad on top of the counter, a few millimetres to the left. Now it was in its proper place.

His phone buzzed.

Come on son, what's the harm in meeting up?

Mouth dry, heart pounding, Jay stared at the screen. Put it away. Distracted himself by contemplating his photo, which peeped out from among the others on the staff noticeboard. He traced a finger over his image. Checking that Esther was still out at lunch, he unpinned his photo and slid it behind hers. His boss's image was watching what it could see of the real him.

The door '*beep-boop*'ed, but this wasn't a customer; the man coming in didn't have keys or shoes in his hands. What a grin, though. His T-shirt looked brand new, and hugged the muscles on his arms and chest, and his little belly. Jay tugged at his Timpson polo shirt, which clung tight to his own muscles.

Jay stopped shuffling as the man came up to the counter.

'Any jobs going, buddy?' the stranger asked, looking up at Jay.

Jay ran a hand over his left arm, self-soothingly. Planning his words before he spoke. 'You can apply online. Or there's a paper form.'

'Sick!' Another flash of that cheeky grin.

'Paper forms do get more attention from the manager because there are so many online ones,' Jay let slip, reaching for a form in spite of himself, and pushing it across the counter. 'You can fill this one in now and leave it with me if you like,' he offered.

'Are *you* the manager?'

Heat crept across Jay's cheeks as he shook his head. What nonsense. He remembered his training, and smiled encouragingly at the young man as he handed him a pen. Remembered to put on his front. 'Not yet, mate!'

The stranger's tanned hand moved across the page, the warm brown of his skin tracing up his arm, ending abruptly at a pale white territory of bicep. Jay pushed away the urge to ruffle the man's thick curly black hair. He distracted himself by reading the stranger's name upside-down, from the box he was slowly filling in. *Noah*. About five years younger than Jay, going off his birthdate. Jay tried to relax. His heart rate and breathing didn't entirely comply.

Noah slid the completed form back across the counter, pursing his full lips and looking right up at Jay with warm, hazel eyes. Jay shifted his gaze down after a moment too long, a smile invading his face.

'I'll pass it on to my manager when she's back from lunch,' he stuttered.

'Cheers, nice one, buddy.'

Noah treated Jay to another cheeky grin before turning

to the door. Jay looked at the form. Would Timpson be Approved by Noah's probation officer too?

The door '*beep-boop*'ed again, announcing Esther's return. She smiled at Noah as he held the door open for her. Placing her lunch on the counter, she turned her head to get another eyeful of him as he walked out. When she turned her head back, she pulled a face at Jay, eyebrows raised, chin dipped, mouth open – thirsty. Jay shrugged, telling himself he had no idea why she was implying, not for the first time, that he might be gay. But … His heart beat frighteningly fast at the thought of how he'd seen gay peers treated when he was younger.

He involuntarily glanced over Esther's frizzy hair, and peeked through the shop window.

Noah stuck his tongue out. Jay started at the tease and turned away.

'He left this for you.' Jay indicated the form on the counter.

Esther glanced at it. '*Noah*. Nice name,' she conspired. 'Looks alright, I'll get him in for an interview. Give him a good roasting.'

Her wink was unnecessary.

'Sick. Cheers, buddy.' He caught himself imitating Noah too late, but his boss didn't seem to mind. Esther only laid the papers on the counter. Tapping an area of the form where Noah had written additional content outside of the tick-box, she made knowing eye contact with Jay.

'Oh, don't know actually, two of you who didn't do what you were convicted of?' She laughed throatily. 'Can't 'ave two innocent souls working here!'

His toes curled up.

'Gotta keep the faith,' Esther said as she moved away towards the back office.

'Yeah, no worries, only a month to go!'

Esther shook her head, and shut the office door behind her.

The shop door opened and a familiar face rolled in, the buzz of her wheelchair providing a comforting bass beneath the intrusive beep of the door.

'Hi, Margaret,' said Jay.

'Alright, Jakey.' Margaret nodded as she came up to the wooden counter.

He grimaced, and rubbed the side of his beard at the nickname. Even though she must be close to retirement, she always greeted him as if he were still a small boy. He leaned forward on the counter to make his height feel less intimidating.

'You can have this, I'm done with it,' Margaret said as she hunted around in her bag.

She slid a crumpled copy of the *News Shopper* onto the counter. His chest tightened at the headline she'd left exposed. Was she going to bring up some rumour about what 'really' happened that day, as she usually did?

'Freezer Killer' Flanagan: 1 Year Until Release

Jay took a deep breath, remembering to act professionally. Not too much of a smile, only as much of one as would come naturally with the words. Not so much that he would crack.

'Collecting your man's shoes, Margaret?' He hid the newspaper under the counter.

'Yes, just the shoes please.' She rummaged in her bag, and dropped a note and some coins in front of him.

'The soles were worn out unevenly. Boots up the road might sell insoles, no?' Jay suggested. He stroked the shoes' brown leather as he handed them over.

Margaret smiled but shook her head as she left. Jay couldn't hear what she said over her shoulder, but laughed along anyway. He scraped the coins into his hands. Maybe he shouldn't have presumed to give a nurse advice about something health-related.

He paused in the middle of closing the till.

Most people paid by card; it was understandable he'd made a mistake. He stared at the segregated gold, silver and bronze discs. The lone pound coin he'd meant to give her as change didn't look away, reminding him how much Margaret probably needed every penny she could get.

He should have checked her receipt, should have counted the coins she'd dumped on the counter while she'd still been in front of him. A memory of Esther giving him a bollock-ing grabbed him round the throat; he'd owned up to making a similar mistake before, after someone had left their store a scathing two-star review. 'We've got to beat the big super-markets on customer service!'

The metal of cut keys winked at him from behind the counter.

No one need ever know what he'd done.

He grabbed the coin, slammed the till shut, and ran out, pulling the door of the shop closed behind him.

Margaret hadn't gone far. She was all smiles as she turned her wheelchair to face him. 'Oh, Jakey, you didn't have to do that.' She leaned familiarly towards him as she gripped the much-needed coin and ensured it made its way safely into the empty space in her purse.

Other people were staring. A woman on the other side of the road lifted her phone to get a clear shot. The would-be witnesses moved away once they'd seen Margaret had car-ried on.

Embarrassed, Jay shoved his hands in his pockets and

rushed back to the shop. Shoulders hunched in an attempt to make himself disappear.

Esther was waiting, paperwork in hand.

'It's not quite your lunchbreak yet, matey.'

'Sorry, I had to give a customer something they'd forgotten,' he panted, taking the papers and picking up the pen on the counter. As he held it over the place marked for him to sign, he looked up from the counter and through the shop window. All kinds of people moved along the high street outside, at their own pace; a flock of birds flew up from the pavement and out of sight. It would be kind of sad to move away from where he'd grown up and lived for over thirty years, but then he wouldn't have to worry about people recognising him. Then, he could get rid of this beard, and wouldn't have to disguise himself with this messy hair.

He scribbled his name at the bottom of the page.

Esther took the store transfer request form back, her broad, gappy smile shining out from her dark skin.

'Have I been that bad of a manager?' She winked, and cast an eye over the form. 'Isle of Wight, is it?'

Timpson had shops all over the country. The Isle of Wight's branch was dead in the island's centre. Living and working there would be a world away from being here in South London. So much open space around the few cosy towns, with only sea surrounding the island. Bright, sandy beaches; quaint, winding roads; and friendly, welcoming people. The air would be fresh, the noise pollution would be non-existent, and no one would know what he'd—

'Remember, now,' Esther continued before he could reassure her, 'if Timpson House approves this, you just go on a list for possible vacancies. Don't guarantee you'll move anytime soon.' She frowned.

He knew how precarious his freedom was. *An offender*

must: (f) not undertake work, or a particular type of work,
unless it is approved by the supervising officer, and notify the
supervising officer in advance of any proposal to undertake work
or a particular type of work.

'That's fine, I'm not that set on moving, I just want to have the option.' Jay put the pen back where it belonged, and straightened the glossy Timpson leaflets promoting their work recruiting ex-offenders. Wasn't always a good thing for customers to know about that.

When he was off licence, he could get whatever job he wanted: he wouldn't need his probation officer's permission. He could become a digital designer again, and put his degree to good use; he wouldn't have to feel guilty about moving on. No need for an Approved Address: he could move away, somewhere cleaner. Would it really be somewhere totally different, like the Isle of Wight? Or somewhere still seaside and fresh, but nearer, like on the Kent coast?

Wherever he ended up, what would he change his name to? *'Dan Lane'* still took his fancy. Dan Lane could wake up feeling like he wanted to go to the beach, and just go. Dan Lane could walk down any street, any time of day, and be happy to see any familiar face. Dan Lane would be a man with no past.

A tap on his shoulder from Esther.

'Go and have your lunch. Don't be late back.'

He ate outside, in the Eltham churchyard, because it was warm, because it was summer, and because he was allowed. In prison, everything had been confined, no space or time to rattle around. The other prisoners kicking their doors, screaming for spice, setting off alarms. The noisy threats bouncing off the walls. The walls, the doors, the locks, the routines keeping him in. Keeping him in with the toilet in his cell, the stench of unwashed men, the windows that didn't ventilate. The things other prisoners might do to him. *'Because.'* Or the things they might get him to do. *'Or else.'*

Jay breathed in the scent of the open, natural space. He savoured the taste of the sandwich he'd made for himself. His bench enjoyed the protection of a few trees and the low stone wall around the churchyard's boundary. Most days it was a good place for staying away from familiar eyes.

But sometimes there were days like today.

'Oi oi! Long time no see!'

Jay's sandwich tasted dry in his mouth.

'Jay Ginige, you remember us? From the estate!' One of the youths sat to his left. It was always worth not looking up at first.

'Jay Ginige. Moved away to live in a fancy flat.' Another shaven-headed young man cuddled up at his right. When in pairs, sometimes they circled his raft for a bit.

'Not even man enough to get done for a proper crime.' The third voice came from above, as its owner, the tallest of the three, stood over Jay. When there were more than two sharks, he stayed still, in case it was true that they could smell fear.

The Lynas brothers: he'd decided soon after he'd got out of prison to cross the road whenever he saw them back in Woolwich. Hadn't they lived in the same block as his family? They were different sizes, but all had blond hair shorn down to sour stubs. Physical hunger, lack of opportunities, and feeling they were looked down on, through no fault of their own, gave them something to prove to a society which had treated them so badly.

As the eldest leaned down, getting into Jay's face, a wave of deodorant smashed into him. Not Lynx. But something still spicy and struttingly masculine. At least they were pronouncing his name correctly, the 'Gin' of his surname sounding like 'Be*gin* to feel uncomfortable', and the 'ge' like '*Get* the hell out of here'.

He was determined. Determined not to give in, determined not to be sent back inside, determined not to undermine his chance to live.

The middle brother called attention to his uniform with a whistle from one side. The youngest flicked Jay's maroon name-badge from the other.

'Alright for some. Go to prison, get a job,' said the middle brother.

'Fair enough. Kill your neighbour, get off benefits?' sniggered the youngest, as he mimed his hands being around someone's neck.

'I didn't kill anyone,' Jay protested. 'Perverting the Course of Justice—'

'We know what you did, Ginige.'

Jay didn't look up. His chest tightened. Just more people who believed everything they'd read about him online.

A sharp shove to his left shoulder. He breathed deeply and tensed his upper body, still not looking up. He imagined the keys on the counter shining like red, pointing fingers in the sunlight at the end of the day. Esther shaking her head and kissing her teeth. *Just watch yourself. It's all well and good you being a nice guy, but someone puts in the wrong word with your probation officer ...* ' He couldn't escape the fixed rules upon which his freedom hung. *An offender must: (a) be of good behaviour and not behave in a way which undermines the purpose of the licence period.*

'I don't want any trouble, I just want to get on with my—'

The brother on his left waggled his fingers in front of Jay, mimicking someone manipulating a puppet. 'Right little Pinocchio, aren't you?'

The brother on the other side laughed. 'Yeah, Flanagan pulled your strings good. Guess that makes him Geppetto then, don't it?'

'Don't even joke about Shaun Flanagan!' The eldest Lynas brother slipped a look down at something on his phone. A message from an *Uncle*, the name snatched away as he turned and summoned the others: 'C'mon, let's go.'

The youngest slowly knocked Jay's lunchbox to the ground as he got up. 'It was an accident.' He raised his hands in a show of innocence. 'Do you believe me and all?'

Jay watched them enter McDonald's across the road. His appetite didn't come back.

He checked his phone instead. Reread Tony's text.

Come on son, what's the harm in meeting up?

He couldn't afford the risk, could he? Knowing what Tony would likely be after. *An offender must: (b) not commit any offence.*

Jay put in his earphones. All he had to do was get to the end of his licence period. He daren't believe he was only four weeks short of his final supervision session. The last five years – two and a half inside, almost two and a half out – spent burrowing up through the damp soil, groping towards the light. He knew what followed him, closeted in the dark.

He shook his head three times to get rid of the thoughts.

He wouldn't let anything stop him emerging from Probation.

2

Jay

Margaret was waiting patiently on the pavement as the bus's yellow ramp beeped towards her. Other passengers were sighing and shuffling in their seats. Jay checked the time. Was he late for meeting Olu? *(d) Offenders must keep their appointments with their probation officer.*

Margaret buzzed up the ramp and into the space Jay had vacated for her, as he swapped seats into the row behind the wheelchair space. He sat at an angle, and stretched out his legs. Reached up to and opened the window to get some air. The sinister, secretive hum of electric vehicles mixed with the louder roar of vans and cars still powered by petrol as they passed by the bus. Tapping his foot, he checked his phone again. Low credit, and a mental image of the receptionist telling him off for calling to say he might be late, made him put it away without dialling.

The bus driver impatiently gripped the lever retracting the wheelchair ramp. His short-sleeved shirt was tight around the coiled snake of his bicep. How often did he go to the gym? Jay would work out in his room after his appointment.

The bus's digital display showed the time in blurry orange.

Jay shuffled in the seat. Thought about putting his earphones in.

'Fancy seeing you again, Jay! My old man will get jealous!'

Jay smiled at Margaret in spite of himself. Her joke gave him some release. He sank back into the cushioned seat, his muscles relaxing, his breathing slowing down.

Sitting side-on to him, Margaret got out a tablet. She peered at its screen, nodding as she read.

26 per cent of miscarriages of justice involve a false confession

Seriously? Jay looked away.

The bus moved off. Would he make it on time? The trees of Eltham Common scrolled into the brown bricks of Greenwich Free School, which then scrolled into the flat grass of Woolwich Common. When he looked back, Margaret had moved on from the news article to Facebook.

She shifted her body, and turned her head to face him. 'Are you alright? People treating you OK?' Her voice was warm, caring.

A flash of memory invaded his mind: football hooligans threatening him as a teenager, the same way the Lynas brothers had in the churchyard earlier. And doing worse to him.

'Yeah, yeah. Great.' He shrank in on himself.

'I still think you were hard done by.' Her voice was low, intruding.

Had Margaret kept count of how many times they'd had this conversation over the past two and a half years? He glanced at the thread she had up. Playing along was the best way to get this over with quickly.

'Yeah, it's mad what people say.'

'So, there was no … you know?' She mimed with three fingers.

He baulked at her typical bluntness and glanced around, making 'shushing' motions with his hands. 'No, fake news.' The effort of forcing a thin smile making his eyes feel tired.

'This post says you were the victim's boyfriend?'

Margaret loved to gossip: Jay remembered overhearing her chit-chat with Amma and Dad after her home visits during that particularly bad time of Amma's mental health.

'Didn't even know him, he was only a neighbour.'

'Were you' – peering at the screen – 'the *killer's* boyfriend?'

'I was no one's boyfriend!' Too loud: anxiety ramping up the volume. Jay glanced up at the other passengers, and then reiterated in an insistent whisper: 'I was *no one's* boyfriend.'

Margaret scrolled to investigate some more. 'So how come this Shaun Flanagan' – Jay shuddered as she uttered the name – 'said you knew? It says it here. About the *f-r-e-e-z-e-r*,' she spelled out unnecessarily.

She meant well, the NHS ID card on the blue lanyard around her neck and all. Or maybe she felt guilty about how things had gone for him at home, despite her appointments with Amma.

Jay shrugged. Looked around. The few other passengers were all trying to look like they were minding their own business. 'Look, we both said what we needed to get shorter sentences,' he whispered truthfully. 'Doesn't mean any of those rumours are true.'

Margaret tutted. 'Unfair that you had to spend all that time in prison. Just because of what he said about you. After all, he was the one who …' She lay her tablet in her lap. Raised her hands to mime again.

'I'm gonna be able to put this behind me soon. On my way to one of my last … meetings, you know what I'm saying?'

Jay smiled broadly – his expression more fake news – putting his hands behind his head and stretching back.

His phone buzzed. Why had he given his number to Tony after that Probation group they'd been forced to attend together?

> *I'm just trying to look out for you, son*
> *I've got a job that'll earn you a lot more than*
> *Timpo's*

His probation officer before Olu had warned Jay about guys who never went straight. Jay hadn't pointed out this was often not their fault; it could be hard to make an honest living even before going to prison, let alone after coming out. When Olu had taken him onto his caseload a few months ago, he'd said Jay didn't seem like the kind of guy who enjoyed having an identity as a criminal. Jay wanted to prove him right, he really did.

Margaret returned to her screen, her eyes sneaking back to check on Jay every so often. Jay pushed away the mental images of him having embarrassed himself somehow during her latest gossip session. He also pushed Tony's text message as far out of his mind as possible. But caught himself thinking about the bus driver's arms again. Why should he push that away? He was just admiring another guy's discipline and good genes.

An intrusive memory of being picked on in football stadium toilets, for being 'gay' as a teenager, flashed into his mind. He slowly closed and opened his eyes three times to get rid of his thoughts and feelings.

He rang the bell and got off the bus soon after. He'd made it just in time. Lewisham Probation Office awaited, the same as always: unclean windows looking down on him as he skirted around bins to get to the side entrance. He took and released a deep breath as he psyched himself up to stride through the door. He was going to sail through another session, everyone would think he was calm and above suspicion, and he'd be one breath closer to life as 'Dan Lane'.

The dark doorway scrutinised Jay. Why had he had such an exposing conversation with Margaret in a place where so many people could listen in? Could he avoid doing anything else he'd regret until his licence period was up? Would today's be the session when Olu would use his power and turn on him, recalling him to prison?

The bus drove past, leaving him with the smell of the roadside, and his shame. He tried to imagine his anxieties going with it. He couldn't escape Margaret's brown eyes.

He strode through the doorway.

3

The tall man

Across the street from where he now knew they lived, the tall man smiled at how they couldn't hide their dirty secrets in there forever. The red-brick building was as ready to burst as their life. Did they think they could ignore him forever? They wouldn't get away with treating him like that. Get away with making him the one to end up at the bottom. Making his skin pale, like the fur of a cold, white wolf. He ran a big hand over his torso: his pecs might be smaller than they used to be, but he'd still got it.

There was another place worth staking out. He pushed off from the wall, and stalked away.

He wasn't going to spoil his fun by making direct contact with them.

For now.

4

Jay

Jay kept his head down as he hurried home, his uniform hidden beneath his grey hoodie. So frustrating that they'd only told him his Probation appointment had been cancelled when he'd turned up at the office. *'Are you sure Olu didn't leave you a voicemail?'* At least he'd get it over and done with next week.

He glanced behind him, scanning along the busy urban street, but not directly into anybody's face. A smartly dressed woman crossed the road when she saw him coming. Shrinking down further, he tried to conceal his height, muscles, and brown skin. He didn't want to intimidate anyone. He checked down the discreet back alleys he would normally take, then pushed himself along the more exposed route towards the main square. The endless noise – traffic and trains, market traders finishing up for the day, chattering groups cluttered around the square – crowded in on him.

Jay's heart slowed as he approached the cheap Ukrainian food van that served the run-down square on Fridays. No other customers this early in the evening. Perfect. He looked across the main road at the development where he wasn't allowed to live anymore after what had happened five years ago. Coming up to the van, he fixed his face into a hollow, friendly expression.

'Alright. Just some veggie varenyky, please.'

The woman at the front didn't say anything out of the ordinary as he counted out his money. He peeked over her shoulder at the skinny man boiling his order of dumplings. The man's full lips were pursed in concentration as he set his strong jaw. Jay snapped his head away sharply, heat rising. He smiled at the dark-haired woman in an attempt at appreciation. She hadn't caught him looking, had she?

Jay jerked his head at the chalkboard menu that was on a level with his eyeline, where *Kyiv cake* had a line scrawled through it.

'All sold out?' he asked brightly.

The man joined the woman at the counter. 'My friend, we wish! Business is not so good.' He looked across the road at where Jay had been staring, at the chain restaurants thriving around the shiny new station that had been built while he'd been inside.

Jay felt inside his pocket. This was his last cash until payday.

'I'll get a cup of borscht too, please.'

After she'd counted the extra coins and handed the warming beetroot soup over to him, smiling, he turned away and flicked his hood up. He checked the street as he set off to smuggle the brown paper bag back into his room at St Magdalene's Hostel. Tonight, he could see only safe strangers. He wouldn't need to dodge aunties, people from school, or anyone else who might know him.

Tonight.

Soon he wouldn't have to live like this. No funny looks, no mentions behind his back, no being treated like some criminal paperwork that belonged in an archived file. Hidden away between litter-strewn streets.

Jay was exhausted by how his days were filled with the need to put on a front. How every one of his days ended and began at Magda's. He slowed down when he turned onto the side-street hiding the worn-down, shame-red brick building recycled from more charitable days. Nowadays it sheltered 'residents' like him, fallen on hard times but not expected to say why. He was grateful for that, at least.

This chance at freedom was worth too much to risk throwing it away. Jay forced his eyes open to keep out the mental image of being recalled to prison for violating even one of his licence conditions. Even one more week back inside would be torture, let alone four weeks. He replied to Tony's text:

Sorry, mate. I can't meet up right now

The buzz of not-far-off traffic pushed him on, the fumes of the town centre inescapable. He rushed up the entrance steps and past the empty reception. Mounted the creaking, thinly carpeted stairs, unlocked his faded door, and went inside his little room. Smallest room in the hostel, the Probation Service happy to make use of the offer from the charity that ran it. Less admin for them, and a safe place for Jay.

A white envelope lay in wait on his bed. He opened it. What lurked inside was a sore on his otherwise sorted room, which he kept tidy to keep his difficult thoughts and feelings at bay. Who could have sent him this? Why? What were they going to do to him?

The tension in his face, the sickness in his stomach, the buzzing in his ears grew too great to bear. His organs rebelling, he left his food and the envelope in his room, backed out the door, and up the narrow corridor to check on Cathy. He knocked softly.

'It's me, Jay,' he said reassuringly.

The lock clicked open, and the door swung inwards partway.

Shivering despite being wrapped in a dark green cardigan in this heat, Cathy retreated back into the chair on the other side of her room, her tangled brown hair falling forward over her face.

Jay still had the feeling 'Cathy' might not be Cathy's name. He thought she was probably telling the truth when she'd said she was forty.

'Having another bad day?' he asked sympathetically, not entering the room but still stooping down out of habit.

She nodded without lifting her head.

'I slept bad,' she mumbled. 'Nightmares. A man in Sainsbury's looked at me.' She turned her head away firmly. 'I don't want to go out again!'

Her room, like his, didn't hold too much that could give away who a person really was, or what they'd been through. He peered through the chink in Cathy's armour at a lavender-scented candle, and a worn copy of Peter Benchley's *Jaws*.

'Isn't Group tonight?' He stayed gentle, stayed in the doorway.

It was a good sign Cathy wasn't peering out from behind the door, or even talking through it. Those were her worst days. At least Magda's gave Jay the chance to wash off some of his persistent feelings of guilt through trying to help Cathy, whose shaky answer broke into his thoughts.

'I don't feel well. I feel hot.'

'Put on something a bit lighter and you'll feel cooler, you know what I'm saying?' Jay suggested clumsily.

Cathy pulled the cardigan tighter. 'Don't need to go to Group. Not that supportive.'

'Come on now, you always tell me how much better you feel for going. You said it helps you feel safer.'

Cathy's eyes darted around jitteringly at the last two words, then fixed on him. 'And you promise what he did was …'

Jay smiled in what he hoped was a reassuring way. He understood why she might struggle to feel safe around him, given the claims that had been made about him. He didn't feel safe all the time either – staying at Magda's helped. Magda's was much less institutionalised than his last place, although the fact it was similarly shared accommodation made him feel more comfortable. The kind of comfort you got from sinking into the space in a settee hollowed out by your body through repeated presence.

Maybe he would deserve real comfort and safety one day.

'I promise what happened to that poor guy … It was a terrible accident.' He knew what he was saying was true. Didn't know if that made a difference to Cathy. 'I can walk you to the Centre if you like,' he offered reluctantly. 'No pressure.'

'Cheers,' Cathy said, unbiting her lip.

He'd weighed up a few things in his mind to feel able to make this offer: his fear of embarrassing himself, his desire to do the right thing. His experience that people he might bump into would not be forgiving of what they thought they knew about him.

He'd also weighed up his feelings about the envelope in his room. Fear. Shame. Justice. Even though he'd put its contents back inside, and tried to pretend he hadn't read them, what watched him from inside the envelope was a sign that, this close to freedom, he would be forced to pay a price.

5

Jay

Jay hesitated in front of Magda's. He didn't need to worry about Cathy getting back from Market Street: the Health Centre was only two minutes' walk away, and the women always took care of each other. He knew the white envelope and its Note were still waiting inside his room to haunt him with words that made being recalled for four weeks seem like nothing. But he didn't want to stay outside, exposed. Yet another South London summer evening closing in. The day dissipating to night, the blur of dim streets and artificial light threatening to imprison him. He ducked his head unnecessarily as he went through the hostel's doorway, moving quickly to dodge the staff member rustling behind the office door.

Back in his room, he opened his small wardrobe, and pinched the edge of his favourite hoodie, one he'd bought years before prison, rubbing the soft, faded fabric between his fingers. It was lucky he'd found it again in the charity shop across the road, after Amma had given everything of his away.

He wondered what she and his brother were up to now. And Dad.

Jay stripped off his uniform and hung it up in the almost-empty space. When he'd dressed for work that morning, he'd told himself it wouldn't get as cold as the depths of winter, but he couldn't honestly have known whether he'd return to frank rain, ambiguous skies, or a yellow, unceasing eye bearing down on him.

In just tight black briefs he fell onto the single bed and checked the calendar on his phone; until the month was up, he was just looking. Looking at whatever he could get, out there in the early summer evening light. He watched the sparrows darting about on the branches of the street's token trees; they brought the hint of a smile to his face. The street preacher at the junction, extolling the freedom of his spirit, couldn't compete with them, as they flew up and off into the sky, to whichever corner they wished for.

Jay's heart thumped and he leaped up: out of the corner of his eye, beyond the edge of his window, he thought he saw a man lurking near the charity shop. Tall. Athletic.

Jay didn't stop to control his thoughts. Was it him? Already? Was the man tall enough to be Shaun? What would he do to Jay for getting him sent to prison?

The fire escape would be unlocked – get out through there. His hand tightened on his phone as he prepared to run. From the past, from the secret, from the man who could snatch his life away.

The complete stranger threw down his cigarette and limped off up the street.

Jay slumped back onto his bed, mouth dry. He stared at his cold, untouched takeaway, and the resealed white envelope beside it. Cupped in his hands was the old newspaper clipping he'd taken from it. As if holding the stained, smoky paper cautiously could make the words on it any less familiar.

In a shocking end to the case, even though there was no evidence against him, the defendant pleaded guilty to knowing Shaun Flanagan concealed the manslaughter. Jay Ginige has been sentenced to five years. As he's already been in prison awaiting trial for half of this time, he has been put on probation straight away. Mr Ginige maintains he believed Mr Flanagan's claim that the death was an accident, and 'did not know' about the victim's body in the freezer. Whatever happened in flat 401 resulted in …

Jay let the scrap of paper fall into the bin. He went over to the sink and splashed cold water on his face. His faded, torn Isle of Wight postcard smiled at him, stuck to the top corner of the small mirror above the basin. He ran his eyes neutrally over his muscular, slightly hairy torso. He couldn't see himself clearly through the grime. Could he get something to clean it with from the duty worker? No. That would involve going out the door. Somehow, it was easier to leave his room in a role: *'Timpson Employee'*, *'Cathy's Would-be Rescuer'*, *'Reformed Man Attending Probation Appointment'*. Activities without a role left him feeling exposed.

He knew he'd been right to worry about being exposed.

Before, Woolwich had been home. But now, he was trapped here by charity. Surrounded by places he used to go, places he couldn't go, and places he daren't go. He daren't google his own name: it was bad enough when people who knew it muttered it at him, along with other words, in the street.

Jay dared pick up the envelope.

Somehow, by putting the simple Note that had come with the clipping back inside, he'd thought he could make it like it had never happened. Like it had never been read,

26

never been sent, never been written. Never caused his chest to feel tight, his heart to beat fast, his stomach to push the taste of sick up into his mouth. Forcing the envelope shut hadn't been enough to push its true contents back down into the dark where he wanted them to belong. Needed them to belong.

Everyone is going to know what you <u>really</u> did.

6

Amelia

Amelia looked away from the landing upstairs. The sight of the door of Steffan's childhood room was too much, like a reprimand.

On the other side of the open front door, Peter was still hovering. He rubbed his palm over his black beard, which was a few shades darker than his smooth skin. 'Just … You could give your parents a break, you know?'

Amelia smiled guiltily and insincerely. 'I guess I'll see you on Monday, then?'

Peter looked deflated. 'You could come back to mine. It'll be easier to commute. I can show you the way.' He smiled, his bright teeth lighting the way for her.

Amelia held on to the door. She wouldn't be drawn to the flame of her feelings and be destroyed like a moth. There were so many things she could do. Needed to do.

'I'll see you Monday.'

She closed the door behind her, went into her parents' living room, and sat on the edge of their beige, faux-leather sofa. The ruin of a ripped-up polling card for this address she no longer lived at was buried in her pocket – ties to this place being another thing Peter wanted her to move on from. Everything here as it had been for years. The TV on the news channel, the kettle boiling in the kitchen. Faded, unchanged wallpaper.

Mam came through with teas for the family. One for herself, one for Dad, and one for Amelia. They all sat on separate seats, sipping silently. Dad stared mindlessly at the television. Mam arranged herself on her armchair.

No fourth cup.

Amelia was drawn back to one of the endless saved articles on her phone. God knows how many times she'd revisited this over the past five years.

Mr Ginige maintains he believed Mr Flanagan's claim that the death was an accident, and 'did not know' about the victim's body in the freezer. Whatever happened in flat 401 resulted in the tragic death of Steffan Evans, a twenty-nine-year-old gay man who worked at an animal sanctuary. Speaking outside the court after the sentencing, Mr Evans's sister stated: 'Because of Jay's and Shaun's conflicting accounts, we still don't know what really happened that day.'

Half the sweet, milky tea was gone by the time Mam broke.

'So, what exactly is this job Peter has arranged for you, dear?'

Amelia described the dynamics of being a receptionist at a shared office building again. Mam's eyes slowly drifted to the smiling photo on the mantelpiece. Soft face, popular, cute. No hint of trouble. Dad changed the channel to nothing in particular. A tap dripped in the kitchen.

'Peter said the only sticking point might be when I have to do the locking-up routine by myself.' Amelia tightened her resolve as she continued. 'Security guard issues. But otherwise he said it's just cleaning the coffee machines on all floors, managing conflicting room bookings when people in the same company can't talk to each other.'

'It's still such a shame you had to give up teaching,' Mam murmured at the photograph.

Steffan's photo looked down at her. Amelia and her brother had the same fine dark hair and golden skin inherited from their mother, and were equally petite, but the old photo was another reminder that he'd always looked more like Mam, she more like Dad.

Dad pressed back further into his chair. His white skin grew redder. The dripping tap struck louder and faster.

'Management didn't give a toss! I worked myself to the bone.' Amelia chewed the inside of her cheek. 'Things at the house are pure grim too.' She breathed in, and raised her eyebrows hopefully at her parents. 'I was just thinking, you said the tenant is moving out of the flat ...'

Mam stirred her tea. There was a diplomatic clink as her spoon was put to rest on its saucer. 'Dear ...' Mam began, her voice soft.

'Haven't got the money!' Dad barked, his Welsh accent turned hard.

Mam bit her lip and kept her eyes on the contents of her teacup. Amelia fanned her face with her hand.

'Spent it all on keeping your idiot brother in "the lifestyle to which he'd become accustomed",' Dad barked again, not taking his eyes off the news.

'Don't call my boy an idiot!'

'Only an idiot would end up like that!'

Here we go. Here we bloody go.

Dad gestured with the remote. 'She's not going to attract

30

any special attention, is she, Mei? Not going to put herself in a stupid position.'

'Hywel! How dare you blame our son for what happened!' Mam wiped away tears. 'You're as bad as Amelia!'

Amelia finished her tea. She didn't care that the slurp was unladylike. Her parents were still arguing as she collected their cups. She took the fragile china back into the kitchen, where she could wait for silence to return. This would normally fall when Mam had retreated to her bedroom. A five-year tradition.

Placing the cups on the kitchen table, she caught sight of the open brown envelope, and the letter inside poking its NHS heading out of the top.

She burst back into the lounge.

'What's this?' she demanded, waving the letter.

The TV chattered in the background. Mam wordlessly pulled at some knitting. Dad stayed sunk in his chair, not making eye contact. Amelia stared at Dad, breathing hard, occasionally looking back at the appointment letter to check what she'd read, to check that she hadn't made it up, that she hadn't gone mad in adding this to the pile of family tragedies.

'Were you going to tell me?' she demanded.

Dad stayed sullenly silent.

Mam eventually responded. 'We just thought, you're going through so much trouble at the moment. We didn't want to burden you with something else. I even left you a drumstick in the fridge.'

'If Dad has cancer, I want to know. Getting upset isn't going to achieve anything: I want to do something.' She threw herself onto the chair. Busied herself with reading through the NHS website. 'How far along the assessment pathway is he? Has he met the consultant yet?'

'Amelia,' Mam said softly, 'maybe we should talk about this.'

She googled symptoms, diagnostics, treatments, prognoses.

'It's OK, Amelia. Your dad's being taken care of.'

Amelia ignored the well-meaning words. She was already bookmarking links for fundraising events so she could later share them to her social media accounts. Clicking on and on, clicking away from the fear and sadness, she registered for an online forum for relatives of cancer survivors.

Mam tried to distract her again. 'Amelia.'

Amelia came to a dead stop. *Probate is the legal right to deal with someone's estate when they die.*

She kept clicking.

'Oh dear, Amelia …'

After ensuring her parents were going to follow the action plan she'd devised for them, Amelia went upstairs. She stared at Steffan's bedroom door. Her brother wasn't inside, would never be inside again. She wished she weren't alone with supporting their parents. She wished she could face up to what had happened to him.

She opened the door. Everything inside was almost as it was before he moved out. The paling of the blue-painted walls gave away how much time had passed. His possessions from flat 401 were still in the corner, bagged and boxed up from when they'd been released by the police a few years ago. A shrine to her parents' dead offspring.

Amelia shut the door and sat down on the bed. Impotent tears rose up in her eyes.

His thirtieth birthday present was still where she'd hidden it underneath his bed. Leaving it where it was, she picked up the Tamagotchi that lay on the bedside table – one of the few things Mam had permitted her to unload from the mouldy police storage boxes. She endeavoured, again, to bring the translucent purple plastic back to life. But the buttons did nothing. One day, she would actually bring one of those tiny screwdrivers and a flat, circular battery with her.

She put the toy back in its resting place.

She'd been working hard, she'd even had friends five years ago. But none of it had registered on her parents' radar. None of it had been good enough. Now, nothing ever would be. But even if he had been paying that psycho creep Shaun Flanagan for something (no doubt with money their parents had gifted him), Steffan hadn't deserved to die. Her family didn't deserve to be stuck like this. One of the men responsible was already strolling around, able to move on, yet her family would be imprisoned for the rest of their lives. And now Dad wouldn't even live to see what would have been Steffan's thirty-fifth birthday.

A sound. It wasn't the Tamagotchi.

Amelia followed the notification on her phone to verify the account she'd set up downstairs on a different kind of online forum. As the anniversary of Steffan's— of Shaun's and Jay's convictions approached, she figured a website for friends and family of LGBT+ crime-victims would be a good place to find trustworthy allies. She composed a post to introduce her past suffering, and present plans of shucking Jay. Whatever Peter said – she couldn't put it behind her. Jay was her best chance of changing that.

Shaun claimed it was consensual.

She could feel that her plan, which had intensified since the news about Dad's ... about Dad, would make everything better. People who'd been through a similar experience would give her the understanding and help she deserved. Jay would be forced to tell her what Shaun had really done.

She kept typing, going back to check what she'd written was correct.

When she was done, she opened the door a crack. Only the dripping tap could be heard from downstairs. Spiteful water drumming against hollow metal. Relentless.

7
Then

Steffan

Another moth bumps against my window. I dismiss the three 'missed call' notifications from the animal sanctuary that I ignored during the day. I know they are only trying to find out how I am, and are looking forward to me going back when I'm well again, but talking about my health and my fears just feels too much. I'll message them tomorrow. Now, with darkness emanating from the homes around me, I scroll through attempts to lure me out into the night.

Are you sure you're not a total btm?

It's when I land on another Grindr profile with 'that' phrase that I switch to my emails, but passive-aggressive implications from my parents that I wouldn't be in this position if I'd pursued a 'proper job' aren't much better.

Still no apology from Amelia.

Wasting time on my block of flats' Facebook group can't sustain me either. I flick back to a favourite photo from my trip to Tromsø with Tejinder – how I'd shivered at the darkness at the centre of the Northern Lights. I stroke myself with encouragement from her:

We all know how claustrophobic an extended period of isolation can be

You'll be travelling again in no time x

As the vanilla scent of my candles fills the flat, I reread the rest of her latest messages. So devoted to taking care of me: Tejinder is like a second mother – prepared to do anything. Anything for me, and for other people, that is – although she can be a bit pushy at times.

Respecting me not medically transitioning for religious reasons isn't quite the same thing, Stef

I know you're afraid after how he treated you, but you've got to learn to trust again. Not every man will be as bad for you as your ex

At least start to get out of the flat a bit more

OK, I'll try 😊

I finally drag myself up from the threadbare sofa and over to bed, looking beyond my reflection in the small window next to it, across to the neighbouring flats. During the day I am comforted by their position. Sometimes I get intrusive thoughts about my condition getting worse and causing me to pass out, so imagining a neighbour seeing, and calling an ambulance, relieves me. But at night it disturbs me how close the opposite flats are.

Especially the studio on the same level as mine.

Jay Ginige's window stares back at me: a dark, unfeeling

eye. I know where he is when he's at his desk, but when I can't see him, it's like taking my eyes off a spider.

I close the curtains.

8

Now

Jay

Doing press-ups, not fully hearing the beats in his ears, not fully seeing the worn-out carpet of his room, Jay went over everything again.

Who could find out?

Everyone

How could they find out?

is going to know

What would happen if they found out?

what you really did.

His mind raced through acquaintances he'd had before prison; other inmates from prison; officers at the National Probation Service; residents and staff at Magda's; other shop workers at Timpson; family and former friends. Times like this, he regretted bottling it and pleading guilty just to get it over and done with.

Slumping on his bed, Jay checked the bookmarked pages of online news outlets: tariffs, Sentencing Council press releases, Crown Prosecution Service guidelines; news reports on completely dissimilar cases spanning the past twenty years; legal firms' pages with accessible information about sentencing.

And what was the crime he'd committed, anyway? Shaun had admitted to everyone he'd hidden the body in that terrible place after the accident. That's why he was still inside, and Jay was almost free.

Google couldn't tell Jay for sure, but by the time the twilight had closed down into a darkness lit up only by his phone screen, he'd convinced himself: nothing could be worse than the penalty for anyone finding out what he thought only he and one other person knew. It wouldn't be just a few more weeks in prison. It'd be life.

The salty taste on his lips was his own sweat. Were there unknown witnesses? People involved with the investigation or the prosecution who'd worked something out? Had he let something slip since he'd been out of prison? Had Shaun let something slip inside?

His penultimate supervision session was in just over three weeks: there was still time for Olu to exert his authority. Jay's latest probation officer was a young man, maybe he'd be keen to show Jay who was boss? Jay was shanked by a mental image of walking into the NPS office. One of Olu's colleagues, rougher-looking men Jay saw through glass, would be there; they always seemed to mock his PO as he attempted to work. Police officers would appear and take him straight back to prison. He'd be there forever.

The walls of his room closed in, grey, as he gagged at a toilet that couldn't be there—

Jay opened the window. The outside air brought him back to the present. He groped his way to the kitchen along the corridor. Made some supermarket own-brand camomile tea, clinging to the hot mug as he retreated with it to the safety of his room. The bitter taste and smell reminded him he was out. He was at St Magdalene's Hostel, 45 Pembroke Street.

For now.

His door opened. Jay jumped. The tall South Asian woman coming into his room froze when she saw him. But his face relaxed into a smile.

'Tejinder? What are you doing here?'

'Oh, hi, Jay. Sorry, didn't know you were in.'

Jay's desperate happiness at seeing her faded into suspicion. If she didn't know he was in, what was she doing in his room?

'I meant, here at the hostel?'

'Oh, right. I've picked up a few hours here.' She sighed. 'Meant I could give someone else a very part-time job at the café.'

After she didn't volunteer anything further, Jay coughed and asked, 'Did you spot a white envelope arrive for me?' He noticed her eyes flick down to his bed.

'Afraid I only just started here.'

Jay lowered his voice. 'You sure none of the other staff mentioned someone handing a letter in especially for me?'

'Only post I've seen arrived in the usual place.' She gestured down, to the ground floor. All the post fell into the wire cage under the letter box in the front door, and was eventually pushed under residents' doors. 'Are you expecting something?'

There were rarely problems with taking each other's post or parcels, but Jay had seen how some of the residents' trauma-informed territorialism meant staff probably had a script for dealing with questions like his.

'No, I ... Someone sent me a card but forgot to sign it, so I wanted to know who to thank.'

'Oh, is it your birthday?' Tejinder asked brightly.

'No, I ... It's nothing.' A new cold wave hit him. 'Has anyone been asking about me? Anyone who doesn't live here?'

Tejinder stayed silent for a bit.

'Sorry, I need to call my girlfriend about locking up the café.'

Jay watched her close his door behind her. He felt like he'd said something wrong, but told himself that was all in his head. He reminded himself to keep his attention focused on what was really going on around him, not ways he was imagining he'd embarrassed himself.

He scrutinised the envelope again. No stamp, no postmark, no smell, no visible fingerprints. Jay didn't even have access to a fingerprint database, what good would fingerprints do him? He tried to picture whether the handwriting on the application form of that guy who'd come into the shop, Noah, had definitely been different from the writing on the Note, but this only flooded him with more uncertainty.

The dark was still outside. What else was out there? Other people's lives; his life was still just about existing inside the window and looking through. Two and a half years ago, his window hadn't even opened: it had only looked out at groups of men huddled along tribal lines as they paced, counting down. The window from five years ago had been high up, modern and double-glazed, and had let the outside in.

But he didn't want to remember ... It had made sense for him to plead guilty to what Shaun had falsely accused him of. What might the police have found out if they'd investigated further?

Jay flinched at the reflection in his room's night-darkened glass. The spots creeping in to his vision obscured who might be out there, watching him malignantly. Even when he flicked the switch, annihilating the light around him, he couldn't discern anything but disaster in his failure to wish away the reality of the Note. Would the threat mean the undoing of his vision of new place, new name, new life?

The identity of the sender was lurking out there, threatening to drag him to the seabed. The endless weight of the ocean, cold, pressed on him; he was totally alone down there. Except for a single pair of eyes watching him in the dark. Gradually getting closer. As he strained towards the choppy surface, only an empty, airless bubble scraped over his lips in a soundless, futile moan.

Before his conscience could overrule his desperation with warnings against having contact with an offender who might have 'bad behaviour' in mind, Jay sent a furtive message to Tony.

9

Cathy

The women at Group were dressed all different, but had the same look. The room they huddled in had just enough space for eight chairs. Two comfy, one office, five brown plastic with black metal legs. An old NHS computer whirred on a faded wooden desk in the corner. Cathy imagined the Health Centre didn't let the charity use the room for free. Never did see that £350 million for the NHS. The kind of thing Ant used to take out on her. Drawing himself up to his full height as he loomed head and shoulders above her. She pulled the cardigan tighter.

Cathy didn't say nothing about the empty chairs. None of them did. But she bet they were all thinking the same.

Someone's missing?

What's happened to her?

Am I gonna be next?

Cathy clung to her tea in its cheap cardboard cup. One of the other women whispered to another, nodding at Cathy. 'Yeah, that's the one! Can you believe, she lives with him?'

Cathy closed her eyes and massaged the side of her forehead with two fingers. Jay'd been so friendly since she'd taken refuge at the hostel. Maybe what that Shaun Flanagan did *was* an accident? At least Ant had never tried on anything that kinky. But even her ex always said he never meant to hurt her. Google hadn't given Cathy answers about why Jay believed Shaun. But the charity wouldn't house him if he was dangerous, would they?

Louise, the organiser, settled on the black office chair. 'Nice to see everyone,' she said. Same as every session. Only one new person tonight. Cathy felt embarrassed remembering the woman who'd come a few weeks ago. She'd got right into her reasons for coming before realising she wanted LGBTQ Mental Health down the corridor. Funny that she'd started working at the hostel this week. Tejinder, right?

Martha was telling her story first tonight. Almost in Sunday best, like this were a church meeting or something. Maybe that's what she told people. As she talked, she looked around the group, and stroked the cross around her neck.

Cathy saw it as both reassurance and a choking risk. She put a hand around her own throat.

Martha got to the point. She explained how she was much more confident these days, but still wanted to be careful. There was a new man at church who kept sitting next to her. What did the other ladies think she should do? She had made so much progress, and didn't want to be set back.

Cathy flattened herself against the back of her chair, a pale fish against a dark reef. She honestly wanted to believe it was safe for Martha to meet this man. To form a new life with him.

One of the less regular members, a posh lady, was talking about her on/off relationship. 'It's hard, bringing up two children on my own now. It can be hard to make ends meet. I feel like a terrible mother a lot of the time.'

44

The group, especially Cathy, murmured support.

The woman went on. Cathy found it hard to remember her name, hard to concentrate. 'My new *beau* doesn't help out that much anymore, but I tell myself it's the good times that matter most. Isn't that what they say?' Cathy knew what the posh lady meant, but didn't say anything. 'Cos clearly this new guy was taking advantage of her. Starting to control where she went. Who she saw. The broken bits of jealousy already showing up, the sex not always wanted.

Cathy didn't look anyone in the eye. She jammed her hands into her cardi's pockets. Kept perfectly still. She thought about how her circle of friends had shrunk. Too many 'Soz, I can't make it' texts. Too much nervously looking at Ant to check whether what she was saying was OK when they did meet up with her mates and that.

Bang!

Martha went rigid, hands scrunched in her lap. The posh woman knocked over her chair as she and the newbie exploded to their feet. Cathy was desperate to swim away.

The noise had come from outside. They were the only other people in the building at this time of night. The women camouflaged themselves against their chairs.

The ticking of the clock suddenly seemed deafening. No footsteps in the corridor.

Louise went out to check. Sometimes the external door banged shut when the LGBTQ group left. A chair scraped as it got set on its feet. One of the women laughed nervously.

'Imagine if it were one of our exes, out of prison,' a voice said.

Cathy didn't know if the laugh and voice had been her own.

Martha fiddled with her cross and Cathy stared at the little Jesus. Shame he'd been busy when most of the women here really needed Him. Louise came back, all reassuring smiles.

'All fine. Why don't we have another tea or coffee before we start again?'

The women all reacted differently, but Cathy bet they had the same thoughts racing inside.

Am I ever gonna feel safe?

You expect me to believe that?

Not taking any chances!

Cathy's turn.

She was all sweaty now. She remembered her mum telling her not to air dirty laundry in public. She also remembered Jay telling her, *'Secrets keep shame alive.'*

The cup of tea was cold in her hands. She sat up slightly straighter and made eye contact briefly. She could afford to take a risk, couldn't she? Here. With other women. It was just talking.

'I had this dream. A plan.' She cleared her throat and looked down. 'My ex, Ant … He ain't a bad person. But he weren't keen on me trading at craft fairs.' She teared up. 'My mum said some of the candles I made were quite good.'

Jay was right – she did feel a bit better for sharing. She was lucky to have met a man she could trust. And she was lucky Ant was still in prison. She could outrun her ex. She was so sure that she would.

The tall man

On the street, the tall man ran his tongue over his teeth. The dirty glass panels on the door of the Health Centre hinted at what went on behind the blinded windows. The whole place looked beaten up. It was a place for the sick and weak.

He started back to the bus stops by Woolwich's main square. He checked himself out in the window of one of the pound shops: he was satisfied by the green eyes admiring him from a lupine face. He flicked them away from the faded-athletic body that reminded him of how he'd been confined, crushed and corrupted by his time inside.

The herd moving out of his way on the back streets pleased him.

The darkness surrounding them was the same as that at the bottom of the human heart.

II

Amelia

Amelia couldn't make sense of all the bloody browser tabs she had open, with the noise of the men digging up the street outside. The drilling and shouting blundered in through the open window, accompanied by the fumes of tarmac, marched up to the reception desk, and demanded attention. Couldn't she be left in peace?

She scoured the articles for clues. They were no different from all the others she'd read over the past five years. Hints of the crime, brief mentions of Jay Ginige's background and involvement, the controversy over sentencing. All as unsatisfying as the crumbs she'd been fed by the police.

The door buzzed a second time. Amelia remembered she was supposed to let the visitor in, that was part of her job. Opening the door made the disturbance from the digging even worse. Jay got to live normally while her life was ruined. None of these articles acknowledged that. Some even implied he'd been the victim, because he'd been in prison for so long without a trial.

Yet another email arrived in her work inbox. Fifty-six unread.

Bugger off.

All these people starting up their gossiping on social media again, getting attention from the anniversary of her family's tragedy. Amplified by mentions of *Shaun the Sex Strangler*'s release next year. Amelia still shovelled the tweets, status updates, comments on pages and the like into her brain. Making herself sick with knowledge. But even she could tell some of it didn't make sense or wasn't true. Stereotype-fuelled speculation about the role of chem sex in the cause of death. Comments-section 'experts' who swore the criminal justice system was colour-blind. Cyber-crime conspiracy theorists. Perverts. None of this helped her find the truth about what Shaun must have had on Jay for him to have turned a blind eye to Shaun covering up his crime.

But at least Jay being out already meant he'd be an easier target for her need to get at the truth. She finished off another online forum post:

> Why would you lie to police about helping a stranger conceal their crime, and delete your messages to the victim, if you were going to plead guilty anyway?!

Nothing the police had told her from their lackadaisical investigation made sense. So they were equally to blame for Amelia and her parents being stuck without answers. But it was because of Shaun and his accomplice Jay that Steffan had died before Amelia had a chance to—

The phone rang.

'Hi, Janice. No, I haven't done the post yet.'

Bollocks to Janice.

Amelia threw the last of the deliveries onto the trolley. The roadworkers outside kept drilling down into the earth.

Amelia started at the top floor. She'd plough her way through the shared working spaces as fast as possible. Each floor one step towards being able to get on with her search. She checked her phone for messages from her latest internet forum. She felt hot, her heart beat faster, her breathing rate increased. Another one from the woman whose username was *EmeraldSiren*.

Until she'd heard from EmeraldSiren, Amelia had been alone with this. She couldn't count on anyone: the police didn't understand, Peter didn't understand, her parents didn't understand. It was just like growing up. Like with all those school bullies she'd had to handle on her own, who'd been making fun of Steffan over his care for animals and not being like other boys. Her teaching him how to give a hard stare when people told them they couldn't be from Wales. So what if standing up to the bullies had got her in trouble? She'd distracted herself and her little brother from their tears.

The lift stopped suddenly. The lights went out. The emergency lights came on. Parcels spilled onto the floor. This was enough to get Amelia off her phone and out of her head. As she edged round the trolley to the alarm button, the safety mechanism lowered her gently to the next floor and the doors opened.

'What's happened to the power?' Peter asked from in front of his dead computer, through the open doorway of his office.

'How should I know? I was in the lift!'

Peter stroked his hipster beard. 'You can talk to me, Ams.'

'I don't want to talk: I want to do.'

He retreated back into his office as Janice appeared around the corner of the stairs from below, hi-vis in hand.

'Those workers cut through a power cable.' She paused.

Amelia looked down at the parcels on the floor of the lift, and her phone.

'Quick word in my office, Amelia?'

Amelia followed Janice, pushing away the dread. It was like the time she'd been summoned to the headmaster's office after telling on that boy who'd been bullying Steffan online. At least it was dim – the migraine-inducing artificial light in the office had been cut too.

'How are you finding your first week, Amelia?'

Express concern for the employee's wellbeing, check.

Amelia shrugged.

'How do you think your performance has been?'

Elicit the employee's view first, check.

Another jerk of Amelia's shoulders.

'I believe there are a few items of concern, based on my observations of your work.'

Give factual feedback, check.

'I appreciate you only want to work part-time here, but tenants have complained their visitors haven't been let in promptly, their emails haven't been answered, and their parcels not delivered on time. All of these are a vital part of the role.'

Amelia pressed back into her chair as Janice continued.

'As a valued tenant said that losing your last job hadn't been your fault, I gave you a chance. I imagine losing your brother was hard, but you need to get on with your life. If you're not prepared to do that, you won't be able to continue working here.'

Make a clear plan with the employee about how to move forward: not sure about that.

Didn't matter. She could imagine, could intellectualise away the loss and the guilt with a fictional, unsafe certainty, made up of her fears, her fantasies, her attempts to piece together the broken testimonies of a liar and a murderer. All the time her only brother lay buried in the ground, never coming back, never returning their parents to her, never being able to hear her say everything she'd wanted to say before it was too late.

Amelia would make it right. No matter what Janice, Peter, her friends, or anyone else said: if there was a way to compel the men responsible to tell the truth, she could free her parents to love her before Dad died. EmeraldSiren was going to bring her dream to life. Finally, she'd found an ally.

Outside, the digger started digging its hole again.

12

Jay

The waiting room was filled with the sound of clicks pressing in from the office behind reception. Clicking of pens, clicking of trackpads, clicking of keyboards – the oppressive bureaucracy made Jay's head tense. He fiddled with his earphones: would having them in when his probation officer came out to collect him make him look disrespectful? At least Olu was definitely here this time.

Jay distracted himself with the posters and leaflets that cluttered up the already tight space. Took a photo of one about mental health. It lay next to fliers advertising another protest about cuts to the over-stretched justice system. He couldn't focus on reading. He stared at the rough brown skin on the back of his hand. Turned it over to face the lighter palm. He spied one old Police Watch leaflet, and pocketed it so no one else could read it.

Bang! The door to one of the interview rooms up the corridor slammed shut. Another offender stormed past Jay to the lifts, and jabbed the call button.

'I'm just doing my job!' shouted a woman – must be his probation officer – from the doorway of the interview room.

'You're supposed to keep me *out* of prison!' the man

shouted back. 'Not threaten to send me back just 'cos you're too busy to do your job properly!' He hit the lift button again, kicked the metal doors, and then stomped down the stairs.

Jay shrank down. Tried to control his restlessness. Everyone was looking at him and the other offenders who were waiting, just trying to get on with their lives.

Out of the cloud of officers who'd clustered at reception, Olu appeared.

'Jay?' he called out, not looking up from his clipboard piled high with papers.

Jay stood up. Smiled but not too much. Tried not to tower over his short, chubby PO as he was led to the interview room the other offender had just stormed out of.

'We're in here today,' said Olu, elbowing open the door. 'Oh, sorry,' he said to the female PO who was staring blankly at a wall, red-faced and red-eyed. 'I've got this room booked now,' Olu added apologetically.

The woman pushed past them without saying anything. Olu looked after her, a concerned frown squashing his face. Jay squeezed around him and sat down. Olu sighed, came in, and let the door close behind him.

Sitting opposite Jay, Olu balanced the clipboard of forms on his lap. Placed a white envelope onto the low table between them. The tension from the waiting room burst back into Jay's muscles. His heart raced. *FAO: Jay Ginige's probation officer*. What was this about?

'I thought this was just going to be another routine appointment?' Jay stammered.

'Got to make sure your file is in order, Jay,' Olu said, looking down at his stack of forms. He flipped through them. Jay had seen all these headings before. *Risk of Reoffending. Accountable. Appraisal Goals. Departmental Targets*. He zoned out while Olu went through his questions, as if he were still

54

and the rest of the room were moving quickly past him. The sweating younger man was mostly ticking boxes, sometimes writing down Jay's answers. How many times had he had to confirm he was 'White and Asian – Mixed'? Not that Olu's forms cared about the reality of his heritage. Still no box for 'White English and Sri Lankan'.

'And you're not having any contact with no-good people?' Olu asked without looking up.

Jay slipped his hand inside his trouser pocket, wrapping it around his phone. Tapped on it three times, as if he could minimise his guilt about the message it concealed.

'No, nobody explicitly forbidden by my licence conditions,' he answered honestly. Olu might not approve of the meet he'd arranged, but who else could he turn to about the Note, other than Tony?

'That's good. I wouldn't want you falling foul of the "bad behaviour" clause. That's important.'

Olu looked up, earnestly, at Jay.

Jay flicked his eyes down to the envelope on the table. Next to it, a note addressed to Olu: *Discuss at next performance review.* The rest of Olu's questions seemed more-or-less the same as he was always asked, so there was nothing out of the ordinary going on here, right?

The gold of a cross glinted at Jay through a gap in Olu's shirt.

Jay swallowed.

'Actually, I was denied bail, and spent several years on remand,' he corrected, when his probation officer summarised his sentence incorrectly. Olu sighed at this, and shook his head, tutting. Had Jay said something wrong?

'Unfortunately, when there is a lot of media interest in a case …' Olu shrugged – 'they tend to be harsher.' He glanced down at the envelope.

'Yeah, well, that was only because of the headlines,' Jay blurted out defensively.

Olu smiled thinly and nodded.

'Yes, yes, I know, Shaun Flanagan was the killer, and you just got mixed up in it. Maybe the police would've gone easier on you if you'd told them why you deleted your Facebook chat with the victim. Especially as it was just after the crime took place.'

Someone knocked at the door. Olu got up and went out.

Looking over at the closed door, Jay reached down for the envelope. A drop of sweat fell from his trembling hand and marked the table next to it. His fingertips made it to the smooth edge of the paper.

The door opened.

'I wanted to ask you about getting a new Approved Address and new Approved Job,' Jay said as he snatched his hand back.

Olu shook his head as he sat back down.

'Sorry, Jay. It's just too much— There aren't the resources for that at present.' Same answer Jay had been given for the past two and a half years, by every PO he'd had. 'But you are almost at the end of your licence period.' Olu laughed awkwardly. 'Just make sure nothing comes out that breaks one of your licence conditions!'

Jay choked on his own laugh.

Olu drew his questions to an end, and completed his forms.

'One last thing,' he said, reaching down for the envelope. 'Do you know what this could be about?' He slid another envelope out from the first, also white but much older. The handwritten name on it had faded. From the older envelope, Olu removed a sheet of paper, covered in small printed text, broken up with crease marks. He held it out to Jay.

'Looks like the instructions for a Tamagotchi,' Jay said hoarsely.

'Yeah, I googled what that old toy was,' Olu said. 'But why has it been sent to me? What's it got to do with you? Not even your name on it.'

Practical joke? Something random from the crime scene? Coded message?

'No idea,' Jay volunteered.

'OK, well …' Olu scrutinised the sheet. 'Well, I'll just stick it in your file. Probably got mixed up with your trial documents.'

Olu showed him out to the lift, keeping an eye on him until it arrived. 'Stay out of trouble, Jay.'

Jay stroked his arm as he descended. One more session over. The lift shuddered as it reached the ground floor, and the doors creaked open.

The man who'd stormed out earlier was standing by the entrance, smoking. Jay nodded at him.

'Maybe you should have a word with your PO?' Jay suggested, gesturing to the worn-out building. 'Don't want to make things worse for yourself.'

The man looked like he was about to cry. 'I just want a decent job, you know? See my kids? Make them proud of me.'

Jay didn't know why this man had been threatened with being recalled to prison: something he'd genuinely done wrong, or a burnt-out PO overreacting? He rested his hand on the man's shoulder. 'I get you. It's hard to trust the system.'

The man bit down on his cigarette, nodding.

'But this is the only way we can move on. They don't need to know the ins and outs of our business, you know what I'm saying?'

The man nodded again, blowing out his cheeks.

'We can do this.'

'Cheers, man.' The other offender wiped his eyes, stubbed out his cigarette, and went back into the Probation Office. The doors slid shut automatically, locking Jay out with a final click.

Jay slipped the Police Watch leaflet out of his back pocket. His own mugshot stared back at him. *In 2020, 2 per cent of the UK population was Mixed. But 4 per cent of those placed on custodial remand, rather than being granted bail, were Mixed.*

Jay whispered, 'We can do this.'

In his pocket, his phone *dinged* with a calendar notification: it was time for him to go and meet Tony.

13

Jay

The cigarette smoke was sharp. The bricks of the wall the two of them were sitting on were rough on Jay's palms. He threw his barely smoked cigarette onto the ground.

'So you're sure the Note's just a wind-up, mate?'

The crumbling concrete of the council estate was like fists held up in his face outside a pub at closing time.

'Yeah, man,' Tony said casually. 'What could they have on you?'

Even though Tony was only about ten years older than him, Jay craved this solid reassurance from a man who'd had multiple goes at the Probation Service. Not wanting to humiliate Tony by forcing him to admit he was another ex-inmate who couldn't read or write too well, Jay read the Note aloud again. *Everyone is going to know what you really did.*

'But how did they find me?' he repeated.

'Seriously man, listen: some people are just dickheads. What can you do? Ask the police to check for fingerprints?'

Tony's dry laugh at his own joke metastasised into a cough. He banged a fist against his pecs.

Jay wasn't sure about Tony or his advice. He wasn't like

the ex-offenders Jay knew through work. Seeing him now, the first time since they'd finished their mandated Probation group sessions together, was a disappointment but not a surprise. The earnest person from back then had since been replaced by the real Tony. Like a bottle of cooled water allowed to heat in the sun: it looks like what you need, but as soon as you taste it, you realise it's no good.

But maybe Tony was right; maybe the Note was just a wind-up, or even a scam – nothing had ever come of it, but over the last few years a couple of individuals had threatened to make a big deal out of his conviction, either at the hostel or work, thinking they could get something out of him. Lucky Magda's and Timpo's had stood by him.

But something about this Note felt different.

'I mean, if you're that bothered, I can get some of my boys to ask around,' Tony offered slyly, looking up at Jay out of the corner of his eyes. A van pulled out noisily from the warehouse opposite, and drove away. The concrete towers watched. Jay had just wanted to ask Tony for advice, for reassurance, not so that Tony would investigate. Not so that Jay would owe him.

'Listen, I've got a job coming up,' Tony said.

Jay's mouth dried up and his heart banged. Tony took another drag on his roll-up, the sucking-in motion of his cheeks drawing attention to how pale and clammy they were. His dirty-blond hair greasy despite being shorn. Even his clothes seemed washed-out. Jay looked sideways.

'I'm doing alright. The job is good for me. Helping me get back to a normal life, you know what I'm saying?'

Tony's hand settled on the wall next to Jay's, who moved his to a safe distance. Didn't want to give Tony the wrong idea.

'Yeah, Timpo's are alright. Much money in it?'

'The thing is, Tony, I—'

'Nah nah nah, hear me out man, hear me out.' Tony's hand leaped up as if it could dispel the few inconvenient splashes of moral qualms. 'It's a straight-up job. We know the time, the place, the security. We just need an inside man. I put in a good word for you, seeing what we shared in group and all.'

Jay looked into Tony's eyes. They were watery, and he didn't want to see himself reflected in them.

'Now isn't a good time, Tony.' Jay tried to be gentle with his tone. Tony's face was having none of it. Shame and loneliness turned inside-out into contempt. Hadn't Jay felt some of the same because of Flat 401?

'Seriously mate, I'm trying to go straight.' He refused to let Tony's exclaimed scorn throw him off course. 'I made mistakes, but if I don't stay out of trouble, that's it for me. You know what it's like.'

Tony cracked his knuckles, looked to the side, and spat. Jay freaked out, inside, at the reminder of Dad.

'You ain't never gonna have a "normal" life.' Tony gestured to two women walking by. 'See the way they look at us.'

Jay nodded and smiled reassuringly at them. They kept walking.

'People like that ain't ever gonna accept us. You think you can get a normal job, a decent place to live, a boyfriend?'

Jay's face grew hot. What did Tony know about his sexuality? What did all those labels matter, anyway?

'We ain't gonna make anyone proud!' Tony laughed. '*The Freezer Killer's Pimp*? Don't matter it's not true! You're screwed, son.' He crushed the smouldering end of his roll-up against the wall. 'The only way you'll ever be allowed to live, to earn a decent living, is by breaking the law.'

Jay felt sick at the thought Tony could be right. He didn't

deserve to meet Amma's maternal Sri Lankan expectations of becoming one of the 'golden child' professions: doctor, lawyer, or accountant. His hands retreated into his pockets. One found his phone. Only four numbers were stored in it, the rest deleted after their owners ghosted him, or made their excuses after awkward small talk in the street, or asked him not to contact them because of … *you know*.

'You think I'd be doing all this if I had a choice?' Tony gestured at his depressing-looking workplace. 'I just want to get my ex back. Get her to let me see my kid. You know? Money makes the world go round.'

Tony got off the wall and walked towards the warehouse. The lanky man didn't wait for Jay to follow, but at the entrance turned to look back, adjusting himself before going in.

Jay looked away. Were the two women he'd smiled at staring at him from outside Sainsbury's? He tensed as, behind the women, two police officers walked past the end of the road; they didn't 'randomly' need to come down this side-street, and ask him what he was doing.

This time.

The tower blocks stared Jay down. Arms crossed, chins up, sucking their teeth. No way they would let him past. What if Tony was right, and there was only one way out? He checked his Facebook Messenger account to make sure any old messages had been deleted, and then dived off the wall. Started to walk towards the warehouse.

Cathy's voice made him jump mid-walk.

'Who … who was that?'

Jay turned. Caught in the act.

'What are you doing here? I mean – Just someone I used to know.'

Jay smiled awkwardly, rubbed the back of his head with

one hand, and hid the other in his pocket. This time, as his pulse raced through his fingers, feeling his phone reminded him: maybe 'Dan Lane' wouldn't need to throw it all away to go with Tony. Maybe he could relax on an Isle of Wight beach. Especially if Tony was right, and there was no need to worry about the Note. If Tony was right, and Jay didn't need him to use his connections to dig into it for him.

'Lucky you showed up.' Jay knew he was clutching at serendipity.

Cathy didn't say anything more. Her face had gone pale and tense.

Jay looked behind him at whatever she was staring at.

Tony had disappeared, for now.

14

Amelia

'Amelia, you've got to stop this. You could bring down the whole campaign.'

Wow. Lina hadn't wasted any time after bringing Amelia into her office, together with Nicola, the other co-director of Police Watch. Amelia bet the other volunteers, sitting out there in the charity's beige office space, were feeling sorry for her.

'How d'you mean?' Amelia wasn't playing dumb. She'd been doing The Right Thing, using whatever she could dig up to get at Jay. Surely a few emails here and there couldn't hurt?

'If Police Watch is linked to illegal activities, that risks losing funding, bad press, putting off volunteers: we don't want to go the same way as Fathers 4 Justice,' Lina continued.

'Yeah, but I'm not doing anything illegal,' Amelia lied. She grabbed a Police Watch leaflet from Lina's desk and waved it at her. 'What happened to nailing the police for their mistakes? Getting justice for the families of victims even if we can't, even if we can't bring them back?'

'This is *the police* we're talking about! We can't risk acting like vigilantes.' Lina's voice shook as she emphasised the end of every clause. Her face gnarled up like one of the men's rights protesters who were regularly demonstrating outside the Crown Court.

Amelia couldn't see any reason she should back down.

'I'm not being a vigilante! I'm only trying to contact two perpetrators of a specific crime – one is already free – to make them pay properly.'

'"Pay properly"! Can you hear how bad that sounds?'

'You know what I mean.'

'This is also dangerous,' Nicola contributed. 'Shaun's already killed once. Imagine what kind of unstable man takes a life like that? What if he finds out you're looking for him, and he has you hurt?'

'He couldn't hurt me more than he already has,' Amelia said bitterly.

Nicola looked down and brushed some invisible dirt from the desk in front of her.

Lina jumped in. 'Police Watch isn't here for you to pursue your own personal vendettas, Amelia. Obviously the circumstances in this case were particularly disturbing.'

'A freezer in a chip shop,' Nicola murmured, shaking her head.

'Which "raises the profile of the issues"!' Amelia exclaimed, throwing the leaflet back onto the desk. 'That's good that is!'

Lina rolled her eyes, snorted and ploughed on.

'But that doesn't make it OK for you to use campaign resources to track down anyone involved. It's probably a massive data protection violation. I'm going to need to ask our compliance officer about this.' Lina gestured to her office door, which Amelia took to indicate her unbelievable lack of understanding. 'Given your background, I would have thought you'd be more understanding towards this Jay Ginige.'

Amelia gritted her teeth, and marched out.

Back at her desk after her final warning, Amelia swallowed the unfairness and completed some tasks to get those two off her back: responding to queries that came via the website, checking the inventory of their online store, writing up a press release about the latest progress on securing funding for their 'police complaints clinic'.

A poster on the flaky wall stared down at her. Its yellow font reminded her of the campaign's mission to scrutinise and eliminate police injustice.

It wasn't even like Police Watch had made such great progress. The police were still getting away with their rotten core of 'heartfelt apologies' and 'systematic failings', without any individual officer ever being held accountable. It was easier for them to believe cases like Steffan's were open and shut.

Steffan ... It was his ex. It was his fault Steffan hadn't taken the proper precautions around the animals. It was his fault he'd got sick and ended up stuck in flat 401, where he'd ended up meeting ... She'd told Steffan to be less generous, less trusting. For his own good. Just like when she'd had to get all those Pokémon cards back for him, after they'd been 'traded for fairly' by that boy in his class. Steffan had been so upset, and she'd ...

Why should she get upset about these kinds of memories? She made herself experience the cold feeling again. Like crushing muddy ground in her hands. It gave her something to cling on to.

Amelia knew, if she could confront Jay, she would be able to get him to publicly admit why he'd done wrong, instead of hiding behind his lawyer. What did Shaun have on Jay that had made him agree to cover it up?

Her thought trailed off at this point, as it so often did. She reread the messages Peter sent after that disastrous first week at his co-working space. Apparently, her *reasoning doesn't make sense*, she's *convinced of something that feels true but isn't*, and *using a fantasy to avoid grieving*. She shoved her phone away. Some boyfriend.

EmeraldSiren's messages, on the forum she'd joined for the families of LGBT+ crime-victims, had shown she was different. People like that don't understand people like us. You're such a great daughter. Moving to a shared house so you can afford to spend time tracking down that bastard Jay. Can't believe your parents are still renting out the flat. So unfair you've had to move while Jay strolls around free.

EmeraldSiren was right: the truth from Jay couldn't escape her for much longer. She remembered when she was nine years old and found a distinctive beetle in their garden. Holding it up to the light for inspection. Her desire to learn everything about the insect drowning out Steffan's cries that she was scaring it.

Amelia pulled her phone towards her, and scrolled through some saved posts:

This Jay guy was definitely in league with Shaun.
I reckon Jay was Shaun's jealous boyfriend.

She'd dismissed them previously as conspiracy theorists. What had been the weirdest thing Steffan believed? Odd thought to have. Guess it didn't matter now. Amelia brushed the salty liquid on her cheeks away with her sleeve. Some of these people thought Jay had helped Shaun conceal the body, or videoed it to put on the internet, or been part of a threesome that somehow—

'A few of us are going to the pub after our shift. Want to come?' Nicola always tried to be friendly and helpful.

'No thanks.'

Amelia didn't want to have to deal with talking to people right now. Yes, she'd always thought it would be easier to get at the truth of what Shaun and Jay really did by going for the one that was already out of prison.

But now it looked like that fantasy was going to become a reality.

She double-checked the notes she'd made at the trial, the summaries of the social media and news coverage she'd collated on a spreadsheet, the latest brief but sympathetic text from Wanda, a female police officer at the Witness Care Unit. Messaging her had been a good hint from EmeraldSiren. Her suggestion of revisiting someone Amelia had ignored throughout the trial might turn out to be a good one too, if Amelia could bear to go through with it. She checked the name to make sure she had it down correctly:

Tejinder Kaur.

15

Cathy

The enormous Sainsbury's had looked empty. This had made it easier for Cathy to brave the impulsive need to venture inside. The memory of unthinking encouragement from Group had pushed her out of the hostel in the first place. Confectionery did have its own aisle, towards the far end of the shop. But Cathy could make do with the single shelf opposite the self-service tills. Near the double door and the security guard.

Bumping into Jay outside had been a pleasant surprise. Then she'd taken another look at the tall man he'd been talking to as he'd walked off over the small railway bridge. Athletic. Like a wolf.

No time or thought to talk to Jay. Was it Ant? Already? Had he been released on bail? *Clara Place looks empty – get out of here.*

Cathy's hand tightened on her keys as she turned left. She'd make a break for Monk Street. Wouldn't risk getting trapped down a side road. Her throat tightened. She stumbled in front of a silent electric car. Nerves about to explode, she sped up. The footsteps behind made her pulse race. Running off hadn't worked.

He'd spotted her.

The streets were empty.

He got closer.

Cathy's eyes blurred.

Her memories had got all mixed up when she'd seen his figure. He was coming up behind her. She wasn't going to reach the hostel.

She was going to die.

Cathy's voice screamed. Memories of Ant doing her head in. He was at her side. She was bent over, her curled-up hands covering her face.

Why did I turn left instead of turning back?

Why did I think I could ever be safe again?

Why aren't I in pain yet?

Cathy's eyes opened. Her bladder had leaked when she'd thought this was it again. He was looking concerned. She was daring to look, her legs not moving as liquid slid down them.

'Cathy? Cathy! Are you alright?'

Jay's voice. Not Ant's.

She looked around her. It was a warm summer evening in Woolwich. The smell of the town centre. The buses turning right at the roundabout ahead of her. The buses were red. Double-deckers. Like the chocolate bar she'd wanted.

'Come on, let's get you back,' Jay said kindly. Despite his muscles, he didn't touch her. She could feel the wet patch on her cargo pants.

'Sorry,' said Cathy.

'Ah, you've got nothing to be sorry for,' Jay said as he began to gently guide her back to the hostel.

'I'm such a total mess, Jay!' She wiped her nose and cheeks on the sleeve of her cardigan. 'I can't even go out for a stupid bar of chocolate!'

'Hey, come on now.' Jay's voice was warm. 'You're trying your best. You'll get over this one day.'

'How?!' Cathy's voice was broken. 'I keep going to that stupid group. Nothing changes. I can't even make it to Sainsbury's without having a total breakdown 'cos I imagine seeing someone who looks like Ant. How do I just "get over it"?'

They stopped at the zebra crossing.

'I know what it's like. Not being able to get away from your past. The other day I …' Jay pulled out his phone, and showed her a photo of a poster. 'I saw this at the … when I was at my … after an appointment.'

'"Research participants wanted?" *Internet-delivered cognitive therapy for P-T-S-D?* What's that when it's at home?' Cathy read off his screen.

'Maybe it could help you. Email them. It's free.'

'I don't know …' Cathy remembered her mum's saying about dirty laundry.

'Tell you the truth, mate, I was going to contact them myself.' A slight blush showed up on Jay's cheeks. 'You give it a try, tell me if it's any good!'

As they arrived at the hostel, Jay mimed '*call them*' with his hand hovering by his head in the shape of a phone, his eyes and mouth wide, like a hopeful guy hitting on her. Cathy laughed a little as he went into his room.

Cathy eventually slid her trembling key into the lock of her room on the third go. Stupid thing. Then the handle wouldn't turn right. She managed to open the door without bursting into tears. She shut it, so she could clean herself up straight away.

Her phone pinged: Jay had sent her the photo of the poster.

*I'm sorry for whatever this Ant guy did to you. You
don't need to keep paying for it. You can make
things better.*

Jay was so kind. There was no way he knew what that sicko
Shaun Flanagan was being paid for.

But she didn't know whether to believe Jay about her
own chances. Her grey face was reflected in the window,
her hand pressed briefly against the glass. Other people were
getting on with their lives out there. A woman was walking
down the street, holding her little girl's hand. The child was
holding a balloon.

She remembered a candle-making workshop she'd gone
to for a friend's hen do. Some clumsy woman had knocked
over a stack of wax and wicks. Almost set them all on fire,
stupid cow. Cathy had been the only one together enough
to grab the fire extinguisher. Back home, Ant had said he
didn't want her hanging around those friends any more if
they wouldn't protect her like he did. Said it was a 'dog-eat-
dog world'.

The photo of the poster stared back at Cathy.

'Yeah,' she whispered. 'I can make things better.' She
could get Ant's voice out of her brain.

16

The tall man

Leaning back, careful not to bump his recently clippered head, he surveyed the latest scrawled note he was the victim of:

> *I think of a time. If what I do now can be called thinking.*
> *Fluttering moths of thoughts bumping into each other*
> *through the fog left of my brain.*
> *Everyone does know. I remember the court case.*
> *If you don't know you're heading towards the ground,*
> *falling probably feels a lot like flying.*

He crumpled up the pleading warning, and tossed it aside.

Making the physical journey had been hard enough, but he'd got what he wanted to help him right some wrongs. It was bad enough this scrap of a letter had reminded him how unfairly he'd been treated: he didn't need the guilt trip as well. Reminding him how he could never have a normal life. Could never get his ex and his kid back.

17

Amelia

Even though the Wellness Café's chair was cushioned, Amelia shifted uncomfortably at Tejinder's latest question, about what Steffan had been like as a child. The middle-aged Asian woman kept on wiping down tables as she waited for Amelia to answer, the café devoid of other customers now it was past closing time.

'He liked to play a lot. Centre of attention. Always performing,' Amelia answered eventually. 'Is that how he ended up—'

'He was maybe a bit much sometimes,' Tejinder interrupted. 'But always so kind to me. Really good when my mum ...' She brought her face close to a table to scrub at a particularly difficult spot. 'And so kind to animals. I remember how much he was looking forward to getting back to the animal sanctuary after his illness.' The surprisingly tall woman stood up and looked into the distance for a moment, before moving on to another table. 'He had a real energy to him, you know?'

Amelia's fingers curled around the sachet.

'Yes, he was always very popular,' she said bitterly. Seeing Tejinder fix her with a stare again, she delicately placed the sachet on the table, smoothed it out, and added: 'Maybe if our parents hadn't gifted him that flat—'

'Look, you can't blame someone who ended up ... Envy is a poison. I remember telling Steffan that. Not long before ...' Tejinder looked away and into the distance again.

Amelia felt hot but didn't argue. This is why she'd avoided making contact with Tejinder. But EmeraldSiren had suggested she might have information Amelia could use.

'He was always kind to animals. Not that we had many in London.'

'How do you mean?' Tejinder tilted her head.

'We grew up in Wales. I grew up in Wales. We moved here when, when he was about four. So he could go to "*bettah*" schools.' – Tejinder raised an eyebrow but didn't chastise Amelia about her resentment of her parents' differing treatment of her and Steffan – 'He wouldn't have remembered it.'

'Oh that's interesting. Steffan talked about being mixed-race, but he didn't mention that.'

'Yeah, well, most people looked at us and saw "Chinese" not "Welsh",' said Amelia bitterly.

'I was born here but I loved hearing my mum talk about growing up in India. What was Wales like?' Tejinder asked smoothly.

*

The wind smelled foul as it penetrated the family car. Mam had insisted they left gaps at the top of the windows because it was such a long journey. The draught was messing up Amelia's hair. Steffan was happy playing with his bee plushy.

'Are we really living here now?' Amelia asked.

Dad gripped the steering wheel, as cars crowded around them. A dirty red bus loomed. He braked sharply as a black taxi cut them up. Horns beeped. Amelia shrank back in her seat, pressing her hands over her ears.

'Where are all the trees?' she asked loudly.

'They have better schools here,' said Mam from the front seat, face forward. 'Be logical about it, Amelia. We want to get Steffan off to the best start in life now we can afford it, don't we?'

Amelia thought. Her eyes stayed dry.

'Remember, Amelia.' Mam turned to look at her, smiling warmly. 'You have to be a good older sister.' She nodded at Steffan, who was now playing with his moth doll.

Her younger brother giggled, wriggling against his seat belt. He smiled at Amelia, and blew her a kiss.

This conversation had been going on too long; Amelia hadn't come here to have painful memories stirred up.

She dropped the wrinkled sugar sachet into its jar.

'I actually wanted to talk about Jay and … Steffan.'

Tejinder fiddled with her apron. 'I still think about him a lot.' She gestured with her cloth around the humble café. 'Steffan. He never got the chance to see this place fully up and running. Well …' She looked down at the cloth, folding it up carelessly. 'I'm not running the groups I'd hoped I'd be running. Haven't felt up to it.'

Amelia clenched her fists. 'And what about Jay?'

Tejinder wiped her eyes and sat down opposite Amelia, who pushed her own chair back a little, uncomfortable.

'Jay? Jay Ginige?'

Amelia nodded. *Now we were getting somewhere.*

'Poor boy. Thank goodness he called the police when he did!'

Amelia did a double-take. 'Excuse me?'

'You know, to let them know he thought it was Shaun. I

76

mean, I thought it was Shaun, but the police didn't take me seriously. Somehow Jay's anonymous message got through to them.' Tejinder's face hardened as she said this. She looked away and twisted her rag.

Amelia sensed something they could agree on. 'Yeah, weren't even treating it as a missing persons, right? Because Steffan was gay.'

Tejinder nodded violently, squeezing the life out of her rag.

'Didn't you think it was odd, though,' Amelia continued, 'That Jay didn't call straight away? He waited until weeks later, like?' She was impressed with how diplomatic she sounded.

Tejinder shrugged slowly. Looked down at her cloth in her lap, and untwisted it. 'It can be hard to do the right thing when you're used to not getting a fair hearing. And then: people think, no social media smoke, without the fire of a crime.'

'I just want answers. He kept quiet because of what Shaun had on him.'

Tejinder rubbed a hand around the base of her throat, and swallowed. 'Is it only a year until Shaun Flanagan's out?' She checked the street through the window in the door, which she locked. 'Can't believe he got away with claiming it were manslaughter! Especially not after the situation with his actual girlfriend.'

'I know there's more to it. There has to be. I mean, do you really believe my brother – out and proud – was paying a straight man for kinky sex, and that …' Amelia sniffed. Tapped her notebook from the trial, which she'd pulled out and placed on the table. 'If only we could know what really happened that day.' Amelia didn't have to force these tears. 'For my parents.'

Tejinder stopped faffing with the snacks. She turned her back to Amelia, adjusted a green photo frame from the shelf behind the till, and slowly stroked her duster over it. The photo was of an older woman who looked like her. She wiped at her eyes with her free hand. 'Nothing wrong if he had been paying for it. But he didn't need to.'

Mumbling something about '*Restorative Justice*', she tore some paper from the till. Scribbled on it, and handed it over.

Amelia put Jay's number into her Contacts.

18

Amelia

The desk's white paint was faded and chipped, and its shelves were lopsided. Amelia couldn't afford to splash out. She got up and kicked some of her dirty clothes off the middle of the floor and into the wardrobe's jurisdiction. It wasn't even a wardrobe, just one of those clothes rails with some drawers under one half of it. She couldn't face doing anything about the unmade bed.

Amelia checked she'd entered Jay's number correctly into her phone, and pressed *New Chat*.

He appeared in WhatsApp as *online*.

She'd reasoned with herself that it made sense to go home, let EmeraldSiren know, and think things through. Although she'd been searching for this opportunity for so long, there was no need to rush into anything. She felt like it was the night before an exam: she'd done all her revision, she was expected to do well, what was there to worry about?

Amelia breathed out. Her stomach heavy like slate.

Jay Ginige?

Her mouth went dry. Her eyes drifted, not for the first time, to her hockey stick poking up from the side of the bed. She scanned the jar in which she was keeping the infectious ticks she'd been studying. As if analysing the source of the illness that had made Steffan so vulnerable could help her think away her grief. She reached down to the unread self-help book on the floor.

A near-instantaneous reply gave her no chance of backing out.

Noah?

Her chest grew tight. She looked over at the small cluster of birthday cards on the window sill. There wasn't one from her parents.

No. This is about Steffan.

Typing …

Who is this?
You got me mixed up with someone else, mate. I don't know a Steffan

The tension in her head and neck drowned out her dry mouth and tight chest. How could you claim not to know the name of a person whose death you'd been linked to? Not revealing her identity would compel him.

Pure lies, that is.
I know about the Facebook messages to him you deleted.

Who is this?

Still playing the innocent. She would force him to make everything alright for once.

Tell me the truth.
What really happened when Steffan died?

I'm sorry about what happened, but it was an accident
Manslaughter, not murder. The judge said so
He was vulnerable because of his condition

The police had used Steffan's tick bite-induced anaemia, amongst other things, to justify treating his disappearance as 'non-suspicious'. All these people trading in words, not cold facts. It was alright for them. How could they live with themselves?

Is that really true?
I won't tell anybody.
Why'd you cover up for Shaun Flanagan? Was what he claimed true?

Her head pounded. She dropped her phone on the chipped desk. Someone had to be responsible. But what if he really had been nothing more than an innocent bystander?

I didn't. I pleaded guilty because I didn't have a choice

Her justice, his peace: there could be no attempt to reconcile the two if she accepted what he said.

Who is this?

19

Jay

The heat and humidity on the upper deck of the 161 ganged up on Jay, together with his guilt: he couldn't ignore the WhatsApp messages. He had felt panic like this before – he'd been, what, seven years old? A rare trip to the local pool, a change from football with his dad and brother. He'd ended up out of his depth, struggling for air, reaching for an inflatable that might save him. The rainbow plastic toy had cruelly bounced up out of the water the moment he'd hoped he had a grip on it, hurling him back in. He'd feared he would never breathe again.

He'd felt that panic again after what happened with Flat 401.

He felt it again now.

No. This is about Steffan.

At first, Jay genuinely didn't recognise the name – he'd pushed it out of his mind for so long, forcing himself to think of his former neighbour only as written initials on post: *S. Evans*. Too painful to think of him as a real person, someone Jay had—

I know about the Facebook messages to him you deleted.

Then he didn't want to believe it could be related to him.

Is that really true?

The police had been the first to put it so bluntly to him: 'So this Shaun Flanagan, a straight man you've never met, strangles your gay neighbour "accidentally" during a sex game gone wrong. *Which* Mr Flanagan had been paid for. He hides the body. And you had no idea what was going on in the flat whose window was right opposite yours?'

'No comment.'

'But then, for some reason, weeks later, you call to tell us that this Shaun Flanagan might be a murderer. Now, he says you knew all about these payments for sex, and so had agreed not to tell anyone about it.'

'No comment.'

'And we're expected to believe you weren't in on it? After you've deleted all your Facebook messages to the victim?'

'No comment.'

'What was in those messages, Mr Ginige?'

Jay wasn't proud. He'd had his reasons for delaying, and for not telling the police everything he'd seen that day. Telling the world about it wouldn't have made any difference. Wouldn't have saved a life. He glanced down through the window at a couple arguing on the pavement as the bus passed them by.

Wouldn't make any difference to change his story now.

Only Jay and one other person knew the unseen, grasping truth. He thought and dreamed about it every day and night. For a moment, he could see the tears on a woman's face as he left the courtroom. But he, too, knew what it was like to suffer. And he *was* sorry about how it had ended up. Unbearably sorry.

Jay squirmed on the uncomfortable bus seats, hard and scratchy right up against him. Were other passengers looking at him?

Who is this?

Jay looked up as the bus went across a roundabout. All these houses ... Who knew what happened behind their closed doors? Did anyone living there have a secret like he had? But he'd been scammed like this before: it was just someone chatting, winding him up. Just someone with nothing on him at all.

He tried to escape the emotions he'd let take over. He looked into the distance through the window again, not taking in the growing buildings as the bus plunged further into Woolwich.

He'd learned it was easier to keep quiet about his mistakes; a memory of Amma surfaced in his mind. Her screaming at him when she'd found the pieces of the vase he'd bumped with his elbow while dancing. She would have screamed at him even if he'd owned up straight away, instead of hiding the fragmented ceramic at the back of the wardrobe he'd shared with his brother. It was impossible to be good enough as the '*useless child*'.

Ugh. He'd missed his stop. He rang the bell, and jumped off at the next one.

Jay walked around the Woolwich Exchange construction site. The skeleton of the old covered Public Market, with its gleaming girders of criss-crossed and arched steel, would be reborn as the home of the new PictureHouse. The cinema screen itself was going to be underground. Jay looked down at his work clothes. He loved the thought of being able to escape underground. He'd have left Woolwich, though, by the time that was all finished. He'd be *Dan Lane*: creating his own life, his own story, just like the animator whose name he planned to copy.

Jay quickened his pace as he moved away from the newer part of town. The future was an open space. Solid, outside ground under his feet. The scentless open air washed over him. Ignoring the people out and about in the town centre, Jay rested his palm against his stomach. There was nothing in his way. Nothing that could expose him, nothing that could hold him back, nothing that could stop him flying forward into a fresh, sunlit, shimmering future.

He blocked the unknown number, and put his phone away.

He'd had a rare great shift at Timpson that day. So many customers smiling, giving him positive feedback. The best were those three blokes from Burrage: 'Haven't seen you guys for years! You remember that neighbour who kept trying to get people to join the neighbourhood watch? *"Please request a copy of the minuets via me."*' They'd all fallen about laughing.

Jay couldn't ignore the fact that the clock to his freedom was still ticking away, but now it felt like the countdown to New Year's instead of to the end of another exam he could never do well in, regardless, or perhaps because, of teachers' assumptions.

Noah being in the shop for his induction had been good too, Jay admitted. He was a friendly guy. *'So you work out, buddy?'*

Jay smiled as he turned on to Pembroke Street. Magda's was waiting for him with her warm, open welcome, her solid bricks compassionately waiting to take him in at the end of another British summer day. Her bright windows looking at him kindly, not penetrating too deep into his conscience.

Tejinder was sitting on the steps. Tejinder, who'd been one of the few people who'd visited him in prison. He guessed saving someone's life counted for something. Tejinder, who'd understood why he'd had to plead guilty. He guessed she'd appreciated that if he hadn't, he would have been on remand forever, locked up and waiting for a trial that would never have come.

Even someone who'd been on his side was shielding her eyes to look up at Jay on his approach. Was it the sun? Or mistrust?

So much for his second chance.

Even if the person who'd sent that Note and WhatsApped him was a troll who didn't know anything, Jay knew. Could never stop knowing. He knew what he'd really been doing at the time of the manslaughter. And what it meant about him.

His face deadened into an unwilling mask as he halted. He stared uneasily at the waiting figure. He couldn't escape the feeling of Tejinder's shadowed eyes.

Jay turned and walked away.

20

Then

Steffan

I feel a smile creep across my face as I see Jay again, re-treating into the isolated anonymity of his unlit apartment. I don't begrudge him what he must have seen through the window. Especially given what we've been chatting about on Facebook.

I actually feel a glow from having a bit of fun on FaceTime with a guy off Grindr. I'm not ready to meet anyone in the flesh yet. I'd feel panic. A panic that, somehow, it would end up like those nightclubs Tej told me about. Men pushing her up against the wall, their faces turning from fawning to feral, no longer full of desire but of self-hatred turned on her.

But I'm safe here, inside flat 401. No one can touch, control or hurt me.

My phone *dings*. I reply to Jay's guilty message:

Honestly, it's fine. I knew I hadn't closed the curtains.
It doesn't count as gay if you're just watching 😊
But you can't live your whole life just watching!

The icon teasing me with his strong-jawed face drops below my message almost immediately. *Typing* ... appears.

> *That's a relief. I really don't want to make you feel uncomfortable.*
> *Not going to go all Rear Window on you!*
>
> *Alfred Hitchcock, right?*
>
> *You know it? Such an awesome film, amazing piece of cinema! Those beats at the end ... You really don't know if he's going to kill off his protagonist or not*

I don't reply immediately; I'm struck by the passion he displays, and not sure how to meet it. Is he going to suggest watching it together? My chest feels tight, the room starts to close in.

> *Anyway, you don't want to hear about that.*
> *Tell me something about you, one of your trips?*

My breathing slows. Tej would tell me I should give him a chance: chatting like this is a good way to learn to trust men again. I type something about how I would like to hear more about his interest in old films. Then delete it.

> *Tromsø was one of my favourites. The Northern Lights aren't like how they show up on film.*
> *In real life they're like glowing dust cascading down.*
> *The light in the sky summons feelings out of you*

I stop, embarrassed at my OTT description.

You write so beautifully.

I wipe a tear from my eye at the memory of that trip with Tej and look out of my bedroom window. Jay presses his hand against the glass of his. From here, it looks as if he's smiling.

I scroll back up to some older messages.

So did they do that study on the Isle of Wight?

Wikipedia tells me a similar moth study was carried out on the Åland Islands, but that's Finland.

I bet all those researchers wore the proper kit in long grass!

Wish I'd never told you about that tick bite!

As I think about how going along with my ex and sleeping together outdoors led to my condition, I wonder: are there some mistakes so wrong, we cannot forgive or make them right?

21

Now

Jay

Jay watched the ducks lazing on the surface of Mulgrave Pond. Weird little body of water, tucked away behind tower blocks only ten minutes from the town centre. Better he'd come here than gone back into Magda's, the way he was feeling. Today, the silent pond was giving away a slight stink thanks to the sunlight burning down on it.

Who'd sent him those WhatsApp messages? Was it really the same person who'd sent him that Note?

He'd gone over what had happened five years ago so many times – police, lawyers, judge, prisoners, prison officers, probation officers – he didn't even know what he remembered, and what was made up by talking about it.

Jay kicked the dust uncomfortably. It wasn't his neighbour's fault Jay had been kept inside. Must have been awful, dying like that. Shaun's man. No, Shaun's ... *victim*. Hard to get the words right. But his neighbour had been a victim.

S. Evans. Still easier to think about him as just a set of initials. All that post delivered to Jay's flat by accident. Strange how the odd numbers had been in one tower, the evens in another directly opposite. Must have been a pain in the arse for the postman. It had been difficult for Jay to psych himself up and venture out into a world full of people waiting to judge him, just to put a few envelopes through the right letterbox.

'Jakey? It is you! Thought so.'

Jay jumped at Margaret's voice. He grabbed his hoodie: he couldn't deal with her gossip today.

'I didn't come over to pry. I like to feed the ducks after my home visit.'

Jay eyed her suspiciously. She was scooping up bird seed from a bag hanging off her wheelchair. He lowered himself back down on the bench. The wood was warm. Margaret scattered handfuls of seed liberally over the ground by the edge of the pond as the ducks sped towards her. She looked happy. The noise of their quacking quarrelling even made Jay smile.

'So who are you visiting here?' he asked, eyes on the ducks. 'One of your patients?' He guessed the clue was in the job title: *Community* Psychiatric Nurse. He wished her visits had done more for Amma; now, she must be approaching the end of her career.

Nodding, Margaret waved the bag over the ducks, emptying out any last treats for them, before packing it away.

'Jakey, listen… Have you ever thought about sharing your side of the story? I know someone who works at the *News Shopper*.'

Jay laughed.

Margaret was looking at him earnestly.

Seriously? Jay shook his head.

'I haven't got some burden to get off my chest. Thanks though.'

He contemplated the ducks for a bit. A while after the sceptical buzz of Margaret's wheelchair had faded into the distance, he took himself back to Magda's.

Everyone is going to know what you really did was the only one waiting for him again. The Note an unwanted guest he couldn't get rid of.

Jay felt dizzy at the uncertainty. What Amma, his brother, his few friends from before thought of him could change like *that*, if they knew the truth. If they knew what memories still toiled in the basement of his mind, still banged on a door he desperately held shut, still screamed to be released into the searing light – the image of him they had in their mind would degrade even further. What they must think was already bad enough.

He pushed against that door in his mind the only way he knew how: telling himself he *hadn't* been responsible for a death. He hadn't been responsible for a *death*. He hadn't been *responsible* for a death. Saying it to himself three times to make it feel more real, as if by magic he could tidy up his own mind and feelings the same way he tidied up pens and paper on the counter at work. Shaun had said it all happened so quickly. And Jay never actually touched him. Jay's mind and body slowed down as he injected this reassurance into himself.

And even if he'd known that what he'd seen would prove fatal, what could he have done? If he'd called an ambulance, it would have been too late – especially given how long it took them to come now. And what could he realistically have achieved by getting involved? Shaun had looked like a pretty strong guy – tall, with tight muscles bulging all over.

'*The evidence suggests death occurred within seconds,*' the prosecution had said.

Jay remembered how Tejinder had done door-to-door before the police had. How bitter she'd been, turning away when Jay told her he didn't know anything, saying the police weren't taking it seriously. Jay could believe that.

Going online when he felt like this was automatic. *#LGBTRights* was a good one. Easy to find good people's posts to like. Assuage the guilt, by association.

Will I ever be able to walk down the street at night holding my boyfriend's hand without having to check who's around?

Like.

I hate that guys like me need to think about this stuff. Exhausting.

Like.

Was out with my son, he looked at another guy the wrong way, got catcalled. Grim.

Like, despite the hint of '*as a father*'.

As a woman and as a mother, I just don't want my children being exposed to—

This sounded like a job for the downvote button. See? He was a good person, too; every post he responded to wasn't just signalling his virtue – it was the same as if he'd carried out a good deed himself.

The white envelope wasn't buying any of this. It knew. It didn't matter that it had lost its stickiness due to how many times he'd opened, removed and reinserted the Note. Its contents said what they'd said. He'd done what he had done. He didn't want to know what kind of person that made him. What kind of person people would see if they knew. His rotten guts spilling out onto an unforgiving gravestone.

His memory collided with times he'd been told off for something he hadn't done, or all his friends did, or he knew his brother had got away with. None of those past punishments comparable to the aftermath of that football match at thirteen – Dad happy to let the sharks surround him. Sticks and stones breaking his bones. Cowering on the dirty, wet floor of empty stadium toilets.

He shook his head, and clenched his fists, to get rid of the memories.

Go. To. Hell.

He sank down on his bed again. Wiped the spit from the side of his mouth with a trembling hand. Began to pick up the pieces of the Note he'd shredded in his frenzy.

The bin area stank as the doubtful setting sun peered over the back wall. At the recycling centre, did they sort through the glass, the plastic, the paper? What if someone picked out the pieces of the Note and put it back together? What if they followed it back to him? A broken magnifying glass over a broken man.

As he scattered the evidence into the scarred grey mouth of the bin, even the empty air spilling his secrets, the black metal gate that opened onto the street behind him squealed, and footsteps entered in. But the Note was gone. He'd buried it. Same as with those prank WhatsApp messages.

Turning, he drew a slow, uncertain smile. Sagged against the side of the bin.

As Tony lit up a cigarette, Jay wondered what he'd need to do next to keep his secrets safe and his freedom alive.

'Alright, mate,' Jay said. 'You got my message, then?'

22

Amelia

Amelia watched as Mam made the tea. Before actually trying to flush Jay out, she'd been able to imagine her parents crying, hugging her, speaking Welsh again. She'd fantasised about them finally accepting that, despite Steffan being gone, she was still their child, and just as worthy of their love. But now, she struggled to even picture Jay in her parents' lounge, saying how sorry he was.

She could still picture that last email to Steffan. I told you not to trust him.

She felt guilty. Despite all their parents' preferential treatment, Steffan hadn't had a perfect life either. But what could she do about it? Her own ignorance and powerlessness had thrown her into a pit, where the intuition she'd been sure was solid now cursed her like broken glass in her back. The problem of actually pursuing a dream was what to do when it didn't come true.

Amelia looked at poor, long-suffering Mam, waiting for the kettle to boil. She looked tired. Straggly hair, badly applied make-up, red eyes.

'I messaged him,' Amelia said.

Her parents' kettle needed descaling: it made a crackling noise as it heated up. That wasn't right.

'I messaged him yesterday,' Amelia repeated.

'Who, dear?' Mam looked up.

'Jay Ginige, the guy who helped Shaun Flanagan …'

Mam flinched at the name.

'The other guy who was involved.'

'Why?'

Every time Amelia was asked this simple question – whether it was a colleague, a friend, an ex – she felt like she was drowning.

'We can't go on like this,' she choked. 'Dad said after the trial that he'd been let off too lightly. I thought if I could speak to him he'd at least tell us what really happened.'

She was doing her best. Why didn't the words make sense, why couldn't they communicate how she felt sure that being able to understand what had happened would make things right?

'Before the trial, you said you felt sorry for him being locked up for so long,' chided Mam.

'That's when he'd claimed he'd not been involved in a crime!'

'To be honest, dear, the police didn't exactly do a great job by our Steffan.' Mam stared at the grey surface of the tea.

At his trial, Shaun had looked defeated. Heartbroken. But none of that from Jay.

'I thought if I could get him to tell us what really happened, you and Dad would go back to the way you used to be' – Mam made a strange noise: half sob, half exhalation – 'Not just sitting in here all day waiting for nothing. I've tried so hard.'

Mam hunched over the chipped counter, her back to Amelia.

'Amelia, your father's treatment, he—'

Bang! The window shook. A pale, ghostly outline watched them. Mam clutched her chest. Amelia went over and looked into the garden. There was nothing below the window – the bird that had crashed into it must have survived and flown off. Sometimes they flew with such force that they injured themselves, their pitiful bodies broken on the patio. Amelia looked at her ashen-faced Mam.

'I'll get the tea Mam, you go through.'

Alone in the kitchen, Amelia checked her phone again. Nothing else from EmeraldSiren. She doom-scrolled through tired-out conspiracy theories about Jay's deleted Facebook messages to Steffan.

DEFINITELY financial. One time, I got scammed by this 'masseuse', through a fake PayPal account.

My mate deleted some to his ex. Just a normal argument, but he didn't want her gossiping to her mates, you know?

I'm not racist, I just think, statistically, it's plausible the two of them were involved in that kind of working arrangement.

Their parents had never approved of Steffan pursuing his dream of caring for animals. She rummaged in her bag, dumped on a kitchen chair, and pulled out a plastic tube which housed one of the diseased ticks from her collection. Held the disgusting, wriggling bug up to the light for inspection. Had the consequences of an encounter with a pest as small as this really proved fatal? The pathologist's report had been so factual. Could barely tell them about the biology. She needed some certainty to push the other scenarios out of her mind.

Amelia removed the brown NHS envelopes from the tray before loading it up with teacups and sugar.

Even with the safety and power granted by anonymity, was pursuing Jay the right thing to do now? Peter kept saying she should stop focusing on being right, and do what was right for her and her family. He was trying to be a supportive boyfriend, but what was right? As she carried the teas into the living room, she scanned the old man. Wondered how long he had left. She didn't want to imagine how she'd feel if she wasted their last months trying to find out what Shaun and Jay really did that day. Maybe she should give up on her vendetta?

23

Jay

Jay had felt uncomfortable talking in the bin area after Tony had let himself in through the black gate: it was weird to think this about a hostel but, after how good she'd been to him, he didn't want Magda to see him with the other offender. Especially not after what Jay had invited him there for.

'Let's take a walk to the square,' Tony had suggested.

They'd passed the new cafés and restaurants near the square, the ones pushing out the bookies, 'ethnic' super-markets and pound-shop variants. The restaurants were busy that time of the evening. On the giant TV in the centre of the square, a scrolling screen of local news cast its doubtful light over the patches of grass, turned-off water feature and polished, angled stone.

Tony lolled easily on the bench next to Jay, face red and sweaty. The stench of alcohol rolled off him and over Jay. Jay checked but no one was looking. It wasn't completely dark, but in the dim light people focused on those closest to them, so as far as anyone else knew or cared, he and Tony were just two more bodies enjoying being outside. No reason to think they had a past, and a present purpose, which meant they shouldn't mingle.

'It ain't easy, it ain't easy for sure. At least you got good old Timpo's.' Tony waved his Carlsberg at Jay as if to cheers his employer.

'Yeah, it's alright. My boss Esther is good.'

'Ooh, Esther!' Tony giggled and then belched. Took another sip.

Jay frowned. Fiddled with the ring-pull. 'I can't betray them, Tony. I can't be in on this job.'

'Who said anything about a job?' Tony held his hands up, one innocent, one holding a pretty much empty can. 'I'm just saying, the Council still haven't got round to installing CCTV here.' He coughed. 'After they "modernised" this part of the square.' He drained his can, crushed it, pulled another out of the six pack and ripped off its ring pull. Tossed the metal tab away, a slight clatter on the grey stone. 'Just like outside of Timpo's.' He took a satisfied gulp from the new can.

Jay's eyes darted to Tony's gaunt face. The experienced criminal glugged down half the can, looking out at the phone shop opposite, and continued:

'Although, if you're saying that note's been followed by some nasty WhatsApp messages …'

Jay's heart froze in his throat.

A moth had become caught in a web suspended across a corner of the bench. It was about to free itself when a massive spider darted out from the side. The moth struggled but the predator manipulated it quickly, pulling more and more web from its back until the moth was completely smothered in the white thread. Jay couldn't take his eyes off the slaughter.

He swallowed tepid beer, turning his attention back to Tony. 'Didn't you learn anything from Group? We've got to take responsibility. Got to get ourselves straight.'

Tony cracked his knuckles, looked to the side, and spat

backwash. Jay shrank back at the similarity to Dad. He swore Tony had never done that in Group.

'There's people like us, and people not like us, that's it. What does it even matter which "category" you're in? People gonna treat you the same. You're gonna die at the end anyway. Just don't get caught. That's my motto.'

Tony gestured around the square.

'We're free now. Who cares what we're *supposed* to do? You only got one life to live, do it. Specially when you already screwed it all up.'

Another flash of memory. Amma getting him ready for a rare Sri Lankan family gathering, telling him to be a good boy, to be like his brother, to be normal. Jay shook it away.

'I just want to be like other people,' he mumbled.

'Me too, son. Me too. It's not like I treated her that badly.'

Jay shifted uncomfortably on the bench. 'I'm sure you'll get to see your kid again one day. But maybe you—'

Tony crushed the now-empty can in one fist, and tossed it aside. 'She's got him! She grassed me up to the police and ran off with him!'

Jay rubbed the back of his head awkwardly. Tony snatched up his final can. 'Just don't end up a grass, son. Nothing worse.' He sighed, holding up a palm to ward off Jay's attempt at an interruption. 'What you did to that bastard Shaun weren't grassing. He's a killer. He deserved it. And I know the police fitted you up alright. You need to have less of a tan, like me!' He coughed. 'You saw something suspect, and put two and two together. Fair play to ya.' He cracked open the can. 'You seemed up for it when you texted me.'

A memory of Amma again, laughing with the rest of her family, Jay on the outside because the funny story had been in Sinhala, not English. He was always on the outside. Even his English cousins, on Dad's side, had asked him things like, *'So do you celebrate Christmas?'* They'd never meant anything by it, but it hadn't helped the feeling of being outside a window, looking in.

This life wasn't all he could hope for. It had been an accident, hadn't it? He didn't deserve to be lumped in with real criminals.

He got his phone out. East Cowes looked like a good place to live. The free air, the birds coming and going from whatever country they pleased, the salty, vinegary chips. Changing your name by deed poll was still only a couple of hours' pay. His heart rate and breathing slowed. Just three more weeks, and two more sessions with Olu. Yes, his anxiety about someone being out there who knew the truth about him had compelled him to contact Tony again, but if he wanted to become *'Dan Lane'*, he couldn't risk anything that might cause Olu to have him recalled.

A snatch of conversation snapped his head up.

'... not worth the danger of messing with Shaun ...'

'... Don't matter he's still inside ...'

'... Yeah. He'd find a way of getting us. We'd be ...'

The Lynas brothers were crossing the square. Jay flicked up his grey hoodie, hunched over. The youths looked at him, pointed and talked, but moved on. Must be easier to bother him when he's sitting alone on his lunch break.

Tony drained his latest can, eyes narrowed.

'You sure you're doing alright? If anyone's giving you hassle, I can get them off your back.' He shook the can like a collection tin, checking to see what was left inside. 'For old time's sake.' He slumped back against the bench.

Jay shrugged, kept his hood up. Took a sideways glance at the drunk ex-offender. Eyes closed and mouth open, clothes smelling shabby in the dark, empty hand hanging limply over the fallen can: Tony didn't look like much of a threat to anybody's licence conditions. And he always knew someone who knew someone.

Jay scrolled through the image gallery on his phone. Way back to the photos of his induction material.

Zoomed in on the details of Timpson's security arrangements.

24

Cathy

Cathy put her phone down. Couldn't believe she'd just had her first ever therapy session! It still felt strange to be able to use her phone whenever she wanted. And for it not to be full of threatening messages from Ant. She looked around her room. Peered out at the signs of life through the window. A group of lads drinking early. A suited and booted defendant clearing off after court up the road. Old ladies going in and out of the charity shop.

As Cathy peered out, the bright light hurt her eyes. The sounds were loud and overwhelming. She could stay in, safe. Didn't need to do no more than survive.

Cathy's phone beeped. *Your next session will be on …* When her therapist, Alice, had described how they'd have one brief call every day for one or two weeks, she'd said this way of delivering therapy was 'intensive'. No word of a lie.

Cathy logged in to the website. Some of it was hard to understand, but the videos and exercises made sense. Even if they were a bit scary. Not trying to be funny – they were terrifying, to be honest. Explaining how, to overcome trauma, she had to work through it. Not go around, or away from it.

But Alice was right: being allowed to text her therapist made Cathy feel like she could push herself.

She snatched up her phone, and a chocolate bar for courage.

Only a few hours in to therapy, and now she was stood opposite a school. In a walled-in corner opposite but not near the main entrance. Standing right outside would look weird. The green branches and poisonous orange berries overhead shaded her a bit from the summer heat.

Maybe Alice had been right about not rushing things. What if it all felt too much? *'Sometimes, when we have been through a traumatic experience, places that remind us of the trauma can bring on feelings similar to those we experienced at the time.'* School hadn't been the worst. But it reminded her of the life she'd lost because of Ant. This place brought it back. The uniforms, the noises kids made – laughing, screaming, chattering – the parents, the signs.

Despite the agitation, she was building up the courage to stay. **You can do it!** Cathy hadn't known there could be a 'cycle of trauma'. Alice was giving her the strength, and the tools, to break it.

Cathy peeled sweaty hair away from her eyes. She started the breathing exercise, following the instructions her therapist had sent, but couldn't focus on it.

Ant had been so into her looks at school. Liked to keep his own hair clippered short. Ant had said, if she'd loved him, she wouldn't have gone out to celebrate her own GCSEs when he'd done so badly. The markers probably had been unfair on Ant.

Ant, Ant, Ant.

Suddenly, screaming. It wasn't her, it wasn't Cathy, it was some of the kids. Cathy froze to the spot. She felt like she was being held down, dragged by her hair. Fear soaking her body, unsafety bleeding through her guts. She wanted to run back down the halls of her school and pull her younger self to where she could never be hurt again.

In front of the school, a boy was towering over a girl, shaking a brown paper bag at her. Ant and his little brown bags, with his little green pills, and his little pink … Cathy would remember nothing afterwards. She would always just try to turn a blind eye to the sore feeling between her legs.

Cathy ran across the road, over to the group of children. She pulled the boy away from the girl and slapped his paper bag onto the pavement.

'Don't give her those! That's dangerous!'

'What the hell do you think you're doing?' One of the mums stepped right up to Cathy.

Alice had said if anything triggered her, she should look hard for what was different between her flashbacks and what was really happening. This would help put the memories away. The girl was a little girl, Cathy had been a teenager, the kids were sharing sweets, Ant had made her take the little green pills in the—

'I'm so sorry, I thought …'

Cathy found herself crying before she even got close to the hostel. Her tears were hot as she jabbed her hand at her face to get rid of them. Alice was right. She'd been so scared. She'd been in danger. After one really bad time with Ant, even her mum had said she needed to go to hospital. The doctors had been like: *'those drugs could've killed you if you'd had a medical condition.'* But that was in the past. Now, she could move on from what that man had done to her.

Cathy popped her head into the kitchen on her way back to her room. Jay was standing by the hissing kettle. At least there was one man she could trust.

'Alright?'

He didn't answer. Cathy ran her hands over her face again, making sure it was dry. She stepped through the doorway.

'You alright, Jay?'

He turned to her, pale. Wordlessly, slipped his phone out his pocket. Showed it to her.

Need to visit you at home. Come to office first. 0900 tomorrow?
Need to review the conditions of your licence.
Olu

'Jay … What did you do?'

25

Amelia

'That's an outrageous accusation!'

Janice adjusted her glasses. 'People have seen you, Amelia.'

'I went into the stationery cupboard. Doesn't mean I'm stealing envelopes!'

Janice pulled at her jacket. 'And you came in late again today.' She gestured at her screen.

'I needed a mental health day: my father's cancer treatment isn't going well!'

'Bit early in your probation period for a mental health day— Sorry, that came out wrong.'

Amelia boiled as Janice continued:

'Of course, we value staff mental health as much as physical health. That's why we have free resilience training, mindfulness apps, the lunchtime walking group ...' Janice's face took on a glazed-on rapture as she recited. 'But we also need to take into account the needs of the whole company. You're letting the team down, Amelia.'

'I've delivered a load of parcels this afternoon. And let all visitors in after no more than one buzz.'

'Too little, too late, Amelia. I'm sorry, but I am going to have to bring the review of your probation forward.'

So unfair. She'd been doing really well, this week.

In response to a tenant request, she hurried up to the third floor. Wrenched the top off the coffee machine. Tipped the pot full of used grounds into the composting bin, the caffeinated smell hitting her. She allowed herself five minutes next to the machine as it ran through its cleaning cycle, hot air and water steaming through various pipes, before popping into the stationery cupboard on her way back to the front desk.

She was getting annoyed about only knowing her contact as 'EmeraldSiren'. What could her job be that she couldn't even tell Amelia her real name? Still, this was useful info. From looking on the internet, she hadn't really understood exactly what a probation officer did. But if what EmeraldSiren said was true, if Jay failed to meet any of the conditions of his probation, he would be sent back to prison.

Maybe she could use that fear of his probation officer.

If Janice would let her find the time.

Was it worth going through all that?

Another buzz on the intercom.

'I'm here to see Janice.'

Amelia looked the tall, slim, blonde over. Very well turned out. Like for a job interview. Amelia had never seen Janice being so friendly.

Janice caught Amelia looking. 'My friend wanted to see where I worked.'

Amelia kept looking even when they withdrew to the other side of the ground floor. Waited until they were at a safe distance to pull out what she'd been writing from under its hiding place of legitimate post.

'No power failures today, then!'

Amelia slid a hand over the paper she had been writing on, before looking up at Peter in confusion.

'From the other day? When the builders dug through the cable? Come on, Ams, let's call a truce.' He stuck out a hand. His body still slim but toned under his lumberjack shirt.

She was still pissed off at him for not being supportive enough. Dealing with his request for a room-booking (which could have been made by email, if you asked her) didn't stop her from overhearing Janice: 'Yes, that's the current receptionist.'

After they'd all left her alone, Amelia went into the post room. She shut the door behind her and kicked the cardboard box of recycling lying at her feet. She'd never really got on with her father, but he was still her dad. She couldn't remember her early years, but things had been a bit better when she'd been an only child. He'd still been gruff, but there had been the odd pat on the head, or kind word for a gold star or good report. Now she could hear the rattle in his chest. See the way his skin looked greyer. Hear through his gritted teeth and her mother's dried-up tears how the father she'd never had was going to die. Amelia didn't know whether to believe Mam saying Dad had a good prognosis. It wouldn't surprise her if she was cut out of death as well as life in that family.

She smothered a scream into sullen silence. Dad had given up smoking before Steffan had even been conceived. Would she be able to get him closure before— She kept her mind busy and her emotions at bay by sending EmeraldSiren another message. Her doubt about pursuing Jay sank beneath the weight of her need to act, not to accept: Jay was the person who could tell her what she needed to raise the truth up into the light. There was no way he only told the police to investigate Shaun because he'd seen him at a fish and chip shop, and recognised him as someone in the building around the time of Steffan's disappearance. Jay must have known more.

She slipped the white envelope in amongst the office building's post. Everyone used office stationery for personal needs, didn't they?

III

26

Jay

Jay couldn't wait to finish work, and get away from the sun, as he slaved away under its gaze in the shopfront. The shop's open door let in the noise of the high street but not much air. His sweat marked his uniform. The smell of leather and shoe polish was oppressive, and the heat ganged up on him with the exhaustion from another night's sleep that had had holes poked into it by unforgiving nightmares.

'Yeah, sometimes Probation has to tick a few boxes. Don't let it get to you,' Esther said.

'But seriously, it was such a waste of time.' Jay's recurrent anxiety about being recalled on the spot had eventually dispersed like dust in a beam of sunlight when *nothing had happened* at Olu's last-minute appointment. All that dread following the message about a home visit and reviewing the conditions of his licence, and *nothing* had happened. Nothing had *happened*. The relief threatened to overwhelm him. 'Thanks again for letting me come in late, boss.' Jay was on his knees, restocking the polish.

'No problem. Noah covered your arse.' Esther looked at Jay meaningfully.

'I mean, when we had the interview at the Probation

Office, you got it, he was literally ticking boxes. Printed off this massive form – heard of climate change, mate? – took an hour, most of my answers were 'No', and he must have known what I was going to say already.'

Jay moved on to the laces. Shoved them and their plastic packaging onto the rail.

'Not like I even did anything. Over once a month for two and a half years I've had to go in there, tick their boxes, attend their groups, do whatever. And for what?'

'We've both been in prison, Jay. We were put there for a reason.' Esther wasn't angry but was firm. She bagged up a set of two-pound coins.

Jay slowed down as he restocked the chamois. Who had he seen in the last week? Tony, Olu, Tejinder, Cathy ... He remembered the nearly-empty list of contacts in his phone. One of them was Esther's number. He felt relieved he hadn't given Tony any info that could hurt Timpson. Even if that had frustrated the older man.

'The thing is ... Do you think I'm a bad person?'

Esther stopped bagging coins up.

'You made a mistake.' She sighed. 'Don't make you a bad person. Like I said, we've all been there. We just need to do the right thing now on.'

Most of the soft cloths looked the same but Jay took his time dividing and sorting them onto the low shelves. He laughed.

'I was like, it's so basic, I've met my conditions. I'm going to make it, I'm going to get out of here, you know what I'm saying?'

Unusually for her, Esther didn't laugh. 'Olu seemed like a good guy.' Jay quietened down, as if he were listening attentively to an aunty. 'This "urgent" session, and then coming back with you for a home visit? Probably just his

113

boss pressuring him. I remember when I was on licence, my probation officer always had so many targets to hit. And they still in that cramped, smelly office block?'

Jay felt guilty; he remembered Esther warmly meeting Olu when he'd visited Timpson to review its 'Approval' when he'd taken Jay onto his caseload. Olu's attempts to form a connection with him had been intermittent but more noticeable than those of his previous POs.

Esther went on: 'Getting to the end of licence is only the first bit, Jay. You've got the whole rest of your life.'

'Yeah, and that's the good bit!'

There had been a point at their meeting when Olu had asked about details of Jay's 'crime' again, and Jay had had to repeat what he'd come up with before. Olu wasn't really listening, searching through his paperwork … But Jay had destroyed the Note and blocked the message sender. He had nothing to worry about. Nothing was going to keep him down. He was safe.

He laughed again.

'When he came to the hostel? I'll tell you another thing! Cathy was there. You know my friend Cathy? I tell you, the way those two looked at each other!' Jay mimed goo-goo eyes.

He and Esther laughed; this gossip was more up her street. He'd never felt this free at work before – maybe overcoming wariness could be worth it. A customer entered the shop before he could fill Esther in. A man asking about watch-strap replacement. Esther served him, racing through his questions, and then replacing the worn-out, black leather band.

As soon as the customer was gone, Esther jumped back on the gossip train. 'So what happened, then?'

Jay sat back, giving his knees a break. The shared laughter was intoxicating.

'She came round when he was in my room. He was supposed to just examine the room, check I lived there – for real, where else was I going to be living? Then Cathy came by. They stared at each other, real close. Then stopped. Started talking at me over each other, looked so embarrassed.'

'Maybe she thought he was a … "friend" of yours?'

'Nah, she was interested in him. He's so much younger than her as well! And I reckon your probation officer shouldn't be checking out your mate!' Jay started laughing again.

Esther smiled as she finished totalling the till. They both smiled at the Asian man entering the shop. But when Jay saw who he was, his cheeky grin disappeared. He snapped his eyes away. Kept them on photo albums, frames, keyrings. Jay concentrated so hard on lining the stock up just right, he didn't hear what the customer was after. Just the sound of his voice, and Esther's cheery patter as she helped him with whatever he wanted. The faintness of Jay's vision, and the buzzing in his ears, obscured the man right up until after he'd lingered at the doorway and then left the shop.

The muscles in Jay's thighs burned from squatting down. Sweat tormented both exposed and concealed parts of his body. Last time he'd seen the customer's face – his brother's face – was Christmas 2018. He'd been dressed more like an adult this time, trying to look proper. Funny how much Jay had copied him when they were kids. Getting into the same music, the same games, the same TV shows. It hurt not to be a part of it.

A different man was entering the shop now. Golden skin, dark hair. Jay froze, his gut churning as the new customer went over to Esther to get served. It wasn't him. It wasn't S. Evans. It wasn't: the customer just looked like him. He was asking for something. Something to do with mobile phone repairs. Esther could help him with that, just give her a moment.

It had been hot that day five years ago too. Sticky. Everything seemed quiet now. It was only the three of them.

Jay regretted thinking and acting as if he could just enjoy himself at work like a normal person. Whether he wanted these memories or not, they were going to come back. Day or night, he had no control over what he was feeling, thinking, experiencing. Pushing his neighbour, including his name, out of his mind couldn't make him come back, wouldn't stop him from coming back. Would he keep going on like this forever? That look on his face, that airless cry for help. *Help. Help me.*

'Help me get this down from the top shelf, would you, Jay?' Esther repeated.

Jay looked up from the raw, intrusive memories to the here and now. The customer was actually a lot older than he'd misperceived. Unsteadily, still not seeing clearly, he got up and helped Esther slide the cardboard box of flat batteries off and down. He stayed behind the counter to warily watch as his boss replaced the battery, charged the customer, and sent him off, good as new.

Esther pushed the box back up onto the shelf unaided.

'It's bringing it down that's the tricky part. Tip it too far and the batteries go all over you.' She sorted a few more things at the till. Wiped the counter down. Checked something on her phone.

'He looked a bit like that Steffan, didn't he?' she asked carefully. 'The man Shaun Flanagan strangled?'

Jay barely nodded. Esther checked the till again. Collected up today's five job applications with a sigh.

'For years I couldn't go back to Deptford High Street. Where I had my road rage? First, I didn't want to admit

I'd hurt anyone. Then I was too ashamed.' Esther gave him a sad, understanding smile. 'We all done something. You got to make up for it and move on. But you can't do that if you pretend like it never happened.' She put the pile of job applications back on the counter, and leaned towards him. 'Confessing what I'd done, making reparations … It was …'

Jay couldn't look away.

'Best decision of my life.'

Jay wouldn't let the tears come. He'd been right not to get this happy at work. Not to let his guard down. But he heard what Esther said:

'We're almost done for today. Go home early.'

Waiting for the 161 again. Staring at the pavement. A small brown glass bottle was propped up by the bin. White paper things that weren't even envelopes were starting to catch his eye.

Surely, he didn't have to go back there? How could that help put these memories and feelings away, put this shame behind him? Didn't he risk digging up the secret that Flat 401 and its window could reveal about him?

But then, he did admire the courage Cathy had proudly told him about. He didn't fully understand how going back places could shut memories away, even after she'd told him about her visit to the school, shown him the therapy website. But maybe if doing it was helping her …

'Jay.'

Jay slowly looked up to face his brother.

'I can't be seen talking to you. Amma would kill me. But you good? Your job and that alright?'

Jay swallowed. Felt his eyes prick. 'Yeah, I'm good.' He swallowed again. 'I'm almost at the end of Probation.'

His brother looked around. 'Listen … I can't promise

anything, but you know what Amma's like. Five years is five years, whether you're inside or out. Just get to the end of that, don't stir up any more trouble for yourself.'

Jay stepped towards his brother, arms spreading.

His brother stepped back. Raised a hand in farewell, and walked off.

Jay realised the last customer from the shop was waiting for the same bus. He was on his newly repaired phone. He was speaking, he was alive, he didn't sound the same as Jay's neighbour from Flat 401. Jay noticed it didn't bother him so much to see the man for a second time. When he got on the bus, he went up to the sunlit upper deck, holding onto the handrail. His avoidance of what, deep down, he knew he'd seen that day was like a snake eating its own tail.

27

Cathy

Cathy matched her pace to Jay's. He was slowing down the closer the blocks of flats came. They didn't look like she'd imagined. A couple of more normal, smaller buildings, made of original bricks, had character. But this one was a u-shape of painted grey and metal, with a glass-covered foyer in the centre connecting its two towers. Round the corner sat a red building with fancy rectangular windows and black balconies. In the distance lay the tallest blocks, the newbuilds, with their multi-coloured cladding. They spiked up into the sky, threatening to tear the clouds. So this was where the farmers' market and that was? She'd not missed much by staying out of this part of Woolwich until today.

'You used to live here?' she asked, pointing at the red building with her thumb. Jay shook his head. He nodded at the grey twin towers.

Cathy was pleased with herself. She weren't constantly looking over her shoulder, only able to focus on where the next man might be coming from and if he looked dangerous. Her therapist said she was making good progress, despite her outburst at the school. Cathy reread the messages from Alice on her phone.

Well, he's said he wants to put memories of a
difficult experience behind him too, I understand?
If he gets triggered, I wonder if you could use what
you've learned to help him. Sometimes helping
others can strengthen our compassion towards
ourself.

Had Jay been triggered? He was looking all over the place. Kept swallowing and licking his lips. Cathy owed him for showing her the therapy poster and that. And she felt bad she'd jumped to conclusions about his probation officer coming round. She wondered if this would be her chance to get him to reassure her about what he'd really done. Pleading guilty to a crime he hadn't committed sounded mad, especially if he'd never actually hurt anyone. But then, she'd had months of the police shaking their heads at her lack of evidence. The justice system didn't always work how it was supposed. And forget about Social Services.

Jay was staring at one flat, at the top of the right-hand grey tower. A delivery driver was at the block's door.

'Is that where you used to live?' Cathy asked. She'd tried to find out exactly what his plan was, but all Jay had said? *'Moral support.'* She hoped he wouldn't get angry. She pulled her cardigan around her.

'No. That's where it happened. Flat 401,' Jay replied, the words limping out into the air like a woman staggering onto the beach after freshly escaping drowning. Were those tears in his eyes?

The delivery guy gave up pressing the intercom button and rattling the door. He threw up his hands and dumped the tumble of unwanted parcels off his trolley. Muttering to himself, he wheeled the trolley past Cathy and Jay to his van. He stared back at Cathy. She held his stare for a moment but then looked away to the bank of letterboxes inside the foyer, chewing her lip. No need to overreact, he was just a bloke doing his job. No danger. Total short-arse. He hadn't looked like Ant at all. Except in the eyes.

Jay sat on a low wall that housed some red flowers. The kind of flower you'd get in a proper garden. He rubbed each hand with the other, staring at the pavement, his back to his old building. Cathy thought the sunlit older buildings opposite were beautiful. They gave off the sense of people from another time, lives lived. Community. The newer blocks were no different from the area around the hostel: lumps of concrete that people didn't live in, they just inhabited.

Cathy decided to take a risk. She sat down next to Jay.

'One time, my ex. Ant.' She shivered as she said his name. 'He almost drowned me.'

Jay shifted on the wall. Looked at her, then at the pavement again as she kept going.

'We go to Brighton for the day. It's so mad, seeing all them people. So much skin. I swear I didn't mean to check the guy out. His skin was so pale but his abs ...'

'What happened?' Jay was less hoarse, concern for someone other than himself in his eyes again.

'I know Ant's caught me looking but he don't say anything. I think maybe he'll forget about it, 'cos it's such a sunny day. But then he persuades me, right, to paddle in the sea with him. I'm worried about leaving our ... stuff alone but he's smiling and laughing, telling me 'relax' and ...'

Cathy wiped her eyes with her sleeve, her voice cracking. She felt like her face didn't know what to do with itself. She couldn't smile at the warm temperature in the memory. She knew what was going to happen next. Pulled her cardigan around her to keep out the cold, wiped the salty water from her forehead. But looking at her hand, she could see there wasn't any water on it, was there? She was out with Jay in the city, not surrounded by the sea.

'He kept holding me down and pulling me back up. *"D'ya like what ya see? Do ya?"* In, out, in, out. I didn't know when it was going to stop. I was begging. Nobody heard.' She sniffed, stuck her hands in her pockets. '*"He not too doughy for ya?"* All the noise. Kids playing, crowds on the beach, seagulls, splashing, water in my ears. That horrible choking feeling, you know?'

Jay almost touched his own throat but then moved his hand back down again.

'I thought I was gonna die.' Cathy coughed. '*"Cheat"*, he says. And then drops me in the water and walks off back to shore. Acts like nothing's happened when I come back. *"Babes"*, he calls me. Asks me if I want an ice cream.'

Cathy didn't know where this story was going or what it had to do with Jay. But for the first time, she felt something other than shame. She'd always been faithful to Ant. Despite everything he'd done to her. Always going on about it being a 'dog-eat-dog world'. Bastard. She wiped her eyes with a sleeve again. *Bastard.* She was choking on the word, choking on her tears, choking on all them years of fear and hatred and disgust she didn't deserve.

'Bastard,' she said out loud. 'Men are bastards.'

Jay agreed slowly: 'Men like that *are* bastards.'

He put his firm arm around her, squeezed gently, and then let go. He blew out his cheeks and hunched over, hands clasped. 'This is where it happened. He died. Up there.' Jay half turned at the waist, pointed at the right-hand top-floor flat, then turned to confess to the pavement. 'I didn't know what was going on. But I can't forget about what I do know.'

Cathy pulled her shaking head out of her hands, tears splashing onto the pavement, and stared at him. So was he really '*The Freezer Killer's Pimp*'? Had that Shaun Flanagan been telling the truth about him?

'I wasn't involved!' Jay was quick to put his hands up. 'Not like they said.'

Cathy's disbelieving face turned to horror, her open mouth scrunching up, and finally turned away.

'I swear at the time I didn't know anyone would get hurt. I didn't come forward straight away because it was an accident. I know now, I should have acted sooner. '

Cathy had wanted to find out Jay was safe. He'd been good to her. But Ant would always deny he'd done anything wrong, too.

'Men like you. You're all the same. Blaming the victim.' Cathy was shocked by the new words rioting out of her mouth. But then she found she enjoyed them. They tasted like money. Like power. She wanted more.

'What?! No way, I never said that. I—'

'I'm sick of hearing it. I thought you was a good person. Turns out you're as bad as the rest of 'em.'

Standing felt good, the power was in her legs now, spit shot over the pavement.

'You've got it all wrong.' Jay shrunk back.

Cathy raised her voice higher. Louder than she'd ever dared.

'You encouraged it. Let him get away with it, didn't you? Same as the rest.'

'I would never say he deserved what happened to him. Never.' Jay's voice was soft but firm. 'The court said it was an accident. Shaun was the one who said he was paying for it. And he'd had a condition – anaemia. Rare kind, serious – due to infection from a tick bite.'

'Yeah, well, that's no excuse.'

But now her voice was back to sounding unsure. Her

legs were wobbly. This was Alice's 'fight-or-flight' reaction overwhelming her. Causing her to feel weak after feeling so strong. But she'd spent so long fleeing. Like fish from a shark.

'I wasn't involved with any payments. But because he was gay, the judge believed the lies Shaun told about him.'

Cathy lowered herself onto the wall again.

'Oh right, the guy who died was a mate of yours. Sorry,' Cathy said, trying to make peace. Trying not to make him angry.

'What? No, I didn't know him at all.' Jay crossed his arms, his biceps framing his pecs.

'I thought ... 'cos you're gay and that ...' Cathy smiled weakly.

'What? I'm not gay!' Jay gave her a right miserable look, then turned away.

'You what?' When Jay didn't answer, Cathy followed his gaze.

Their side of the street was in the shade. The sun lit up the other side. A laughing boy and girl, football shoes dangling by their laces, waited at the historical-looking entrance of the building opposite. Cathy thought about taking a walk a few minutes further up the street. She guessed the river was where the gulls were coming from. The delivery man wheeled his trolley back from another building. Chucked it in the back of his van, slammed the doors, and drove off.

Jay's voice faintly from beside her. 'My parents thought I was gay ...'

Her insides were soaked in stress. Her head twisted slowly to scrutinise Jay.

'They – they didn't take it too well,' he added quietly.

Jay shifted on the wall.

'I'm sorry,' she said. And she meant it, honestly she did.

Jay had been good to her. So she didn't want to think this next bit. But hadn't Ant's dad mistreated him as well? 'Dog-eat-dog world' and that.

She slipped a look at old messages from Alice:

How we are brought up can set the stage for how we relate to others as adults.

Jay sat on his hands. Glanced at her, and at flat 401 looming over them. Then looked away.

I need to make sure you're giving informed consent to these therapy activities, Cathy.
So, I should tell you that, often, when you take the courageous step of revisiting a traumatic site or memory, it will stir things up.
As a result, you might find yourself remembering or saying things that you've previously tried to keep hidden.

What had coming here dragged up for Jay? Cathy would find out.

28

Amelia

Nicola gave Amelia a wave as she queued for their drinks. Amelia's now-ex charity boss hadn't yet had the chance to give her name to the barista. Was 'Nicola' a name that could get misspelled? Amelia often ended up as *Emily*.

Amelia brushed some dregs off the table. It wasn't quite the end of office-workers' days, but the Starbucks was still busy. Amelia didn't have anywhere better to be – her eyes worn-out, her body sagging, and a thin coldness hovering over her skin, covering up the edginess of waiting.

In her pocket, her phone made a fuss with notifications. She ignored them.

A woman propelled a buggy past her, careering after the screaming toddler dragging its coat. The aroma of the mother's cappuccino slapped Amelia in the face. The child had found a table for them. Amelia smiled despite her state.

She couldn't believe Lina had taken things at Police Watch so far. She hadn't been employed by them, so she hadn't been fired. Let go? Too euphemistic. There hadn't been anything euphemistic about the threat of criminal charges.

'Please sit down,' Lina had opened with, planted on the chair behind her desk.

Nicola had closed the door behind Amelia and stood next to it. Blocking Amelia's escape. Or just standing because there weren't enough chairs? A man Amelia had never seen before occupied the other seat by Lina. Light grey creased suit, an over-large striped, blue tie wrapped tightly round his neck. Volunteers at the campaign didn't wear suits.

Arms crossed, Amelia attempted a confident smile which felt weak on her face. Like the striplight over the stairs down to the basement. It flickered in and out of existence, plunging anyone descending into darkness with fitful sparking sounds.

Lina's office was still. Amelia sensed Nicola watching, with a tingle in the back of her neck. She wriggled in the seat set up for her.

'This is the campaign's lawyer.' Lina indicated wrinkled-suit man. He adjusted the tie, exposing a stain on the cotton of his shirt, and coughed, clearing the way for his sonorous voice.

'Miss Evans, Lina has shared with me some concerning information about your alleged activities here at Police Watch.' He pulled out a tablet from his faded brown satchel. 'Misusing the campaign database and sharing information outside of the campaign without consent' – Lina nodded three times at 'consent', hands clasped on the desk in front of her, golden head and pale fists standing out against her black polo neck – 'are very serious accusations.' He slid the tablet across the desk towards her, keeping his fingers pressed on top of it. 'Do you deny that these emails, asking for trial and investigation details not in the public domain, were sent from your account?'

Amelia's arms dropped to her sides. She gripped the seat

of her chair. She stared, mute, as her emails – to journalists, court officials, lawyers, police officers – stared back at her. The evidence was in white and black on the cracked screen.

'Do you deny that you sent them?'

Amelia didn't understand. Was this a way out? 'Maybe someone else sent them from my account?' The pitch of her voice reaching up for an escape route.

The man pinned the tablet against the desk with his fingertips. His eyes pointedly didn't move from Amelia as she dug her nails further into the hard, unforgiving seat of the chair.

'That would mean you had allowed a person, or persons unknown, access, without authorisation, to the aforementioned email account, either deliberately or by failing to follow cybersecurity procedures as set out in the campaign's Information Governance Policy. Did you allow someone to use your email account unauthorised?'

'No.'

'Did you fail to follow proper cybersecurity procedures, such as by leaving yourself logged in on a public terminal?'

'No, sir.'

'So, do you deny that you sent these emails?'

Amelia shook her head.

The man swiped across to a different document, and then sat back, arms folded.

'Do you deny that these logs, which show you accessing the campaign database on multiple occasions to download details of police officers, lawyers, jury members and witnesses (*inter alia*) related to the case of the death by choking of a Mr S. Evans, are accurate?'

Amelia's chest heaved.

'Would it be alright if we opened the door to get a bit of air in?' Amelia asked quietly.

Nicola moved to assist but Lina interrupted her:

'We don't want anyone else to hear this discussion, Amelia. Don't you think that's best?'

Amelia didn't disagree.

The lawyer lowered his voice. 'Are the logs accurate, Miss Evans?'

Amelia nodded, not looking. She could feel him looking at her, could feel them all looking. Then the tablet snaked away.

'These are very serious charges, Miss Evans. Potentially criminal.'

Amelia looked tearily at him. He was putting the tablet into the satchel.

Lina leaned forward on her desk. 'The campaign has decided not to press charges. But we can't allow you to continue at Police Watch. Your placement here has been terminated, with immediate effect. Your log-ins have been disabled, your security pass has been deactivated, and we have asked other volunteers not to communicate with you about campaign activities.'

'Do you have any questions, Amelia?' Nicola asked after a long pause.

Amelia shook her head again. Stood up.

'The consent form you signed, for your image to be used on our website? To show we value diversity?' Lina said, not getting up. 'That remains valid.'

Amelia was led silently from the office. She was grateful they hadn't noticed the tweet she'd sent from the Police Watch account just before the meeting.

The meeting with Lina, the lawyer and Nicola had felt like being down in the dark of a mine. Now, in the coffee shop, she was like a canary that had escaped. Everything was brighter and lighter. She wanted to reach out, to be connected to another human, to escape the lonely misery that had threatened to cave her in.

Nicola made her welcome return from the counter, white cardboard cups branded with thick black marker in each hand. She put the cup with *Emily* written on it in front of Amelia. Her own cup said *Charlie*, an astonishing mistake which faced her from the opposite side of the table. Amelia thanked her and then was quiet for a while. Nicola watched and waited.

'Why did you follow me after Lina had you show me out?' Amelia asked eventually.

'We all knew what was going down. You didn't deserve to be treated like that,' Nicola said, shrugging her left shoulder. She took another sip of her latte.

'Yeah, well, not everyone agrees with you.' She had no idea how she could move on from this. Was EmeraldSiren her only hope?

'I think it's pretty rough. She could've at least let you finish your shift.' Nicola was looking right at her, her eyes hazel and sincere and human. Amelia looked down at her Americano. The white lid smiled up at her. At least she hadn't been arrested.

'I'm sure you can find another charity to volunteer for. Loads of them out there, and your time's free!'

'I was really afraid you were going to charge me. The lawyer in there and everything.'

Nicola clicked her tongue and rolled her eyes. She smiled reassuringly. Her reddish, voluminous hair reminded Amelia of a security blanket. 'There was no way we would charge you with anything. We'd be in trouble for starters. That was just to punish you for breaking the rules. Lina can be a real … Look, I agree with our mission, but there's so much unconscious bias and microaggressions at Police Watch.'

Nicola pulled a face, and Amelia frowned slightly. She wasn't a fan of everything bad that happened to her being attributed to racism. Yes, there had been times she felt she'd been treated differently from other volunteers, and had panicked about not knowing why, but she didn't need another White saviour.

Nicola slid her hand partway across the table that lay between them. Then stopped. 'To be honest, I'm kind of glad we got this opportunity to talk again.'

Amelia remembered how Nicola was one of the people who'd been especially friendly to her when she'd started at Police Watch. Helping her with the photocopier, asking her out to the pub, going out of her way to show her the trick to getting the basement door to lock properly.

She kept her hands around her cup, but smiled shyly back at the lid.

'I'm glad we got to talk again, too.'

Nicola leaned forward, excitedly bringing her cup down onto the table. 'Really? Because I've wanted to talk to you so much, and you always seemed like you didn't want to.'

Amelia shrank away apologetically.

'I'm sorry, I've … I've had a lot on my mind.'

'About your brother?'

Amelia looked up at Nicola sharply. Only the *lie* side of her cup was showing. Both her hands pressed flat around it. Her eyes locked onto Amelia, bright like a coalminer's lamps.

'How do you know about Steffan?' Amelia's breath rose again, chest tightening.

'Well, that's who you were contacting people about, from the database, wasn't it?'

'Yes. Yes, that's right.' Amelia dared not relax her grip on the cup. The smile of the lid took on a different angle now.

She should have remembered the dark contents behind the saviour's white face: like people, a drinking vessel could seem to promise to do her good, but on the inside it was bitter, and not to be trusted.

'I'd always wanted to talk to you about him. 'Cos he'd paid his killer for sex, hadn't he? Sorry, I don't know how to say it right!'

'I don't like to talk about it.' Amelia's guilt about the last thing she'd said to Steffan when he was alive was still mutating. Speaking her feelings aloud wouldn't help her make sense of them.

'Sure. Of course. I don't want to pressure you.'

Nicola sipped her coffee some more. Looked away.

Amelia followed her gaze. A goth girl, dark clothes, pale face, big nose-rings, out of place in this tribute to conformist capitalism, stirred her drink awkwardly opposite a preppy-looking boy. A first date? The girl's eyes darted around, her body poised to run at any moment. Like a canary in a mine, used to detect poisonous gas. Held in a cage to warn their keeper that death was near.

Nicola broke into her thoughts.

'I know it's weird, I swear I don't know what's wrong with me. What he did makes me sick to my stomach.'

Amelia felt nauseous. Did those canaries down mines know what was coming? Did they know the sick purpose of the man who held their cage?

Nicola pushed her empty cup across the table.

'It's just, there's so many things that aren't in the news stories. Like. What exactly did they get up to together?'

Amelia managed to stumble to her feet. Everyone else at every other table having normal conversations. The mum feeding her toddler. The preppy boy and the goth girl moving on from awkward small talk. The baristas serving and writing and making drinks and '*would you like anything else with that?*'-ing.

'Do you think it's true he might be bi? Hey, where are you going? Amelia?'

Nicola tutted audibly.

'Not my fault Shaun Flanagan's fit. I'd let him choke me any day.'

An avid fan of true crime podcasts, a member of staff at a charity which focused on dangerous men: *of course* Nicola was one of *those* women.

After she'd dazed her way on autopilot to the bus home, Amelia stared at her phone. It was still always about Steffan. Something had to make it all stop, and then start her life again. Even just ending the not knowing would be something. How could you get closure without certainty? Jay and Shaun's remorse would fix her own.

She sent Jay another WhatsApp message.

What really happened to Steffan?

No point messaging EmeraldSiren again – she still owed Amelia a message. Amelia instead sent a text to someone else who might be able to put an end to the not knowing. Then checked WhatsApp.

One tick. Not blue, not read. She couldn't see when he was last online.

Jay had blocked her.

29

Jay

Jay sat in his bed, pillow behind him against the wall. As usual, he had his phone on silent. Just him and his screen, the small rectangle lighting up his face as the rest of the room lay dim, save for the street and building lights spying through the flimsy curtains. He knew he should be going to sleep but he was still searching for ways to avoid the nightmares that would confront him with distorted partial truths about what happened.

His right thumb took him down through other people's lives, bigged-up through their carefully curated collections of photos (filtered or otherwise). He wanted not to think, not to remember.

Observing. Like at school. He'd been on his guard from a young age – never sure how to answer the '*But where are you from* originally?' question. But before it had all gone wrong for him, at least he'd been functional. It hadn't all been just observation. He'd been able to make friends at uni. And socialised a bit on the periphery of work events after graduating. Now, he couldn't remember the last time he'd seen a friend outside of Timpo's or Magda's.

The sink gurgled. The sound of the wastewater stirring

through the pipes below momentarily grabbed Jay's attention, and roused him from one mindless app to another.

Amazing what exchanges you could scrape together online. The masked orange devil of the Grindr logo welcomed them all in. Well, maybe not all: the guys with *No Asians* on their Grindr profiles couldn't be considered that welcoming. Jay had learned through trial and error that a faceless profile, with only his muscular, slightly hairy, light brown torso on display, was best for the kind of conversations he wanted to have here. *Open-minded Chat* did the job as profile title. *Curious* in the bio. *Drugfree* his only tag.

He fired off a few messages into the ether: maybe a reply would come and fend off some of the loneliness, feed his feelings into submission. Maybe someone could provide the dopamine hit he needed to chase the guilt and shame out of his head. Not attaching any pics right then.

He wasn't gay, of course – those infatuations at uni had just been a phase – but he needed someone to talk to. Sometimes iPlayer or YouTube couldn't cut it as a distraction, particularly when he couldn't concentrate on a whole episode or film. 'Chatting' calmed him down, made him feel safer. Despite Tony's reassurance, without anything solid on the Note's sender, and no one else to turn to, he needed soothing right now. Especially after going over what Tony had said about not being able to lead a better life than this. Cathy's freak-out downstairs from Flat 401 had made him wonder if, after all, he would have no choice but to get in bed with Tony and his schemes.

Totally pic-less, nameless, detail-less was online again tonight. '*Nameless 35yo*', Jay called him. A window onto someone else's experiences was better than being shut up in this room completely by himself.

Alright mate

Hey Mr.
Up to much?

Nah. You?

No

Would he ever move beyond these banal openings? Jay examined the damp patch on his ceiling that appeared whenever it poured with rain. Dry for now. The past always threatening to break through. Never the opportunity for him to break out.

I'm still up for that threesome btw

Whatever happened, whatever anyone said, all he had now were words. Until the three weeks were up, he couldn't even stay away from Magda's overnight without Olu's permission. But he could imagine. Jay's mouth went dry. One hand went under the covers. The dull background hum of the city pressed in through the open window. The residue of the damp patch was a grey eye on the white ceiling, still watching in the dark. His fragile curtains threatened to lift on the draught seeping through the window he'd cracked open, and penetrate the room with artificial light.

Yeah I tried something like that before
Didn't go so well

A shadow outside Jay's door covered up some of the light clawing its way through the gap at the bottom. He froze, worried that he might have said aloud what he was typing. Or reacted loudly enough to be heard through the thin-as-skin walls.

You only into chatting?

Jay was conflicted. But he reminded himself that *Nameless* didn't know who he really was. It was just a bit of fun. A fantasy. Not real life.

The shadow outside his room moved away. A door down the corridor thudded shut. Was it Tej going down to the front desk, or Cathy going back into her room?

What if this guy on Grindr had been the one who sent him those WhatsApp messages?

You into poppers at all?

Jay closed the app. He'd be safe here in bed, behind the distance afforded by ones and zeros that were without colour or class. Sometimes contact with the outside world could be a short-lived relief. He closed his eyes: the sound of Dad's boots thudding on the tiles of football stadium toilets, as his own body grew bruised, jerked them open.

He had to learn – being open had a price. He hadn't learned from what happened as a result of Amma and Dad's tough love after that football match at thirteen; Dad's emphasis on toughness, Amma's on an attempt at love. He hadn't learned from what happened with Flat 401, with three lives wasted as a result. He had to learn: another mistake could send him back to prison. For life.

30

Jay

In his dream, it was night-time. The door to Flat 401 was open. The knowledge of what Jay had seen inside was a cold, tight sheet wrapping around him. If he could wake up or go somewhere else, he wouldn't have to relive it again.

But the dead weight of the nightmare inexorably put him in the Flat.

Blocking his view of the bed, the judge from his trial in their bright red gown, fake white hair tumbling down their back, half-turned their face. 'In passing sentence, I take into account your actions following the death of Mr Evans.' The judge pointed at the still-alive figure on the bed. 'Or, at least, what you told the court about your actions.'

Now the judge was Jay's boss from his old job. The puffy man swivelled to face him.

'There's some very disturbing evidence here, Jay, very disturbing.'

His boss was waving a faded white envelope. Fresh ones were scattered across the bed next to the prone figure. They bubbled over onto the floor, multiplying like eyes.

'Says here the death was directly related to your "*disrespect-*

ful, hateful and homophobic"' attitude, Jay. This is going in your appraisal.'

His boss shook his head, then downed his pint.

Jay couldn't stop watching what was happening on the bed. The muscles in his flesh didn't want or permit him to move; it wasn't his fault he wasn't intervening. Shaun was staring at him as he knelt above S. Evans. Jay gazed into his devouring green eyes as the figure on the bed cried out.

'I can't breathe.

'I can't breathe.

'I can't breathe ...'

Jay forced himself awake. The usual dampness drowning his body. He knew he wouldn't get back to sleep – he never could. He peeled the sticky sheet off his body. The streetlights guided him to the light-switch on the wall. He clicked it, and looked around the room that was not his old flat: small wardrobe, small sink. Closed window. He stripped, and dried himself with underwear from his laundry bag. Put on the dry charity-shop dressing gown Tejinder had given him. Only one previous owner was a big step up from prison clothes.

Jay had torn up the Note, but not done anything about the envelope. Fresh white, but crumpled. Yet again, he checked it didn't have anything else in it. Time to throw it out. Jay still felt it watching him. Watching his mind and everything it hid, everything it stole, everything it held down and ripped open.

A knock at the door. Tejinder's voice saying it was her, asking if everything was OK. Jay didn't know why she was bothering him – the nightmares weren't so bad anymore, anyway. Shivering, Jay shuffled over to the door to open it, then retreated back to the hostel-provided chair on the other side of the room.

'Sounded like another bad one. Want to talk?' Tej asked

as she stepped inside, shutting the door and keeping her voice down.

Jay pulled the dressing gown tighter. Looked away.

'It's been over two years, Jay. Maybe you should—'

'I don't want to talk about it.'

Tej's brown eyes widened and grew wet, then narrowed in disapproval like his mother's.

'Well, I'll leave you to it, then.'

After counting nine seconds to get himself out of his head, Jay pulled open his door. Tej had started down the stairs, too far away for Jay to call out 'thanks' without disturbing everyone. He went back into his room and got out his phone.

Websites by ex-inmates. The ones who'd turned their lives around and had a job, a partner, a life they could share with everyone. Was he going to end up the polar opposite: an unnamed, faceless blog going on about social stigma and suicide rates?

You last visited this page yesterday next to every entry.

Jay switched to Twitter. *#ExPrisoner, #DoneTheTime, #JustLetMeLive*. That last one still a bad habit. A guilty pleasure, like reading the Agony Aunt section of the *Sun* in the barber's.

The first time he'd searched for *#JustLetMeLive*, he had meant it. He just wanted to live. Not to hide, not to shut down, not to survive: to live. At first, he'd felt irritated by the content he found: rich young women acting as if criticism of their bad clothing choices was an unbearable cross. But then he'd got sucked into the random posts about the weird food combinations people were trying, the trashy songs they liked and pretended to have shame about, the celebrities they had crushes on, and hadn't felt so alone.

It had made him smile.

But tonight, even the comedy tweets wore thin. People eating salami and jam, listening to the Backstreet Boys, or crushing on Pedro Pascal couldn't ease the emptiness, the heaviness, the waking fear ... Scrolling down, down, down, nothing changing how he felt. A pointless person living a pointless life.

Jay went across to the window, pulled a crack open in the curtains. This time of night, the streets were empty. No one watching. He pulled the curtain closed again. Why did he still feel this way? It had just been a dream. He had them all the time.

One hour of pointlessness on TikTok turned into two. The lack of connection began to outweigh the stimulation. He pressed Twitter's *Home* button one last time. Maybe someone else who wasn't asleep would have put up something new. Retweets from a few ex-prisoner accounts he followed. The usual—

Jay froze his screen where it was. The curtains were definitely shut. The white envelope was still staring at him from its watchpoint on the chest of drawers. Why had Police Watch retweeted itself, an article from five years ago? Why could he not put this behind him?

Slowly he felt his thumb moving towards the link. He knew it would only make him feel worse. It was like how he'd reacted to that time in prison when he'd hurt himself, months of inactivity and slouched posture weakening his lower back until a final push from one of the other inmates left him unable to find any position – lying, sitting, standing – that didn't leave him in agony. He knew he should stop rubbing it.

But he didn't want to. Didn't deserve to find a way to make the pain stop.

At the other end of the link, it was the photo from the

day he'd entered his plea that got him. The pitiful old man
– S. Evans's father – a stony face defiant at the camera. Bent
and gnarled by weathering one storm too many. And the
sister. Jay remembered her tearstained face. Unceasing eyes
petrifying him.

The odour of his shame had haunted the dock. His brother
had not been permitted to attend by Amma, and Dad's side
of the family had been long gone after she'd turfed 'that man'
out in 2016. The choking heat of the courtroom had grabbed
him around the throat, forcing him down, down, head down.
He'd said what his lawyer had advised. Said what he could
bear for everyone to know about why he'd taken so long to
tell the police where his neighbour's body was.

But they could never know what had been in those
Facebook messages to S. Evans.

Messages.

He raced through the anonymous WhatsApp messages
he'd received. Zoomed in on the photo from the Police
Watch article to get a closer look. Her dark eyes fixed on
him through the lens, across time and space. Unforgiving.
Just like when they'd bored into him in court, as she'd read
out her Victim Impact Statement. She'd stopped herself
crying, like a robot crowning itself with a skull-like mask, to
drive home her point about how awful it was for the family
not to know what really happened that day. She'd used the
same term back then as in the messages: 'pure lies'. And
only a family member would refer to S. Evans by just his
first name.

It was her. The sister.

Amelia.

Even though he couldn't see her WhatsApp profile pic,
he was sure it was her. Fear and shame mixed with confusion and relief; she couldn't know anything, so what had she

wanted to get from sending him those anonymous messages?

Jay was like a robot too. Unable to resist, operating automatically. The dead weight of his shame forcing him to act. Pushing him face-down, drowning under the urge to do the right thing.

He opened WhatsApp, and unblocked the 'unknown' number.

Started typing a response.

31

The tall man

He was approaching Woolwich, legs and torso confined by the narrow bus seats, grinding his sharp teeth at the latest handwritten ramble.

> *I think of a time.*
> *Not everything is how you would like it to be. I shouldn't have let you rope me into covering up your wrongs. I believe you can still be a good person. We're all suffering, it's not a competition. Sometimes we just have to admit we've not got what we wanted. But you can survive that. You are not small, empty, or defective. I love you.*

He choked back a cough.

> *I tried my best with you. Our shared, shame-fuelled anger always seething inside. Do you remember asking me 'What does "forgiveness" mean?'?*

He hadn't got doughy; he still had his strength. He would show them he understood forgiveness – and its limits.

32

Amelia

Amelia dodged the white van that sped out of Catford McDonald's car park. She stared impotently as it drove off, then picked her way across the poorly signposted crossing to the entrance. The stubby building, like a dark green metal witch's house, was fronted by smeared glass on all sides, save the cooking and drive-through area. The office workers on their lunch breaks at the pitiful outside tables provided no cover. Amelia hesitated at the double door. It was mostly car park around there. The nearest shops were the other side of the main road. Only a dilapidated residential street jutting off to the perpendicular offered even a crumb of footfall. She pushed the door open. No one would spot Wanda meeting her here.

She took her place in the queue for one of the self-service screens. As she waited impatiently, Amelia scrolled back through the text messages she'd exchanged with Wanda after escaping from Nicola at the café. This woman she hoped would become her police informant worked at the Witness Care Unit: as someone who'd been involved with the case, surely she'd be able to help Amelia find out more?

The self-service screen glowed at her. The bright HD

menu pushed salt, grease, healthy options, sugar-free options, meals of all sizes and for all ages. Why did there have to be so many choices? In or out, cash or card, individual items or pre-selected meal plans. She would keep it to a quarter pounder (with cheese as a treat) and fries. Diet Coke. Not large.

Amelia kept her eye on the door as she settled down to eat. Checked her phone before getting oily residue all over her fingers. No update. Wanda had asked Amelia not to text on the day so as not to arouse the suspicions of her colleagues. The salty, fatty goodness, the sticky cheese, the tangy gherkins and burger sauce – all made it easier to resist the urge to check and text.

Fingers cleaned on a pre-packed lemon-scented wipe, Amelia tutted inaudibly as the couple two tables over left their tray piled high with rubbish, escaped chips spilling onto the table, and splashes of Coke on the floor. Why couldn't people take more care, be more considerate, do what they were supposed to do? The bin was right there! She frowned at the noise of the schoolchildren the other side of her.

Amelia checked her phone. Past one o'clock. What if something had come up and Wanda couldn't make it?

Nothing new in WhatsApp either. She stared again at the message from *Jay Ginige (THE Jay)*. Sent in the early hours of the morning. And then a missed call before lunch. Well, it hadn't been missed: she'd deliberately avoided it.

Nothing helpful wherever she doom-scrolled to.

She surveyed her now-desolate table. All her waste kept neatly inside the boundaries of the tray and the burger box. Through the window, the surprisingly green hedge the other side of two parking spaces looked plastic, its roots showing above the thirsty dry earth.

She remembered when she'd become preoccupied with what had really happened to Steffan. It had been before Jay had decided to plead. Shaun's defence counsel hadn't said much of use during his mitigation:

'*Mr Flanagan was just trying to earn some extra money.*'

'*Shaun panicked and that's why he hid the body.*'

'*He sincerely regrets misusing a freezer at his place of work.*'

It hadn't mattered to Amelia that Shaun Flanagan had '*no history of violence*' – one death was enough, particularly when what he'd done had been so disturbed and unfair.

And she hadn't cared about the lawyer's plea to '*think of his unborn child*'.

Amelia limply rested her phone on the table. She stared through the dirty windows. Maybe Wanda wasn't coming. On a sick day, with no shift to go to at Police Watch, she might as well stay here. She felt her lunch repeating on her at the thought of the lawyer's tablet and the IT records that had told on her. EmeraldSiren had gone silent. Wanda was the only person from her campaign investigations whose number she'd had in her phone. Amelia needed whatever it was she'd promised to show her in response to her desperate text. Something so secret it had to be printed off, not emailed, because it wouldn't get past the WCU's digital security.

More screaming and laughing from the other side of the restaurant. Their parents had never allowed them to celebrate birthdays here. Wow, was there really a time when they'd stopped Steffan getting something he wanted? The only other time she could think of was the Tamagotchi he'd begged for as a child. At her last visit home she'd ignored the Tamagotchi he must have bought himself, but had retrieved the thirtieth present she hadn't been able to throw away from under his bed. The thin black box preserving the silver ring on a chain was a silent coffin gathering dust.

She wasn't like the hedge outside. She was planted here: a tree, her roots snaking down into the earth, ready to choke whatever they found. Whatever she needed to feed on to give her life.

Amelia put in her earphones to make the video call.

33

Amelia

Jay's video was scratchy and weak. He was wearing a dark red polo shirt with white writing on it. His face was pulling a different expression – eyes wide, mouth open – but otherwise he looked the same as five years ago. No tears yet.

'Hi.' His voice was softer than she'd expected.

Amelia looked over the top of the phone and scanned the restaurant for anyone watching. She moved to a different chair so her back was against a wall.

'What do you want?' Amelia leaned towards the screen.

'What? You called me.'

'You called me this morning. What do you want?'

Jay looked at something off camera, to his right. Amelia couldn't see too clearly where he was, but it looked like he was sitting on a bed. He leaned in. 'Listen, do we have to do this now? I wasn't expecting it.'

Amelia struck the table with one fist. 'I'm in McDonald's, this isn't exactly a great time for me either.'

Amelia darted her eyes to her left to check no one had heard her judgement. Lowering her voice, she continued. 'It's *never* a great time for my family. After what happened to Steffan ... And now my dad has cancer.'

Jay looked blankly at her. A blink gave away that he hadn't frozen.

'It won't change anything. Knowing.'

'It would change *everything*. Right now, all I know is my brother died. Suddenly and unfairly. Was the court even right about it being manslaughter not murder?'

'I can't tell you but you've got to believe me!'

'Believe what? What did Shaun Flanagan have on you? Why did you delete those messages?'

People were still shuffling up to the screens and the collection points, taking their places at spare tables. It was somewhat quieter now, after the peak lunch hour, but this kind of place was never really empty.

'What kind of cancer does your dad have?'

'Why do you care?'

Jay shrugged. 'Maybe he'll get better.'

'I don't know why I bothered. I thought you'd want to make it make sense. Take some responsibility. You obviously don't give a toss.' Amelia made to end the call.

'I am sorry. I'm sorry about everything that's happened to you.'

Amelia let her finger hover. Adjusted her earphones and her hair. 'You should be. Why did you do it?'

'I wanted to let you know that I knew. I knew it was you sending the messages.'

'Not why did you call me. Why did you do *it*?'

'I swear, I didn't know it would hurt him. I just …'

Amelia breathed in sharply.

Jay looked down. 'The judge wasn't exactly sympathetic, because of that lawyer going on about the police not investigating crimes against gay men properly. The police had it in for me, kept telling me they knew my type. You know—' Jay smiled weakly and pressed his skin up against the camera.

Amelia rolled her eyes. She wasn't interested in playing oppression Olympics.

'I'm a mixed-race woman, I know something about being treated unfairly.'

She could see Jay take and release a deep breath before the sound filtered down the cables and through the airwaves and into her ears. The digital extension of her hungry, thirsty roots garbled by delay.

'Look, I called you earlier because I wanted to tell you what really happened. With Shaun. But you can't tell anyone else.'

Amelia leaned in.

'I want to tell you … was in danger … all the detail …'

He was starting to sound robotic.

'… the windows. It was only later …'

His image was breaking up.

'I can't hear you properly.' She hunched over the phone, not wanting people at neighbouring tables to overhear her desperate whisper.

'I didn't know … something bad. They'd done stuff like that before.'

Three harsh beeps. The line went dead, the message on her screen not giving her any answers.

Call Ended.

Amelia jumped up, raced outside, waved her phone around. She had to get signal back.

4G appeared.

She redialled his number.

34

Jay

Jay had taken a pre-work afternoon shower to finally wash off the sweat and fear from the night before. Safe in his room, he'd slid on his tight red Primark boxer trunks. The guilt and disorientation still lingered, only partly due to lack of sleep. He needed to make it through his shift. *Get it together.*

His Isle of Wight postcard reminded him: he could get through this, he had a future. He blew out his cheeks as he examined his naked torso in the small mirror above the small sink. *'Muscular.' 'No Chem Sex.' 'Mixed.'* A human being reduced to a set of adjectives, a set of tick-boxes. Didn't even know why he chatted to those guys anyway, was just something to do, something to pass the time, some way of making a connection with anybody who would talk to him. Online didn't count.

The 'silent' buzzing of his phone warned him he was receiving a WhatsApp call.

A video call.

Amelia.

He pulled on his work top. As she talked, he imagined different ways of dealing with this openly.

The bad connection, at his end or hers, wasn't helping.

'I called you because I wanted to tell you what really happened. I want to tell you the truth.'

Was Amelia giving him a chance to speak, or just breaking up?

'I didn't know your brother was in danger. I couldn't see all the detail. Through the windows. It was only later ...'

Was Amelia judging him, or just frozen?

'I didn't know it was something bad. They'd done stuff like that before.'

Was Amelia withholding forgiveness from him, or was it just a bad connection?

Call Ended.

Jay couldn't believe how much he'd been prepared to tell her. But she clearly didn't know what had really happened that day, so she couldn't have sent the Note. Did that mean he could put this behind him? If he didn't get a move on he'd be late for work.

No. He needed to finish this. Now he'd started, he was tumbling towards the end of the tunnel. He *was* sorry, and he did want to tell her as much as he could. But he hadn't been thinking straight when he'd responded to her unblocked message after his nightmare. He'd wanted to get the night demon off his chest. To tell her what he hadn't been able to tell the police or the court. Maybe a small extra trace of honesty could finally earn him an end to the nightmares, the flashbacks, the guardedness. It wouldn't bring her brother back, but maybe Jay could help Amelia put the past behind and move on. If he didn't do something, he'd become a man who'd contributed to the deaths of two Evanses, not just one. Living like this wasn't living.

Jay waved his phone around, checking the Wi-Fi. Three bars. Relieved, shoulders sinking back down, an *Incoming*

Call showed up again. *Voice Call* this time. He looked down. His bare legs were sweating against the seat.

He started over but she cut straight to it.

'What do you mean? You saw something? Before?'

'I'd … I'd seen them … Before …' Jay launched himself out of the clammy chair, one hand clamping the phone to the side of his head, the other awkwardly rubbing his hair.

'Who is *them*?'

'My neighbour—'

'He had a name!'

Jay gripped his hair tight, squeezed his eyes shut hard. 'Steffan had his bed right at the window. Sometimes he would sit by it, burning candles, looking out at night.'

The silence cut into Jay like a key being used in self-defence. He opened his eyes, checking the call hadn't dropped again. When Amelia's voice returned, it was a shameful whisper.

'Oh my God, I can't believe those people on Facebook were actually right! So that's what Shaun had on you? You *were* his pimp! Spotted a lucrative customer, did you?'

Jay flushed at the memory. Forced his mind from the window he'd been looking through five years ago, to the window he was looking through now.

'No, honestly, I was just … looking. The first time was an accident, I thought he'd caught me staring. Thought he'd close the curtains, or complain, or stop, or something.'

Jay put his free hand out in front of him, palm open.

'But he didn't. He was looking at me while he was, well …'

'He let you watch him? Were *you* paying *Steffan*? Is that how he ended up—'

'No! No … Don't blame him. He wasn't paying for anything. I know why Shaun made that up. What happened to him, it wasn't your brother's fault. I could see Shaun was the one who'd be good for Steffan's loneliness.'

The sunshine was warm on Jay's exposed skin. He kept his hands up, one on the phone, one on the window.

'I don't need to hear this,' Amelia whispered. 'He had friends, plenty of people looking after him. Didn't he?'

'Sorry. I don't know about that. But I need you to know. It wasn't his fault. It wasn't anyone's fault. Shaun and your brother, they'd been good together.'

'What did you see?'

Two policemen were escorting a youth in a suit up the street. Going to the County Court up the road, Jay guessed. A teenage memory of trouble in the toilets after a football match threatened to surface. Feeling like he was being held under water, unable to breathe. Chanting surrounding him. Holding him down. Shaming him.

Killing him.

'But even when it came to my trial, I couldn't tell the truth, because then people would know.'

Silence from Amelia's end. A kind-looking old lady stepped out of the Age UK shop across the way. A middle-aged man stepped in, arms straining under his box of donations.

'Jay. What did you see?'

The light from the window was distracting. It was like the light of his childhood bathroom reflected on the surface of a full bath, dippling and waving, beckoning him into its heat – a soothing embrace set up by Amma. Staring out at the sky, despite the white clouds now in the distance, Jay forgot where he was or the fear of being overheard. It was all going to come out now. It was all going to be alright. It was surprisingly easy to finally admit the truth about himself, without a face looking at him: not on the call, nor reflected in the bright window.

This was it.

Five years, nineteen years, thirty-two years of hiding.

About to be broken open.

'I told myself – I was just watching, I didn't know for sure he needed help. Someone else was with him.'

Breathing ragged.

'Everyone would have found out if I'd called an ambulance. If they'd seen those messages; if they'd found out he invited me to watch.'

Sobs shuddering.

'And I knew what everyone would think if they found out about me.'

Feeling like he was about to drown. But only telling the truth could save him.

'I didn't know he was going to die. And underneath all that, deep down, I'm still the same person. It wasn't my fault. Because I was just watching. You can't be held responsible if you were just watching. It doesn't count as gay if you're just watching. Right?'

Silence from Amelia's end.

'Please ...

'I'll do anything.' Jay wiped the tears and snot off his face. His shaky breathing slowly steadied. The kind-looking old lady made her way from the charity shop to the Chinese herbalist. The sun was still in the calm sky, its warm rays softly hugging Jay as he rested his head against the window. The two policemen were walking back from their escort duty. One gently tapped his feet against litter blown into his path.

Amelia's voice broke. 'You were watching when it happened. You didn't call for help. Didn't even send a message to see if he was *alright*.' Her voice turned slow and cold. 'Steffan died because you have issues about being gay. In this day and age. My father isn't going to last much longer. My life has totally gone down the toilet because of you. You deserve everyone knowing what you really did. And this poor excuse for why.'

'Please, I'm sorry. Shaun is the one who got sent down for manslaughter. I only found out Steffan had died afterwards.'

He had been so stupid to think anyone could understand why he had been so afraid, so ashamed of people knowing the truth about him.

'You're full of it.' Amelia's voice crackled.

Jay barely registered the bang at the window as he stared at the *Ended* screen. He dragged his eyes away to peer out. A scrawny, helpless brown bird twitched and then was still on the pavement below. A man pulled his dog away from the broken-headed corpse. The animal raised its leg up against the railings a few feet away. Trails of urine slunk down to the unwanted carcass.

Behind him. Jay knew he mustn't look at the white envelope. The room seemed to be filled with the roar of a boiling ocean. His mouth was full of sand. He didn't remember covering his nakedness and getting from his room to downstairs, but there he was.

The light as he opened Magda's front door and escaped outside was too bright. The sun was the strip-light in a police interrogation room, the eyes of a father wild with the fanaticism of a Leave victory, the golden necklace of a mother closing the door of the family home. The fresh air beat his lungs like a pummelling from homophobic football fans.

The shoppers' chatter, the traffic's grinding, the ringing silence of the air itself crowded around Jay and overpowered him. He was a worthless scrap of paper being thrown away on the wind. Every cell exposed.

He thought of a bright beach, fresh air, and a smiling face. The name *Dan Lane* printed on a deed poll. The Isle of Wight postcard above his sink. Lining up his thoughts, and trying to magically out-think them; desperate to cancel out his guilty, shameful memories.

The wolfish-looking guy leaning on the black railings at the bottom of Magda's entrance steps wasn't just a thought. The tall man stood up straight. Popped another jelly into his mouth from the paper bag in his hand. Licked his strong fingers, and then used them to offer one to Jay.

The green sweet was like an exotic, venomous spider at the centre of its white web.

Jay was strangely relieved to hear the athletic man still had the accent, although felt an unwanted pang at his hair being cut short now. Jay knew he should be afraid, but the fellow tall man's voice made him feel like everything was going to be alright.

'Hello, Jakey. Green still your favourite?'

Jay found himself opening his mouth. Long, white fingers slid the treat (its colour the same as the familiar face's mesmerising eyes) over his lips.

The sour green candy was also sweet. Jay swallowed.

Shaun smiled, revealing his lickable white teeth.

The two of them. Together again.

One moth, one flame.

Jay smiled back.

35

Then

Steffan

Inside the mirrored cube of the lift as I go down, I check my phone, rereading the eConsult message from my GP.

> *Blood smear (Babesia): no parasites detected.*
> *FBC: haemoglobin < normal.*
> *Treatment for above: Rest. ESSENTIAL to avoid proscribed medications due to nature of this anaemia.*

I also check if Amelia has contacted me again. No: still just her last email about my ex.

> I told you not to trust him.
> Don't blame me if you die in that flat.

The mechanism grinds and creaks above me as I put my phone away and wipe away my tears.

As I come out of the lift, I see my favourite tall young man from the flat opposite faffing around with the door to the rubbish and recycling bins; even though he's not wearing an ostentatiously-tight T-shirt, I can tell he's got muscles. His skin is smooth and clean. He glances at me, and seems flustered, but then looks back at the task in hand. I smile at him, but I don't think he sees, he is so focused on opening the door as he carries a rubbish bag in one hand, recycling in the other.

I start to sashay over, catch myself being OTT, and turn my walk into a relaxed stride. I grab the frame of the door, and pull it wide open for him.

'Hi. Jay, isn't it? From flat 400?' He looks down blankly at me. 'Steffan. From flat 401. We've messaged a couple of times?' I stick out the hand that's not holding the door open. 'About misdirected post?' That's how our messaging started, anyway.

He shrugs, smiles weakly, and gestures helplessly with his hands full of rubbish and recycling bags. Adorable. I smile more, and squeeze myself in-between him and the door, propping the latter open with my butt.

'Your girlfriend not around to help you with that?' I ask unsubtly.

He looks away, his delicious face colouring. 'I ... I live alone.'

My own face grows hot as I imagine that voice saying unmentionable things right in my ear. I cough.

'Here, let me get that for you.' I raise the lid of the bin. He hesitates and then, leaning away from me, deposits his sack in the metal container, and tosses the recycling into the blue plastic one next to it. I check out the broadness of his back as he momentarily exposes it to me. I flick my eyes back up to his when he turns round. The same shade of brown as mine. Hair the same black, but thick and wavy where mine is fine and straight.

Jay licks his lips and breaks eye contact. He shuffles past me and hurries to the lift. He looks back at me as he presses the button, and steps inside.

'Thanks. Steffan.'

The lift doors seal him off from me. I shake my head, and step out of the foyer. It feels good to move outside, its spaciousness against my skin. Even if I'm only walking five minutes beyond the main road.

I feel like punching the air as a customer leaves the fish and chip shop as I approach: another few quid to keep the bank manager happy. I genuinely worry about these small local businesses. The man behind the counter is a bonus. My goodness. Quite the dish! Tall, lean build. Rugged, stubbly face. He smiles at me as I enter. I smile back. He scans his green eyes over me.

'Alright?' he opens with. Do I detect the hint of a delectable Irish accent? I stare at him, licking my lips and smoothing my hair as I stretch my mouth into a smile. A bit too much but you know what it's like, when one hasn't been in this situation for a while. And now twice in one day!

'What can I get for you?' the man behind the counter asks. I realise I've said nothing.

I feel hot under his gaze. I tug at my jeans. Fiddle with the cheap chain around my neck. The greasy vinegar smell overwhelms my senses.

'One scampi and chips, if you please.'

The man behind the counter raises his eyebrows. '*If you please?*' I'm burning up. Is he stifling a laugh? Oh my God, the humiliation.

He busies himself about getting the chips frying, sliding out the breadcrumbed balls of seafood from the tray in the counter, slipping them into the usual polystyrene carry-out box. Getting a bag and newspaper ready. Perhaps he hasn't noticed? I start to retract my wishes for the ground to swallow me up.

'If you please, my lord, wouldst thou like salt and vinegar

onst thy chippes?' His face is straight, but his eyes have a cruel twinkling light in them. I wish for every element to erase this moment: earth to devour me, fire to burn in my cheeks, water to sweep me away, air to be sucked out of my mouth so I can't put my foot in it again.

Then his mouth curls into a gentle smile.

Relief floods in. I cover my mouth with my hand as I give a shaky laugh back. The laugh he returns in exchange is loud. Firm. Confident. The tension leaves my muscles in a giddy rush. Does the handover of my food parcel take just that little bit longer than it needs to? Is his hand resting on mine? The tension comes back.

He lets me pull eye contact away when we are interrupted by the next customer coming in. I'm pretty sure he has given me an extra sachet of tartar sauce.

As I walk home, I look around, but there aren't any homeless people, so I keep my change. I know I shouldn't get too excited; I'm sure a good-looking man like him must flirt with loads of customers. But that smile looked ready to eat me up. So different from my dark-featured, dark-minded ex.

I get in and unwrap the hot parcel, diving into the golden chips and salty, breaded balls.

Blue biro's been scribbled on the grey paper. A number, eleven digits.

And a name.

Shaun

Am I enjoying myself too much? Is it unsafe to be doing this? Memories of how I trusted my ex invade me. Are there some mistakes so wrong, we cannot forgive or make them right?

I look around sharply, but there's no one there. My ex's critical voice and silent treatment are just memories; these men aren't a danger to me.

Another message from Jay bubbles up on my phone; going to end up having to choose between two hotties, at this rate. Perhaps Tejinder's right: perhaps not every man will be as bad for me as my ex.

36
Now

Jay

Even as they made their way to Wimpy's – Jay sneaking, Shaun swaggering – Jay imagined he caught the scent of gossip calling to him. People who were out for early afternoon drinks, or waiting at the bus stop, or just sitting in the square. Stopping and staring. Everyone no doubt knew someone who knew something. The whispers flooded his head.

'He was into chem sex.'
'He was a serial killer.'
'He was someone's son.'
'He better not come in here.'

Despite his swagger, Shaun hid round the corner while he got Jay to order his Halfpounder Bacon and Cheese, avoiding all eye contact with those passing by, and the possibility of anything worse.

'The thing is, I'll be late for work,' Jay protested weakly as he carried out the greasy brown bag.

Shaun flashed him one of those wolfish smiles. 'You've shouted me the food, you can't stand me up now fella.'

Jay tingled and grew hot. 'OK, but let's eat over there.'

He hurried ahead, choosing the long way around the

outside of the square. People there concentrated more on looking up the street at whether their bus was coming than who was rushing past them trying not to be seen.

They arrived at the unfinished development by the river. A few sad trees shielded them from the eyes on the road. Noise of the construction – drilling, banging, shouting – keeping away any eavesdroppers. The development's neighbours, who were supposed to have moved out, still slouched incongruously on the other side of the side-road: spiky chain-link fences, run-down buildings with pebble-dash frontages, pathetic patches of grass covered in piled-up rubbish. Eating there would mean fewer witnesses.

As they slipped into the skeleton of the central plaza through a narrow gap in the construction site fence, Shaun looked up and around, nodding. Giving an approving once-over to the hollow outline of high-rise flats destined to house fancy shops beneath them.

'Good to see they're finally making something of this dump,' Shaun said, gesturing at where the tatty low-rise buildings had been demolished and replaced by neat towers. He took his meal from Jay as they sat at opposite ends of a backless bench.

Jay didn't have much appetite for the regular chips he'd got for himself. He picked at the anaemic strips, half-heartedly poking them into the blood-red ketchup pot. Shaun couldn't get enough of his burger, chips and low-sugar drink. Would be a feast compared to prison food.

'Looking good my man!' Shaun grinned at Jay over the end of his burger. 'Don't get the wrong idea, though.' His grin transformed into a cautioning frown.

Jay hadn't filled out that much: although he'd never been able to meet Dad's sporting expectations, it's not like he'd ever been the nerdy weakling everyone expected of Asian guys. Shaun, on the other hand, had lost weight since the last time Jay saw him. Brought out his cheekbones. Made his muscles more wiry, although his back was less broad. His skin was paler too. Who out of he and Shaun could lift more now?

He should message Noah back about those tips on bench press form he'd sent Jay. He felt his phone in his pocket, picturing the progress pics Noah had shared, unasked for. Well, 'unasked for' – Jay had been squeezing his bicep at the time, during a quiet moment in the shop. Jay shifted uncomfortably and left his phone in his pocket.

'So, what brings you back here?' Jay ventured. 'Surprised you're already on day release.'

'Yeah, who would've thought five years would come round so soon?' Shaun tipped his head back to devour the last dregs from his can of soft drink. 'I guess the last few years haven't been so bad for you, have they, *Jakey*? Out here in the sun.' Shaun leaned back and closed his eyes, sunlight on his face, dark brown hair now prison-clippered short.

Jay looked. Didn't stop looking when Shaun opened one eye. 'I know you've had it worse. But it hasn't been all that great for me either.'

Shaun's face tensed at this, both eyes open but fixed in place, gritted teeth concealed behind his lips.

'*Hasn't been all that great?* Job, friends, freedom?' He crushed the can bitterly. 'Sounds pretty grand to me!'

'Sure, sorry. We never thought you'd end up put away for so long.'

Jay looked down at his hands in his lap. Olu and his checkboxes. The thin hostel walls he needed permission to escape for even a night. How he longed to start over, to be *Dan Lane*.

'But I have to sign in every month. You know what I'm saying?' His mumble grew louder with resentment. 'Only going the places they say, doing the jobs they want, seeing the people they say you can see? Telling them every last little thing about your life? This ain't freedom.'

'Freer than waking up inside a cell every day. Screws "accidentally" rattling your door as they go past early. Stuck inside with a load of guys who reek of BO.'

'I remember the smell from the toilet in the same room as my bed. Going crazy from twenty-three-hour lock-ups. Never knowing who I'd be sharing with next.' Speaking firmly now, the past and the present hurling the words out of him. 'And now I've got to tell someone every single detail of my life, worried they'll send me back if I don't tick the right box.'

'You got any idea what it's like inside when guys think you're a murderer?'

Both of them had finished whatever they were going to eat and drink now. They were straddling their ends of the bench, facing each other. Shaun leaned forward, hands half-way between his thighs and Jay's, his face eight inches away. Jay could smell the bacon, the cheese and the onion. Shaun's meaty breath.

Jay didn't look away:

'People might as well think I'm a murderer! I never knew when I'd be sentenced. What for. For how long. No variety, no meaning. Hours obsessing over canteen orders and keeping my cell clean 'cos there was nothing else to do. Then being forced to come back here. Never allowed to move on.'

'At least you could make your cell your own. Everything I try to own gets nicked. Even Listeners are against me.'

They were both breathing heavily now. Eyes locked onto each other's. Four inches apart. Jay still didn't look away:

'I had no contact with anyone from the outside for two and a half years.'

'I almost died.'

Jay stopped mid-retort. Pulled back. Mouth open. Eyes moving up and down Shaun, whose expression was still defiant but trembling. Shaun pulled up his T-shirt. Jay kept his eyes on the scar up the side of the abs.

'I almost died,' Shaun whispered, lowering the T-shirt, swinging his legs round so he was sitting side on to Jay. He hunched over. 'There'd been loads of death threats. Rumours of a knife smuggled in. All my time on edge, like. Then all it took was—' He took a shuddering breath. 'One. Quick. Shank.'

'Mate I ... I'm sorry.'

Shaun's head was in his hands now. He choked back what sounded like a sob, his body rigid with trembling. Jay reached out, his palm hovering an inch above the other man's shoulder. Shaun kept his head in his hands, his voice still torn up.

'And I'm sorry. I'm so sorry. I never meant for him to get hurt. It was an accident. I thought he was having fun. We did something terrible. Just to earn a few quid. I can never forgive myself. Never make it up to his family.' One more sob for good measure.

Jay let himself lower his hand onto Shaun's shoulder. Let Shaun keep kidding himself that Steffan had been paying him for something they'd both wanted – it would be hypocritical to judge otherwise.

'We both feel bad for what happened, mate. I know it all got ... out of hand. I'll never stop feeling ashamed of what happened.'

'What we *did*,' corrected Shaun bitterly.

Jay's phone buzzed in his pocket. Startled, he pulled it out, his hand sweaty. Big problem. *Incoming Call: Esther (Work).*

Esther's tone was patient but firm through Jay's tinny phone.

'I'm sorry, I'm running late, I'll be there soon.'

As Jay talked, Shaun freed his now-dry face from his hands, and stood up.

'Yeah it's the buses. Cool.' Embarrassed by his lie, Jay barely heard what Esther said as he ended the call. His heart jumped at four unread messages from Noah as he put his phone away. Breathing heavily, he looked up at Shaun, who was standing so close Jay's face was almost at his crotch.

Jay swallowed, and stood up. 'I know it's easy for me to say this, but can't we just do our time and put it behind us?' he asked placatingly.

'Sure, I know we agreed to this, Jakey, but—'

'Yeah, I'm not proud of what we did. That doesn't mean we deserve to be treated like we're worthless.' Jay surprised himself with the strength of his voice.

Shaun clutched at Jay's wrist with one hand. Jay tingled. Shaun used his other hand to pull out a crumpled white note. It trembled.

Everyone is going to know what you really did

Jay stayed standing to read it. Taking it in only once but staring at the page as if he were reading it over and over. Shaun's fingers rested around Jay's wrist as he pulled him to sit down next to him, and then let go. Those words. Following him everywhere, looking over his shoulder, twisting his stomach, clamping onto his chest.

'Did you send one of these to me?' Jay demanded.

'What the—? No, I got sent it in prison. What did yours say? The same thing?'

He was being sucked down into the depths of the ocean

again. Dark, unforgiving eyes watching him. Waiting to devour. He rubbed one hand up and down his arm, but couldn't get warm. He thrust the Note sideways at Shaun, pushing it away like a rotten taste.

'No idea how they got it to me through the prison post,' Shaun muttered. 'Smuggled in with something more innocent. Or maybe those stupid screws didn't bother to check what was in it before they left it for me.'

'Other people have seen this?!' Jay's turn to put his head in his hands, pulling his forehead back, forcing his eyes open. The drilling of the construction work burrowing into his brain. He twisted. Grabbed Shaun's T-shirt.

'Think what would happen! That'd be it for us! We'd both get life!'

Shaun gently placed his big hands on top of Jay's. 'No one has said anything to me. You?'

Jay let his hands drop. Shook his head violently. His mouth shut like a child resisting the foul-smelling medicine they'd been told to trust.

'Grand, grand. That's grand. We can sort this, Jakey. We need to find out who's been sending them. What's the plan?'

Jay thought about Amelia. The video call that proved she didn't know what had really happened that day. The shame that burned him up regardless. He glanced sideways at Shaun, and shook his head. Shaun drained the last drop from his crushed can like a thirsty baby.

'You sure?' Shaun frowned.

'I don't know, mate. You sure it's not a hoax? Tony—'

'Why would he ... Who's Tony?'

'A guy I know from Probation. He thinks it's nothing—'

'Must be nice having a mate who didn't grass you up and get you sent down for twelve years.' The cruel, narrow look was in Shaun's eyes again, his lips thin, curved like a knife, teeth semi-bared. He crushed the Note in his asphyxiating hands, rising to his feet without breaking eye contact.

But Jay could see the tears threatening to pour out.

'I'm not the only grass here, Shaun.'

'Jakey: if you hadn't gone and opened your big fat mouth, think where the two of us could be today?'

Shaun placed his right hand on Jay's shoulder. A flash of memory came to him, an aunty in the same position leaning down to kiss his forehead and bless him, under Amma's approving look.

Another call from Esther.

'I need to get to work or—'

Shaun brandished the crushed Note at Jay.

'Please. I've spent five years in prison, Jay. This is why I've come to find you. I can't do much from inside. But you can. Internet access, going places, speaking to people without a guard handcuffed to you.' Shaun rubbed his wrist. 'Find out who sent these. Could be anyone: someone you opened up to, another witness, a family member. You owe me that much.'

Jay ran for the bus.

'You owe me!' Shaun yelled after him.

His debt to Shaun was coming for him at last. To pay it off, he'd go as far as he needed.

37

Shaun

The alien machines communicated with each other in bleeps and wheezes.

'At least hospital air isn't stale,' Shaun said to his unresponsive audience. Prison air stank. Stank of judgement and humiliation, of boredom and piss. This air was fresh by comparison. Sure, sickness and death did have a scent. The scent of weakness. Humans unable to escape their own worthlessness.

He turned over his hands on his thighs, looking down at his worn palms. A man's hands. He shouldn't think about what they'd done. Not in a place that was supposed to be about keeping death at bay. Death would come for him too, one day. Probably one day soon, the way things were working out.

He clenched his long fingers into his palms, feeling the muscles in his arms working. Gripping tight. *Be a man now.*

'You're lucky! Bed at the end of the ward, like. I guess you can't appreciate the view right now.' Perhaps, even when she was under, Ma could feel the change in the daylight on her eyelids. That's what one of the nurses had said.

Shaun had found the nurse comforting, and hadn't

minded him placing his hand on Shaun's shoulder. Did that mean something about him? Maybe he was just stirred-up from being here. Maybe it was the uniform.

He remembered one of Ma's awkward 'talks' from when he was a teenager.

Now she was nothing but a voiceless, hollow shell. Growing up, she'd been a babbling anchor. No wonder Dad had left. *'You take after your dad. A good-looking man. So charming. Why I fell for him.'* Ma would always look so wistful when she said things like that. When she wasn't looking frightened, because of the son's resemblance to the father.

'What did you do for me, anyway?' he asked her silent form. Sure, she'd worked, cooked, cleaned, supported him through those troubles at school, but he could have done that himself. He hadn't needed her. He hadn't. He rubbed at his eyes with the back of his palms. 'A hospital shouldn't be so dusty.'

He got away from the bed.

The tea from these hospital vending machines was almost as weak as the stuff he'd got used to in prison. Taking a quick shufty to make sure he wasn't caught, he slipped some sachets of sugar and pots of UHT into his tight jeans pockets.

Dad had been fun. When he was round, treating him to sweets with a wink and an encouragement not to tell his mother. Shaun's favourite had been the jelly sweets: wobbling, luridly coloured candy which formed the shape of *'He-Man and the evil forces of Skeletor'* inside small plastic moulds. He kept the moulds so he could make ice-lollies out of squash. Ma helped him. When she was at home from one of her jobs. Never made him wait otherwise.

A memory of wasting a whole day waiting for Dad to pick Shaun up on his birthday. Ma unable to erase the shameful sense of not being good enough. Of being shut out from a relationship he wanted to be part of. Of being nothing but the worthless, hollow darkness at the bottom of a discarded human heart.

He sat back down. Reached over and stroked her pale hand, its skin thin as a funeral veil.

'You still believe I was innocent, don't you, Ma? You always thought I was special. You had the proof, like.'

He cleared his throat. Withdrew his hand.

'I'm only visiting you so I can get out on day release early, you know.'

He'd been a model prisoner inside. He would always have made contact with Jay again, eventually. Ma having a stroke had just helped him out sooner, that was all.

The fading light tiptoed in through the hospital window and rested a hand on Shaun's shoulder. He clenched his fists together, squeezing a knuckle between his teeth. When his chest couldn't grow any tighter, and his eyes threatened to wet themselves, he fled from the ward. He hurried along the corridor, blindly down the back stairs, and forced his way through heavy double doors and into the outside world.

The sun, faded as it was, should have felt warming on his pale skin. The breeze, polluted as it was, should have smelled fresh. The taste of freedom should have been sweet. But Shaun couldn't escape the image of Ma three floors up. The last five years of her life, rotted away in an empty flat, her only son bang to rights.

'She might still pull through.'

Shaun heard the words but didn't realise they were directed at him.

'She might still pull through. Your mum, is she?'

Shaun turned to face the short, pretty woman who was smiling at him. Black hair framed warm, dark eyes. She

174

was wearing a nurse's uniform. That's right, he'd seen her tending to Ma. She looked so unintimidating. He tearfully nodded an acknowledgement, catching his breath. He desperately wanted to be held. To have his hair stroked. To be told everything was going to be alright.

He puffed his chest out and stood with his legs wider.

She smiled at him still, the creases next to her lips and eyes telling him he was safe. Nobody was going to hurt him here.

'I seen lots of women like your mum. Strong women. She's not so old. She's been through a lot, I can tell. We've got good doctors. She's in the best place for care. We'll do all we can for her.'

Shaun felt like the nurse was enveloping him, even though next to her he was like a tree beside a flower. The concrete earth felt more solid under his feet. His skin felt thicker.

'I can't … I can't come to see her as often as I want.'

She didn't stop looking kindly at him. Tilted her head up and on one side. Shaun could see the slow rising and falling of her breathing.

'I'm sure you do all you can. Do your best. It's not easy when a loved one is in hospital.'

Shaun found his breathing slowing down. His shoulders lowering and relaxing. His facial muscles calming. In, and out. In, and out. In … and out.

'I know she must appreciate your visits.'

After enough time for Shaun to let her words sink in and spread comfortably through his body, she looked at her nurse's watch, patted him on the elbow, and went back inside. After the doors slid shut and left him in peace, Shaun allowed two tears to slide over his stubble. He needed Jay to take the threat of the notes seriously. Needed Jay to do what Shaun knew he was capable of.

38

Amelia

Amelia flipped through the printed pages Wanda had brought for her, again. First the call with Jay, now this disappointment. Opposite her, the police officer who'd supposedly been going to help her with dirt on Jay tentatively picked at her remaining chips. Rummaging right down into the empty bottom of the brown bag. The rustling irritated Amelia. The pages were just a straightforward transcript. No new information. Nothing. Useless! Amelia felt sick at the thought that her supposed Witness Care Unit informant was going to let her down.

Operator: Sir, this is a number for emergencies only.

Amelia had been excited when Wanda had showed up shortly after she'd ended the call. She hadn't been able to believe it when Wanda had said, 'Jay being gay too, and maybe having watched a little too much, isn't incriminating. Especially if the victim encouraged him.' She'd sat, open-mouthed, as the police officer who'd been involved in taking Jay's statement all those years ago had said she was sorry if that made her brother seem bad – of course he hadn't deserved what happened to him. But if Shaun had hooked up with him before and it had been, well, anything other than vanilla, then that might make it more likely his death had been a tragic accident.

'Consensual sex acts do go wrong. What Shaun told the police added up,' the mousey woman had concluded timidly before hiding behind her fillet-o-fish.

Amelia spread the loose transcript pages on the table and gazed at Wanda.

'Sorry if I'm being dumb, but how does this help me?'

'Amelia, please, it's the transcript of Jay's nine nine nine call.' Wanda held onto the sides of the brown paper bag, keeping it between them like a barrier.

Amelia slowly squashed the bag flat. 'I know, you said that, but what leverage does this give me on Jay? How can I use it?'

'The call wasn't recorded under caution, it wasn't used as evidence.'

'And?' Amelia chucked a not-quite-empty ketchup pot into the flattened bag. Red sauce splattered up the inside and over the edge. Wanda dabbed at the table top ineffectually with a paper napkin.

'I thought perhaps seeing how he'd tried so urgently to communicate with the police, I know it was after your brother had already died, but it might give you some of that closure you said you were looking for. Knowing Jay tried.'

The scrawny, slimy burger in Amelia's stomach mixed with her growing feelings of contempt towards Wanda. How could she ally with a man like Jay? Amelia considered retrieving her box of Kalms tablets from her bag as she looked down at the meaningless transcript.

Operator: Sir, if no one is in immediate danger, I'm going to have to end this call. I can try to transfer you to the Crime Management Unit. If there's no one available, please contact Missing Persons using the details I have given you if you have information about a specific crime.

Caller: But what if they don't get there in time? I'm telling you, he's planning to kill her for coming after him. I'm sure it was him in the flat, isn't that good enough?

Caller: [inaudible]

Amelia shook her head.

'If he was so sure, why didn't he call the police *when* it was happening?'

'I think, I mean, he only put two and two together later. After he'd recognised Shaun when he'd seen him in person, at the suspect's place of work.'

'I can't believe you've bought all that crap. I thought you were on my side.'

'Amelia, I'm very sympathetic to your situation. I really thought you reading this might help.'

'Well, it hasn't.' Amelia slapped the transcript down on the table. Could this seriously not have been an email? Through wet lashes, she scrutinised the ending.

Flushing red now, Wanda stood to her full height of 5'2".

'I'm going to get back to the Unit. I didn't come here to open a can of worms. I'll take those if you don't want them.'

'No.' Amelia pinned the papers to the table with her fingertips. 'No, thank you. I'll keep them,' she added thoughtfully.

Wanda pulled her handbag onto her shoulder, stared at Amelia, and left.

Amelia traced her finger over the last few lines of the call. Her despair and disgust were thinning, like mist on a valley morning, revealing the path to a summit that would burn under an unforgiving sun. As they cleared, she vaguely remembered some things Jay had said on his call to her. And from her interview with Tejinder. She got out her phone and messaged EmeraldSiren. She still owed Amelia a message, but maybe this latest finding would goad her.

Reviewing the thread of their conversation reminded her about the probation officer. Yeah, that was right, legally he had to act on any information he received about Jay. But was this the right kind of dirt? She needed to make sure she had enough to bury Jay alive. Get rid of his stench from her life.

Operator: Sir, you don't seem to know who's in danger or why. I'm going to end the call now.

Caller: Shaun's got the body stashed in his freezer at work.

Operator: What's that?

Caller: Shaun, I mean the guy I saw. I was in the fish and chips. He had this, this dodgy-looking chest freezer thing. Padlocked and everything. [inaudible]

Operator: Jay, please pass this information on to Missing Persons. You can leave a message if there's no one there when I transfer you.

Caller: How did you…?

Call ended by caller

Amelia wasn't surprised Wanda hadn't noticed the discrepancy: the woman was overloaded in that kind of job. If only this transcript *had* been passed on to the CPS. But the police had been so uninterested in her brother's disappearance. *'Not suspicious, insufficient resources for further investigation.'*

Amelia's burger struck her with a wave of nausea at the thought of how Steffan's body had been folded into the freezer. She laughed grimly into her chest when she realised how, whatever the operator did, this call must have helped, together with what Shaun said, to tip Jay into the muck. Idiot clearly hadn't realised that the police already know who you are when you call from your own phone.

She checked that old article just to be sure.

… and 'did not know' about the victim's body in the freezer. Whatever happened in flat 401 resulted in the tragic death of Steffan Evans, a twenty-nine-year-old gay man who worked at an animal sanctuary. Speaking outside the court after the sentencing, Mr Evans's sister stated: 'Because of Jay's and Shaun's conflicting accounts, we still don't know what really happened that day.'

The day Jay had pleaded guilty, the courthouse had been dark, its solid bricks barely holding up the weighty roof. Almost-black slate pressing down on its bones, guilty and innocent alike coursing through its innards, pale grey clouds gossiping overhead. The clouds had loomed close, threatening to release their downpour, but the muggy air hadn't broken.

When Jay had entered his guilty plea, his lawyer hadn't said anything about the freezer. Denied he'd had any knowledge of what Shaun had planned to do with the body. The deleted messages to Steffan the police had never been able to recover had poured petrol on a fire for Amelia, and for many on social media. They'd all been sure that Shaun had something on Jay which compelled him to help Shaun cover up his crime.

But, according to this call, *Jay* had been the one to have something on *Shaun*: Jay *had* known Shaun, *had* known what he'd done with the body, and, not only that, but *had tried to claim Shaun might kill again.* Why? And who was the alleged target?

Could she only form one conclusion? Maybe EmeraldSiren was right? *Jay is really the one responsible for your brother's death.* Digging into her, buried amongst these doubts, were thoughts about how she'd treated Steffan while he was alive. All that sarcasm and silent treatment. That last email. Whatever she needed to throw away, under the bus, or wherever, to get him justice, she would.

It was worse than Jay having pleaded guilty to helping a stranger conceal their crime, which Amelia had found so obsessively inexplicable; it was worse than him having watched people have sex through a window, and then letting someone die due to his own shame, which Amelia had found so anachronistically implausible.

If Shaun really had tried to murder a woman, surely that would have been mentioned at his trial? That would mean Jay had called the police, not to help her family get closure by alerting the police to where Steffan's body was (as he'd told Tejinder), but to try to frame Shaun for a murder Shaun never even attempted. Who was more likely to try to throw suspicion on someone else – innocent witness or guilty party? Jay had known exactly what happened in flat 401, and what happened to Steffan's body afterwards. Who was most likely to be in the know – accomplice or perpetrator? Shaun had pleaded guilty straight away, whereas Jay had only done so after two and a half years on remand. Who was most likely to 'fess up only under duress – accidental killer or deliberate murderer?

It must have been Jay's crime all along. As horrifying as Amelia found it, she was finally getting to the truth: now she had to prove it. If she didn't get him sent back to prison – who knew what he might do next?

39

Cathy

'Alright?' Cathy kept speaking before Louise could even say *Let's get started*. 'No word of a lie, not sure what to say about this. It's been doing my head in.'

Louise gently laid her tea down. 'Sounds like you've got something important you want to share with the group, Cathy?'

Cathy looked around at them all. 'Don't wanna drag other people down with me. That ain't fair.'

'That's what we're here for, Cathy,' reassured Martha. She smiled, and stroked the cross around her neck.

Cathy took a deep breath, like how Alice went on about in their therapy messages. 'I live with this guy. Jay. In a hostel.'

One of the other women, a regular, nodded like she was so smart.

Cathy went on. 'So he's been in prison, right? I thought he was another victim of the system, like me ...'

The regular rolled her eyes.

'But then I thought: cycle of abuse, you know?'

The regular snorted and shook her head.

'How can the group help you with this, Cathy?' asked Louise.

'I want to know if he's one of the bad ones. Want to prove it. Can't have him living at the hostel if he's dangerous.'

'Of course, it's important to be safe, especially where you live. But how would you—'

'I catch his probation officer looking at me, on a home visit the other day, right? And I think, "If I can get the information out of him somehow, I'll know what Jay really did."' Cathy caught her breath shallowly.

Louise smiled tentatively. 'How would you do that, Cathy?'

The unprepared answer rioted out of her mouth.

'Sex.'

Martha gasped. Bit of an overreaction, if you asked Cathy. Everyone else was staring at her, silent.

'Come on. You know what men are like!' The sex idea was like money. Like power. 'Easy to twist them round our little fingers.' She looked round at the women, who shifted in their mismatched seats. 'Come on. We've all been there.'

'Cathy,' Louise said gently, 'It might feel like this is the only way to get what you want, but it's not worth risking your well-being. Is there—'

'Jay could be a bad man. We're all here because of guys like him.' The heat rose in Cathy's face as memories of Ant surfaced. She put her head in her hands. 'They deserve what they get. Shouldn't be allowed near us.'

Head still in her hands, Cathy thought about the messages she'd exchanged with Alice the day before:

While it's true that victims of abuse (males in particular) can go on to become violent themselves, this doesn't mean that they all will, or that Jay has.

Cathy hadn't been reassured by Alice's little TED talk.

She'd closed the messages and opened Insta. It would be easy to find others who would join in with her feelings. Easy to feel rage instead of fear. Easy to set up another anonymous account. *Following* and *Liking* with no risk of being seen or known.

20 per cent of women have experienced some form of sexual assault.

Ant forcing her when she didn't want to.

Men silence women by blaming them for everything.

She hadn't lied to him, she hadn't. Why was he shouting right up in her face?

Men are ultimately the oppressors of women.

'Weak, cheating, stupid.' His words in her mind.

I can't forget anything Ant has done to me.

The intrusive memories can be put away, in time.

Alice gave Cathy some advice, and directions to the next bit of the website to use. Cathy watched some videos of ex patients talking about how the treatment had helped them. Read a load of information about how unwanted memories come back because they *'haven't been put away properly'*. Typed in how she'd use Group to help her if it got too much.

Cathy spent hours writing it all out. As much as she could put into words. Pages and pages of control, beatings, and other misshapen memories. The worst moments burst into her brain anyway, so why not get them out on paper? A horror story, joining up the broken pieces so they didn't dig into her so bad. She needed to get over this, otherwise Social Services would never get off her case.

Alice said the next task was '*optional*'. Cathy didn't need to send the therapy letters to anyone. But she wanted to say all these things. Things she'd been too afraid or ashamed of before. To her mum, her sister, Ant's parents. His old work. Cathy wanted them all to know. Nothing he'd said about her were true. Everyone would know what he'd done. She slipped the letters into white envelopes, and scabbed stamps off Tejinder.

That would show him.

She stumbled back from the postbox empty-handed. Her muscles were dragging her down, and her head was no help. Collapsing onto the bed, she still cried herself to sleep.

But the nightmares felt more over when she woke up. It was a day for something else. Underneath the hurt, she discovered it. She didn't want to believe it was still there.

But Alice said it was '*normal*'.

Cathy wanted to push it away. Like denying when she'd made a twat of herself.

Alice had said it was *Totally normal to desire physical intimacy. It's understandable that you might be afraid. But I believe you will be able to work out who you can trust. How did you work it out before?*

At the end of the break, Cathy overheard Louise talking to someone. Tejinder? Whoever she was was hidden on the other side of the door.

'That's OK. Must be tough, having run the group, and now attending it yourself. But you're doing the right thing.'

As Louise sat down, and brought the group back together, Cathy spoke up.

'Just wanted to say thanks. For today.'

Everyone smiled at her from their mismatched chairs.

Like they and Alice said – it was normal to want to keep yourself safe. Did they want men like Jay to get away with whatever he'd done? If she don't do anything, she's keeping the cycle going. And like they'd said – it was normal to fancy a bloke. She had the probation officer's number from his home visit. *Olu*. Group didn't need to know she was going to use it to kill two birds with one stone. Like Ant used to say – it's a dog-eat-dog world.

And she knew, from Ant's run-ins with probation: they could get you recalled to prison like *that*.

40

Jay

Streets in Woolwich town centre were as crowded on Sundays as they were on Saturdays. Only the Black families coming back from church made the day a little different. Jay, reminded of Amma, turned away and spied on the entrance to the warehouse, checking his phone briefly. It wasn't time yet. He sat back on the low wall opposite Tony's workplace. After what he'd found waiting for him at Magda's on the day Shaun had showed up, it was worth coming back, as long as Olu didn't find out. He had to be sure.

He'd better gain more here than he had from his door-to-door investigations downstairs from Flat 401 earlier that day. The previous visit with Cathy had made it easier to go back, at least. And the exercise had been almost fun: pretending he was looking to buy in the area, but was concerned about the 'incident' from five years ago.

It had to count for something that he'd eliminated the two flats he was sure were the most likely places to find someone who might have seen something that day. Someone who needed to be silenced, so they couldn't grass him up. At the first flat, opposite the lift up to Flat 401, he'd thought he'd got the wrong door, but it turned out the old man who used to live there had died while Jay was inside. At the second, opposite the lift up to Jay's old flat, he'd gone on high alert when a buff guy opened the door. But then he'd realised the look in the guy's eyes was flirtation, not recognition. *'Sorry, man. Do you want to come in for a bit? I could try to remember if I saw anyone that day.'*

Jay stood up. Tony was coming out of the warehouse, shielding his eyes from the sunlight with one hand, already lighting up the cigarette hanging from his mouth with the other as he crossed the building's boundaries. Jay declined his non-verbal offer of a smoke. The older man looked particularly weak today.

'What's up with you, son? Got a job interview or something?' Tony asked, pointing with his lighter as he put it back in his pocket. Blowing smoke away from Jay but keeping his eyes on him.

Jay looked down, grabbed the lapels of his jacket, then let the ill-fitting, second-hand blue blazer drop. He shuffled, pulled at his tie, smoothed the creased white shirt. 'Nah, I'm going somewhere later.'

'A date?' Tony giggled, although his narrow eyes were watchful.

Jay didn't smell any alcohol. Just the sharp, ashy smoke. 'Nah, just doing the rounds, mate. People who might know stuff.'

'What kind of stuff?' The smile half-gone now. 'Need a favour from me and my boys, do ya?'

Jay took a deep breath and fixed his eyes on Tony as he plunged in. 'I received another one of those Notes. At the hostel. Different wording, but basically the same.'

Tony gave him a sidelong smirk. Shook his head, and puffed out a grey cloud.

'Do you remember the stuff I asked you about? About

people being convicted of one crime but what if, hypothetically speaking, they'd actually committed another?'

Tony's smile disappeared altogether. 'I'll save you the time, Jay. Like I said before – notes, WhatsApp messages, whatever. I don't think you should care. If you told me everything back when we were in Group' – Jay turned his face away from Tony's sneer – 'then you've got nothing to worry about. No one can have anything on you the court didn't already hear.'

Jay grew hot in his suit. Clenched his fists.

Tony tapped his cigarette against the wall, embers sparking and falling to the ground. 'These notes making you see you can never go straight?' Tony ran his tongue across his lower lip. Taking another drag and puffing it out. 'How much does Timpo's make?'

Jay didn't have time for Tony's nonsense. He checked to see how close other people were: he hadn't wanted to put this in a text, but didn't want anyone to overhear. 'I'm serious, mate. I'm not the only one who got … a Note.' Tony's eyebrows rose, and he started to speak. Jay kept going. 'Shaun got one too. Sent to him in prison, in his actual cell, like. So, someone is after both of us. I need to sort them out.'

Tony was shaking his head as he pulled his cigarette out of his mouth. 'You should not be meeting up with that guy, Jay. I know I've done time, but he's bad news.' He threw the smouldering butt onto the pavement and ground it out under his shoe. Put his hands in his pockets. 'I thought you might want some help with the three brothers who've been bothering you. Or in on that job I've got going. Or both. I'd do that for you, Jay, but don't drag me into something with Shaun Flanagan.'

'He's not as bad as everybody thinks.' Jay laughed bitterly.

'Oh, I see how it is!'

Fear flooded Jay at how suddenly and intensely Tony's face burned red. Dad's eyes burning into him as he lay, punched and kicked down.

As if in sync with the memory, Tony cracked his knuckles. 'Everybody always gets given a second chance, but me? You know what it's like not to even know where your kid is? All I wanted was to be a good dad.' Spit splattered against Jay's cheek. 'I tried to do my best for you, Jay. Not just because I thought you might put in a good word for me.'

'I don't even know—'

'You don't know anything. I swear, one more person tries to put me down ...'

Tony lunged at Jay.

Jay backed off, raising his palms, puffing up his muscles.

'What's got into you, mate?'

Tony's heavy breathing slowed down. Staring at Jay, he rubbed the back of one fist across his eyes. Jay kept up his defensive stance, bemused and concerned. Tony turned, and walked back into the unlit mouth of the warehouse. Jay stared after him into the darkness, then walked off into the sunlight.

The sweat from the twelve minutes' walk, and the subsequent wait, glued the back of his shirt to his jacket. He pulled at his collar, straightened the cheap, thin tie. His hands clammy on the phone in his pocket. Still not time. As he waited behind double-parked cars, glare reflecting off the windscreens, he watched the narrow house his mother now lived in. She might still be at Temple. He remembered *dana* ceremonies led by orange-robed, monotonously chanting, bald-headed monks; he couldn't imagine them gay-shaming him.

His only prior attempt at reconciliation had been a year ago. Tony had known someone who'd known someone who knew where she was. Jay had then spent his first year of Probation psyching himself up to visit, only to be hissed at through a crack in the door. *'I was moved because of you!'*

And now he was waiting outside again. What a messed-up anniversary. Another set of shame-red bricks, door to match.

Jay was surprised to see Amma in a sari as she let herself in, alone. She'd get changed into something plainer. He gave her time before crossing the Close, and knocking.

When the door opened only a crack, all sense of hope disintegrated. Amma's face contemplated him stonily. Classic FM floated in from somewhere further inside the house. She was still wearing her purple and gold sari.

'Ah! I have told you. You are not welcome here.'

'Ammi, please, I need to ask you something.'

'What if people see you?' She looked past him to check the street.

'No one here knows me, Ammi. Look, I dressed up.' Jay gestured at himself uncomfortably under the direct gaze of the light: his suit material didn't allow heat to escape, and he was boiling in this spot of sun right in front of Amma's cool, shady hallway. Despite the sleeves and legs of the suit being too short.

'Ammi, please.'

The silhouette of a beer-bellied, pink man in a wife-beater vest lurked behind the frosted glass door of number 23, a few houses up, on the curve of the cul-de-sac. Amma fiddled with the thin, saffron-coloured thread around her wrist; the *dana* ceremony involved them all sitting around cross-legged, holding the long thread above their palms as the monks chanted, and having the *pirit-nula* bound around one's wrist, after being blessed and cleansed with water.

Amma pulled him inside and shut the door.

'Aiyo. Why couldn't you be more like your malli?'

Not waiting for an answer, she shuffled into the small lounge, and sank into the two-seater settee opposite a tired coffee table. As if Jay could ever have measured up to his younger brother.

'Why did I throw your Thatha out? No, that man: "*but you're different, I didn't mean you should go home, just those other foreigners.*"' Amma's face twisted as she mimicked Dad after how he voted in 2016.

'Where is Dad these days?' Jay hesitated at the doorway.

'What's it to me? And his family ...' She made a 'chh' noise and a disappearing, waving-away motion with her hand. Face turning away in disgust.

Jay dared to step into the lounge. Twisting his feet awkwardly. 'I might be in some trouble—'

'Again! Useless child! Haven't you brought enough shame on this family?' His mother turned her face to him now, narrowed eyes full of tears. He lowered his gaze, throat thick, scared to say more. He stood like that for a while, swallowing to hold back his own tears, hearing her sari rustle as she wiped her face.

'The thing is, puthaa ...'

Jay looked up, surprised by Amma's suddenly gentle tone. She was gazing at a photo in a silver frame, of her, and him and his brother when they were kids.

'I tried my best for you. I didn't want you to go through the kind of thing I did. I have told you what I went through when I came to this country, no?' She shook her head.

'I get you were doing what you thought would protect me. There's still prejudice, Ammi.'

She waggled her head from side to side.

Jay stepped closer and went on. 'So you know what it's like to be, to be judged for just being who you are.'

Looking over her shoulder, his gaze came to rest on the

multicoloured wooden demon mask on the side: black cobras for hair, a giant red tongue sticking out between sharp teeth, big black staring eyes ringed with white and red.

Amma jumped up.

'I'll tell you another thing! I am proud of being Sri Lankan. That is not the same as being ... like you. Couldn't you have *tried*? After all I've suffered. Ah! You will go and do what you want.'

Jay lost the connection with her insistent eyes. He looked over the walls of a home he'd never known, and through the window at a street he could never live on, as he turned to go.

'No thank you, I am not buying anything today, good-bye, God bless!' Jay's mother declared loudly as she closed her door firmly in his face. The lock clicked decisively.

Jay thought about knocking again but the shaven-headed man at number 23 placed a tattooed hand on his gate. Jay tipped his head back in slight acknowledgement, faked a smile. Rubbed the back of his head as he swaggered away, half turning to see that the man was still watching. Jay could take him if he wanted.

He couldn't go back. Amma clearly didn't want anything to do with him, nor anything about him to be made public in case it attached itself to her. So, she wouldn't be sending the Notes. He hadn't really expected she'd be willing to help him, anyway.

He stopped at the end of the Close, where it joined the main road. Took in the few trees, bright green in the sunlight, as he sheltered in the shade under the graffitied road sign. If people from his past couldn't help him be sure that the Notes were no threat to him, he'd have to pay an unexpected visit to someone who'd recently reentered his present.

He left the Close, and headed back towards Woolwich town centre.

41

Jay

Tejinder seemed caught off guard when she looked up from taking the previous customer's payment and saw Jay the other side of her counter. Imagine all the surprises he could spring on her … He hoped, today, her expression was pleasantly surprised. Big white teeth beamed out from her brown face.

'Jay!' She grabbed a cloth, and half redried a cup from the shelf before putting it back. She put the cloth down. Hung it up. Fiddled with her apron. She was still smiling but also eyeing the queue behind him.

'Can I get a camomile tea please, Tejinder?'

'Of course.' She jerkily turned away from and then towards him again. 'Sit, sit, *beta*! I'll bring it over to you.'

As Jay waited at his wooden table, which was painted a compassionate shade of green, he stared at the small bag of sweet popcorn Tejinder had bidden him 'eat, eat' along with the tea. It might be telling him it had only *84 kcal per (1/4) pack*, the corn dressed up like an angel to endorse this message, but the bag was still tellingly red. Amma's voice was louder in his mind than it had been for months. Jay wondered if today would be the last time he saw her in this lifetime. He opened the bag and stuffed the sweet, sticky lumps in his mouth.

Tejinder came over when she'd served the queue. Laid the white ceramic pot on his table. Didn't go straight back to waiting behind the counter. Stood there turning the circular brown tray she held flat against herself like a flower-patterned shield.

'I want to talk to you,' Jay said, pushing the other chair at the table out with his foot. 'Didn't know when you'd next be at Magda's.' He stared at her. Nodded at the chair pointedly.

Tejinder obeyed his unspoken command, and sat down with a release of breath, looking like she might burst into tears from smiling. 'I'm so sorry about Amelia.' She placed the tray down on the table and wrung her apron with both hands.

'You what?' Jay sat up straight. Had something happened? Would he get blamed, if it had?

'She told me she wanted Restorative Justice. She didn't call it that, but she went on about sharing with you how she and her family had been harmed by – by what happened. I told her nothing would bring Steffan back. But I thought hearing from you directly, if she could speak to you, that might repair some …' Tejinder wiped her eyes. 'That's why I gave her your number. Once she'd got it, she changed.'

So, it was Tejinder who'd given him away to Amelia. At least he didn't have to take care of that loose end.

Tejinder cast her eye back towards the rich green photo frame which contained the image of an older woman who looked like her. 'It wasn't fair my mum died. But sometimes things that aren't fair happen. We have to make our peace with that.'

Jay gave Tejinder a moment of silence for her mother.

'That's why you're here, isn't it? Did she call you?' Tejinder asked.

Jay stirred his tea unnecessarily. 'Yeah, she did. But that's not why I'm here.'

Or was it? After their call, Jay had changed his mind and ruled out Amelia as the Note sender, because she didn't seem to know anything that wasn't already public. But maybe she had been trying to wind him up: psychological revenge. Or to torment him so much he'd expose his own secret?

'I don't understand.' Tejinder was looking inquiringly at him.

He needed to play this carefully. If Amelia was sending the Notes, he didn't want to arouse Tejinder's suspicions. It was bad enough he'd blurted out to Amelia about watching Shaun with Steffan.

'I've been getting these anonymous messages.'

Tejinder's hands shot up to cover her open mouth.

'You think it was Amelia? What did the texts say?'

Exactly. If Amelia knew where he lived, why would she have bothered getting his phone number from Tejinder?

'No, not text messages. Good old-fashioned letter writing.' Jay flashed a fake smile that dropped into the cup of tea as he sipped at it. 'You didn't tell her where I live, did you?'

Tejinder looked shocked. Or was it guilty?

'No, of course not! I thought that would be too much. Given she was here, and the hostel is right round the corner, I thought she might have already—'

'Here? She was here when she spoke to you?' Jay let go of his cup and gripped the table. Why had he assumed Amelia had spoken to Tejinder over the phone?

'Yes, but, I mean … I don't think she's the type to send anonymous threatening messages. She was pretty direct.'

Jay sank back into the chair. Amelia had been happy enough to be anonymous the first time she messaged him.

Did that translate to written threats? Did it make a difference she'd come to the café?

'So who else could it be?'

Tejinder tilted her head and squinted. Crossed her arms, bit her lip. Then her skin flushed, her eyes widened, and her mouth dropped open. 'I bet Shaun wasn't too happy with you for getting him sent to prison. He's a wrong 'un, that one. Thank God they banged him up. I don't blame his girlfriend for moving away to have the baby. Heard she changed her name and all. And that's another thing: it's just so unfair he got to plead guilty to manslaughter straight away. Didn't even get a trial. But you had to wait all that time, and had to plead guilty, after what he'd made up about you.'

At least Shaun hadn't said worse. Was doing so within the Note sender's grasp? Jay shifted uncomfortably on the padded seat. He remembered his 'no comment' police interview, not believing that a guy like him would be treated more leniently if he pleaded guilty, whatever the duty lawyer said.

Tejinder filled the silence. 'How threatening were the messages? Could they have been from him?'

Jay tried to picture whether his licence conditions forbade having contact with Shaun: he didn't want to take any chances.

'I don't think it's Shaun. It would be hard to send a note like that out of prison. Screws – sorry – *prison officers* read everything.'

It wouldn't have done Shaun any good to expose Jay's secret, given Jay had known the unseen truth about him, too. That had been their deal, their prisoner's dilemma. But, after what Jay really did, Shaun had been sent down for far longer than either of them had thought likely. And why was he on day release so early? He could have faked that 'note' he showed Jay. No proof he'd received it. And in fact, that would explain how it had been 'smuggled' into the prison: it hadn't been.

But wouldn't leaving the second Note on the same day as he showed up at Magda's be too obvious?

Tejinder stood up. More customers. 'Maybe you should talk to your probation officer about this? Aren't they supposed to look out for you, help you make a new life for yourself?' She raised her hands to ward off protests Jay hadn't even intended to make. 'It sounds like this Olu guy might want to do the right thing by you.'

Jay played with his cup. Watched the quality of light morph as the day became late.

Who else could it be?

Jay checked his phone again: it was time. He drained his tea. Left the Wellness Café with a short but friendly wave to Tejinder. She bowed her head slightly and smiled. Jay took himself back to Mulgrave Pond. Part of him hoped Margaret would be carrying out another home visit. But apart from Amma's old Community Psychiatric Nurse, he knew no one would disturb or overhear him there, in the shadow of the trees, by the water. He sat, chest tight, heart beating, mouth dry. Staring at his phone, waiting for it to ring.

Incoming Call: Withheld Number

Finally.

'Shaun?'

'Alright, mate, how ya goin?' It was hard to hear over the background noise, presumably of the wing he was calling from, but Shaun sounded less Irish today.

'I did what we planned. I haven't been able to find out anything.'

Although it was much less intense than when he first got each Note, Jay felt himself wading into the deep; sunk at the bottom, a murky wreck signalled a nameless darkness that would wait for him forever.

'Don't worry Jakey, it'll be OK. We've got through worse!' Shaun's voice was still smooth, accent or not.

After Jay didn't fill the pause, Shaun went on: 'I've been thinking, what about my … the victim's family?' The lightness in his voice trailed off guiltily.

Jay still didn't want to risk Shaun knowing what he'd blurted out to Amelia. And anonymous WhatsApp messages weren't the same as anonymous Notes.

'Nah. How would they know anything? And how would I even get in touch with them?'

'OK, no worries, no worries. Did you speak to' – the next word said as if it tasted bad – 'Tejinder? She thought she were a detective last time, like.'

'She doesn't,' Jay said dismissively. 'She's just running that café, mate.'

'Let her run it. "Wellness".'

Jay didn't think Shaun would like this next part, but he said it anyway. 'She suggested I speak to Olu, my probation officer. Check out whether the Note could be a problem, like.'

A slight pause. Cell doors banging, inmates shouting at each other. A brief breeze ruffled the surface of the pond. It cooled Jay's cheeks and made the trees whisper to him. *Only mention one Note: if Shaun brings up the second, that means he's the sender.*

'That's not a bad idea,' Shaun said sarcastically. 'Ask him what he thinks. Maybe we can earn forgiveness.' The background noise grew louder and more confusing. 'And if you do figure out who sent those notes: get them off our case. Please, Jay.'

Call Ended

Jay didn't blame Shaun for hanging up: he remembered seeing the intimidating queues for payphones on the wing – not that he'd had anyone to call.

His penultimate offender management session was coming up. But he couldn't wait. His mouth went dry and he bit his lip. Despite Shaun's opposition, he would call up and get booked in – no, it was the weekend. He could use one of the tips Cathy had learned in her intensive therapy.

Jay pictured going to *Olu* in his Contacts. He would take a deep breath, smile, and type out a message. Olu would reply in a friendly way, and be happy to see him. Jay mouthed the words as he imagined. The smile on his face, the slowing of his breathing, the softening around his eyes and forehead, were real.

Tejinder's mothering had made his skin feel thicker. Talking to Shaun was a booster: like some of the big man's confidence rubbed off on him. Same with the latest flirtatious messages from Noah.

Yeah. Things would work out. He could do this.

He sent Olu the message requesting an extra session.

42

Jay

Jay was glad Cathy seemed alright with him after her anger outside Flat 401. Her coming with him to this voluntary Probation appointment added to the courage Shaun, Noah and Tej had infused him with.

He'd been relieved when Olu had texted him back, but now it was Monday, Jay's anxiety about what might happen had risen. Nothing was immediately breaking the waves, or visible when he looked down, but what lay in the dark beneath his treading feet?

He nodded 'alright' to the other offenders in the waiting room.

Cathy flipped between looking around and at her phone. She was jiggling her leg. Jay's own level of apprehension built, threatening to bubble out of his throat, spilling out in front of everyone.

He looked up sharply when Olu called his name loudly. But his probation officer was smiling. Some of the tension smoothed away from Jay's face and shoulders. He smiled back tentatively.

Although Olu was at least five years younger than Jay, it felt good to have someone who understood him a little better than previous POs seemed to. Over the past few months, they'd swapped stories about their upbringings: parenting (tough love on both sides), religion (Jay vaguely got the Biblical quotes Olu rarely offered, and tried to reciprocate from his meagre experience of Buddhism), food (Jay definitely preferred sweet, creamy cashew nut curry to the spoon of microwaved egusi soup Olu had offered him one time). They'd both grown up in South London too, so despite different patois surfacing every now and then, they even spoke in a similar way.

Jay depended on Olu more than he'd admitted.

Seeing Olu look at Cathy, he said, mischievously, 'This is my friend Cathy. You remember her, from the hostel? She was just making sure I got here OK.' Turning to her, he added, 'Thanks, Cathy. I've got this now.'

She responded with 'OK', a blank face, and turning back to her phone. The two men went through to an interview room up the corridor.

'What are you listening to?' Olu asked.

Jay fumbled for his earphones. He hadn't noticed he'd not switched off the electric guitars, synthesised drumkits and Sinhalese vocals that he'd been using to amuse himself while waiting.

'Sorry about that.' Jay paused the music on his phone.

'No, seriously, what was it, man?'

Olu was smiling at him. Maybe he really wanted to know?

'Baila. It's Sri Lankan music called Baila. Uncles would put it on at the end of family gatherings.'

Olu reached out a hand. Jay looked at it, confused, and then slowly placed one earphone in the outstretched palm. Olu lifted the earphone to his ear, and Jay pressed play. He put the other earphone in his own ear, and slow smiles gradually dawned on their faces as their heads moved to the cheerful music.

'Listen to this,' Olu said, pulling out his own phone as Jay put his away.

Olu played him a couple of tracks before saying they should probably get down to business; the style was different, particularly the much livelier percussion, but Jay, inside, appreciated the attempt at sharing. Or had Olu wanted to cover up his real motive in taking Jay's earphone: to make sure it really was music playing like Jay said? Would he take Jay at his word?

'So, Jay. I believe this is the first time you've asked for an extra supervision session,' said Olu, his fixed smile faltering somewhat. 'Nothing wrong, I hope?'

Jay took a deep breath in. Let it out, looking Olu in the eyes. Olu was still smiling. He could do this.

'I've been working hard to meet my licence conditions. Meeting with you, never missing a shift at work, not staying away overnight from Magda's, the hostel.'

Olu nodded, relaxing back into the plastic interview-room chair.

'Yes. You've been very diligent. Doing a great job meeting your licence conditions.'

The air of the room was still and stuffy. The over-sized clock ticked.

'Two weeks ago, I received this Note.'

Olu frowned. He looked absent-mindedly down at the paper file in his lap, and then back up at Jay.

'A note?'

Jay pushed on.

'I don't know who sent it. Well, I mean, I might have an idea, but I don't know if it's her or not.'

'What did the note say, Jay?' Olu had taken the lid off his biro.

Jay hesitated. He looked at the pen and the papers in Olu's lap, then up at his eyes. Olu was still looking warmly at him.

'It said I would be sorry for what I'd done. But I already am sorry. You know that. I'm not a wrong 'un.' He looked sincerely at Olu. Tears threatened but he kept them back, clenching his hands over his knees.

Olu didn't write anything down.

'I know Jay, I know. Can I see the note?'

Jay wiped his hands on his thighs.

'I ... I threw it away. Recycled it.'

Olu nodded gently, a few times, keeping his eyes on Jay.

'And you have no idea who sent it?'

'Well, it might be the sister of the man who ... you know.'

Olu nodded again, looking kind of sad now. Then he frowned.

'Why do you think it might be her?'

'She messaged me. On WhatsApp. Got my number from a hostel worker. Said she wanted answers from me. Wasn't satisfied with what I'd officially said happened ... about Steffan.' Jay remembered the mess he'd made of himself on the voice call, and Amelia's response. 'Which is fair enough. But I didn't have anything else to tell her.'

Olu looked at the clock. He was running out of time. Or patience. Jay jumped in before he could say anything else:

'Is that against my licence conditions? Having contact with her? Or, anyone else involved with the case, with the crime?'

Jay watched the younger man's mouth turn down at the edges. Olu flicked through his file.

'Doesn't look like it. Some licences spell out you can't

have any contact with victims. Yours doesn't. The family of the victim didn't make any application for that kind of condition.'

Jay slowly edged the next question into the space between them.

'And what about the other offender?'

The question hung there for a moment. Olu blinked a few times, looked at the clock again, then smiled, a bit more thinly now.

'No. That's not in here either. It's based on what the Offender Manager – that would be me – believes is necessary for your successful reintegration into society.'

It was either Amelia winding him up without any evidence, or Shaun winding him up because of how things had worked out after their arrangement. In either case, his prayer had been answered.

'I asked around a bit, but there's no one else it could be. I even went round my mum's.'

Jay surprised himself with his next reaction, as he told Olu about the visit.

He started to cry.

Not the kind of crying like when he'd begged Amelia to be understanding, which had left his whole face snotty and wet. But as he opened up to Olu, raw tears caught him unprepared. He saw Amma again, face taut, eyes frozen, shutting the door in his face. Pretending he was some kind of repulsive salesman.

'Sorry, don't know what that's about.' Jay laughed uncertainly, and wiped his cheeks. Vulnerability seized hold of him again. He hunched over. His voice lowered. 'Something happened to me that I've only told one other person.' Folded in on himself like that, it was as if he were alone. 'There was this football match.'

*

He was thirteen years old, washing his hands in the empty football stadium toilets. Heart and stomach fighting their way up into his desert of a mouth. Had the other guy spotted Jay checking him out before he'd walked out? No time to dry his hands properly – get out of there.

The lad and his two mates blocked the door. Advanced towards him. His pleas and excuses not fooling anyone. A shove, a punch, a kick. He cowered on the dirty, wet floor. They loomed over him, ready to add to his bruises. The leader of their pack leaned down, fangs bared, clawing at Jay's chest.

Behind them, the door to the Gents opened. Dad's boots thudded on the tiles. His face was a dark thing. Jay looked up, full of hope.

The youth who'd been leaning down, hand grabbing Jay's T-shirt, stayed down but looked at Dad uncertainly. The others took a step back at the sight of the big man.

Dad took in the scene. Cracked his knuckles. Spat to the side. Eyed them all in turn.

And left.

The tendrils of the stench from the urinals pulled Jay down as the door slammed shut and the youths slammed into him.

At home afterwards, Amma ran Jay a warm bath. Made Dad wait outside. She peeled off Jay's clothes, rubbed witch hazel over his bruises, and cleaned up his wounds. He felt her disappointment and anger through the fingers digging into his back. She ran a hand softly over the back of his head.

'It's OK, puthaa,' she soothed. 'It'll be OK.'

Then she was pushing his face down into the bath, wailing, holding his head under the water until he was sure the alien liquid that didn't belong in his lungs would choke him to death.

Her homemade Buddhist version of praying the gay away, cleansing the shame from him, monotonously chanting to free her son of his karmic debt. In, out, in, out. The burning wet slapping him in the face each time he was pushed back under. His tears mixing with the tap-water when he was momentarily allowed back up, his 'please' lost in his gasps for air and the sound of his brother shouting at Dad and banging on the bathroom door. The quality of light strained through the turbulent window of the surface, as his blurring vision warned him time was running out.

You will fail to function, fail to escape. You will be crushed to death, the eyes and minds of every person who knows you holding you down until you die, the alien breath of lungs that no longer belong to you choking you as you beg to be released from the prison of your own body.

Bubbles of oxygen formed the image of death in front of his eyes. Life and freedom awaited. If only he could break free.

After he'd finished getting the memory out, Jay dried his face, and cautiously looked up at Olu.

Olu was shaking his head, gazing softly, a caring smile creasing his face. His eyes and tone were soft: 'I'm sorry, Jay.' He leaned forward and put his hand on Jay's shoulder. The touch rested there like a duvet, Jay's breathing slowing down underneath it. 'You didn't deserve to have that happen to you.' Olu's hand was warm with compassion. 'When I was a kid, I had a friend.' His smile turned sad. 'He got outed on social media. Parents threw him out.'

Olu leaned back and rubbed his head awkwardly. 'I'm sorry I put you through such a hard time recently. My boss, she …' He looked at the clipboard and papers in his lap, lifted up one corner slightly, then set it back.

'I don't think we have anything to worry about,' he said, looking up at Jay, firmly and kindly. 'I don't need to take this further, based on what you've told me.'

'Thank you,' Jay said, keeping his eyes on Olu, clasping his hands in his lap, wanting to make sure this safe harbour didn't disappear. He felt held in Olu's gaze. Like when his brother had tried to look out for him when they were teenagers.

'So I don't have to worry about being recalled?'

Olu laughed. 'Man, I'm not like most of my colleagues. You'd have to do something proper serious for me to recall you. Prisons are loads full! It's not like the Government's been keen on early parole for good behaviour, you get me?'

He covered his mouth, blowing his cheeks up as if he were a hamster concealing food for later, and comically checked the door for listeners with wide eyes. They shared a laugh at authoritarian bureaucracy's expense.

The waiting room was empty as Olu showed Jay out; Cathy must have gone back to Magda's.

'Just keep your nose clean and we'll have you discharged by the end of next month,' Olu said, clapping Jay on the back as he returned to the office.

Jay took the lift to the outside.

No message from Cathy, but one from Noah. That man was cheeky.

Jay held still, ignoring the flutter in his stomach, and gently bit his lip. How much was lies, showmanship and exaggeration? Jay didn't know for sure how much was safe to let out, and how much he still needed to keep in.

He only had to make it to the end of the month.

He messaged back.

43

Then

Steffan

I stare at the blank black surface of my coffee. The golden logo of Tej's café, printed on light green cardboard, stares out between my fingers.

'You have to be careful what you put out there,' Tej continues.

I squeeze the paper cup, my fingers burning. 'Have I ever told you about the time Amelia told on a boy at school? Using Facebook?'

Tej shakes her head.

'I can't remember what he'd done, but something like every afternoon on the bus back from school, for a week, she'd go on at me about him. Not even really talking to me, but just going on about him. What he'd done. How she'd get back at him.'

Tej laughs. 'Hard to imagine the two of you are related!'

I give her a doubtful smile. 'She does take after our Dad more. Anyway, the whole thing didn't end well for her. The boy got in trouble, but no one likes a tell-tale.' The grey clouds through the window are like a horde of eyes bearing down on the jagged skyline.

Tej smiles genuinely and finishes her coffee. 'And how are things going with Shaun?'

I can feel the smile spreading across my face at the question. I know I am perhaps being naïve. But our messages have been intense.

'I am fond of him.'

'Are you fond of him, or who you need him to be?'

'Alright, Sigmund!' I laugh.

Tej laughs along, then smiles compassionately.

'Steffan, after what you went through with your ex … I think you need to learn to trust again, that's important. But it will take you time.'

She's right. The fact I want to slowly move towards something serious with someone who is out is like an acorn in my mind – I promise myself I will send him that honest message.

'It's only been a couple of weeks. I'll admit he doesn't express his feelings a lot. Despite being totally full of "blarney".' My imitation Irish accent is a bit off on the last word.

Tej laughs. 'He's a man, isn't he?'

'And what about you? Any lucky ladies on your horizon?'

Tej shakes her head, sadly.

I think of how having to look after her mum hasn't given her the energy or time for dating.

'And what about this Jay? He seems like a nice Sri Lankan boy,' Tej says, exaggerating an Indian accent. 'Does Shaun know you have a neighbour you care for like one of your wounded animals?'

I take another sip of my hot drink. My eyes land on my 'monstrous' (Tej's word) travelling bag. I know I'm not going anywhere anytime soon, but it's another thing that helps me cope with being cooped up inside; I shall see the world again.

'Honestly, if you only make coffee this good, you won't even need your cakes—'

'Made according to my mum's family recipe!'

'Made according to your mum's recipe,' I clarify. 'You won't even need those for the café to succeed!'

I feel a deeper connection to Jay, but I think he's even less comfortable with his sexual orientation than Shaun, hard as that may be to believe.

'You'll be alright,' Tej says. 'I know you'll make the right choice.'

44

Now

Amelia

'Oh. It's you again.'

Amelia ignored Tejinder not sounding pleased to see her. 'Can I get a tea?'

'I'm a bit busy right now.'

There were other people in the Wellness Café, but they were finishing up. Amelia had come at closing time again, just making it after another day satisfying Janice's demands. The woman was making her work even harder as the early probation review approached. At least she'd enlisted Peter's help with her search.

'I can wait,' Amelia said, taking her tea to a corner table. She kept an eye on Tejinder, distant from the other customers. Checked her phone for messages from Peter: no report from her boyfriend-turned-accomplice yet. Wasted time doom-scrolling through viral social media stories of unsavoury celebrity antics. Tapped her fingers on the colonial green table.

Tejinder waited until Amelia was the last customer left before shutting the door, turning the sign on it to *Closed*, and coming over. 'You used me. I understand you hounding Jay, but I don't want to be a part of whatever game you're playing.' She picked up Amelia's cup, not asking if she'd finished with it.

'Jay accused Shaun of planning to kill a woman.'

Tejinder froze on her way back to the counter.

'Was it you?' Amelia asked.

Tejinder turned, made as if to return towards Amelia, then sat down two tables away. 'How did you find out about that?'

Amelia didn't answer.

'Steffan had told me about him,' Tejinder said softly, clasping her hands in front of her.

Amelia noisily ripped up a serviette in her hands as Tejinder spoke.

Tejinder went on: 'Steffan was sort of dating him. Shaun. He was a bit lovestruck, to be honest. I warned him to be careful. Chasers.'

Amelia shook her head impatiently: no idea what she meant.

'Some men fetishise Asian guys, you know, or use them to experiment with their own sexual orientation,' Tejinder explained.

Amelia pushed the remains of the serviette away from her.

'When I stopped hearing from him, I knew something was wrong. And then when I went over, the whole place was neat and tidy, smelling of solvent and bleach. But empty.' Tejinder snorted angrily. 'The police later told me off for contaminating the crime scene, can you believe it? Bit rich, given how long it took them to actually treat it as a crime.'

Amelia nodded. A scheming smile curving her face. She didn't care about the legal technicalities or social justice sob story. Tejinder was going to talk.

The other woman fiddled with her apron. 'He was missing for days before they let me file the report. We all know why they were so keen to emphasise "*No evidence of a struggle*". And then – do you remember how the coroner ripped them a new one for not having got a toxicology report?' She rotated the saucer of the cup on the table next to her. 'His big travel bag missing. And because I wasn't family …'

Was that a judgemental look she was giving Amelia? She could get lost.

'I kept searching. Even went to confront Shaun at the chippy's, just round the corner from here. He denied knowing Steffan. That made me sure he'd done something.'

'So you thought Shaun had deliberately murdered him?'

On her phone, Amelia switched from the spreadsheet she'd been making notes on to the opening hours of the fish and chip shop. Tejinder nodded violently, kept talking.

'I don't know why Jay sent that message warning me off. Didn't know it was him at the time, he sent it anonymously through my website. I wasn't too good with that thing. I ignored it. Thought it might have been from Shaun's girlfriend. But Jay admitted it was him when I visited him in prison.'

'Did you ask him why?' Had it been because he was the killer, and he'd wanted to frame Shaun?

'All he said was, he'd got a bad feeling about Shaun. He felt sorry for you, you know. For your family. Not knowing the truth, he said.'

Amelia remembered the week of not knowing, of hoping Steffan would turn up safe and sound, back from another of his erratic adventures, like that time with Tromsø. *The Northern Lights aren't like how they show up on film – in real life they're like glowing dust cascading down.* He'd been dead for at least a fortnight by the time the police, bugged by Tejinder, had got around to contacting their family. The unearthing of the body in the freezer in the fish and chip shop had been gruesome. That's when Mam had started making endless cups of tea, leaving them for Amelia to trip over, lying around the house, cold. At the same time, Dad had sunk into his final resting place in front of the TV. Bitterly, aggressively fixed on whatever he'd chopped to.

'Would probably have been better if he'd stopped Steffan being killed in the first place, then.'

Tejinder stopped fiddling. She stood up, and collected the remaining cups, mugs and saucers smartly. Busied herself behind the counter. Wiped the tables down vigorously.

'I wish I'd never encouraged Steffan to … And that the ones really responsible for your brother's death had been punished more. But I haven't got anything else to say to you. Sometimes we need to accept our losses. Carry our loved ones' memories with us.' She looked at the green photo frame behind the counter. 'Please let me get on.'

Amelia hesitated, and then let herself out. Boiling in her frustration, she followed the directions on her phone to go down the high street and into the narrow fish and chip shop. After she'd been served, she took her small order to the back table. She was the only one dining in. She looked around – no CCTV. When the customers getting takeaway had left, she slid over to the counter. She didn't know if the bald, middle-aged man serving was the owner: no name-badge.

'Have you worked here long?'

The red-faced man laughed and said, 'As long as it's been open!' He shook his head, laughed to himself again, and wiped a cloth across the counter.

'Are you the owner?'

'Yeah, who wants to know?' He looked more suspicious now, screwing up the cloth in his hands.

Amelia leaned conspiratorially on the counter. 'So this is the place, huh?'

He stared at her blankly. 'Come again, love?'

Amelia gave up leaning because of the awkward difference between her and the counter's height. She pulled down her jacket and gave it another go.

'Is this the place where that guy Shaun worked? You know, the one who was convicted of manslaughter?'

His smile surprised her. 'Oh, you're one of them are you, love?' He chuckled. 'You bought the wrong order!' Still smiling to himself, he tossed some of the golden chips, bathed in hot light under the steel and glass display.

'What do you mean?' Now it was Amelia's turn to stare blankly.

'Scampi and chips! That was the victim's favourite. Oh yes, he used to come in here, loadsa times. I saw him, flirting with young Shaun. Can't blame him, he wasn't a bad-looking fella.'

He opened a pot of vinegar to fill it from a large plastic container. As the brown liquid slopped in, the acrid smell filled Amelia's nostrils. She looked on in disgust.

'Don't get me wrong, I don't approve of what he did. But he was a decent worker. A bit intense sometimes.' The man quietened down as someone who looked local came in. 'Same as last time, Cathy?' After he'd served the woman and she'd left, he brightened up again. 'Some people dropped off after. Some were into all the gory details. But there's so many people new to the area, it don't get brought up much.'

His tone made her feel nauseous. She tried to focus on why she'd come. There was no chest freezer in the front of the shop: if there was one, it had to be through the back.

'How was Shaun intense?' Amelia swallowed her bile.

The chip shop owner paused in his work and looked up at the ceiling, then back at Amelia.

'The way he'd look at you. Or talk – sometimes he acted like he was the boss here, not me.'

'And did he ever flirt with any of the male customers?'

He laughed out loud, showing off his smoker's teeth.

'Look, I've got nothing against gays, me, but I can't imagine Shaun swinging that way. He was a ladies' man! Of course, his girlfriend wasn't too happy how he'd been earning a bit of extra cash. Seeing as how she was in the family way and all.' Now it was the shop owner's turn to lean conspiratorially on the counter. 'I never imagined ...'

Amelia's heartbeat quickened. Her cheeks burned. She leaned in as the greasy man continued.

'Never imagined he'd draw in tourists like you! You're not the only person to ever ask about him. Can you believe it? Rest in peace and all that, but maybe good old Shaun didn't sink my business after all!' He slapped the counter, and gestured to the door leading into the back of the shop. 'Course, I don't have the original freezer from back then, but I've still got one you can pose on if you like? Hey, you alright love?'

Amelia didn't stop until she was outside and around the corner, the artificial lights of a twenty-four-hour betting shop's sign casting a baleful net over her. Palms flat on her thighs, she bent over to clear the rushing in her head. The sickness swirling in her stomach threatened to overcome the top of her throat. Steffan's dead body like some ghoulish Happy Meal toy. She didn't want to find out how Jay could have known about the freezer after all.

Back on the train, the imperious skyscrapers of Canary Wharf rose behind and to the side of the crowded carriage Amelia rode in. Ahead, the Thames lay constrained by a disjointed mix of old industrial sites and new developments. Scattered around, dusty patches of grass were hemmed in by faceless modern flats that pressed in on the railway line.

Woolwich lay ten stops behind her.

Overhead, low in the sky, the late evening sun made its blood-orange way down to an uncertain, inevitable destination. When the track curved, the light blinded Amelia, making it hard for her to see the way forward. She swallowed a Kalms and buried herself in the dark mode of her phone. Peter had messaged. But he was the third disappointment of the day. He'd run his hand over his hair, and hadn't made eye contact, when he'd agreed to help her *just this once*. Yet here she was – no phone records, no CCTV, no internet search history: he said most were secure, many would have been deleted, and it was hard to know where to start without anything specific to go on. He provided a report on Jay's social media: his posts, things he'd liked, followed and so on. *Refuge, London Chemsex Network, Timpson* ... Skimming through this list didn't help Amelia uncover anything that could hurt Jay. Peter said this **sounded a bit dodgy**. Admirable ethics. She was fine with his suggestion not to come over that night. Really.

She smacked the phone against her leg.

Using up some of her energy to keep her bull-like breathing under control, she deleted her angry reply to Peter. *Start here*, she messaged back, with the link to the contact form on Tejinder's Wellness Café, Woolwich's website. *Look into the message history. Look for something from Jay's email account.*

She checked her forum inbox. EmeraldSiren seemed surprised to learn Jay had admitted he'd watched Steffan and Shaun through the window several times before the day that ended it all. *He's a bad man.* Amelia could tell her contact was pleased she was doing her dirty work for her. She wasn't giving Amelia much to go on that she wasn't learning for herself, but she promised she would deliver something good soon. *We need to make sure Jay gets what's right.*

That was well good, that was, but EmeraldSiren didn't need to keep going on about contacting the probation officer. Amelia had looked up all the details, she didn't need reminding. She had wanted to be sure she was doing the right thing. Even if she hadn't got any more definitive proof against Jay – she wouldn't be fobbed off. He would know what it was like to suffer. She imagined him choking Shaun while he choked, like a human centipede but with death tied to each person instead of—

She set a reminder in her phone for the next day, to call Lewisham Probation Office as soon as it opened.

45

Jay

As he leaned over and into the bottom shelf, Jay slipped his phone out of his trouser pocket. Based on his latest message, Noah would be there soon. Jay grinned.

He looked over his shoulder. Esther smiled as she nodded at him, showing off the gap in her upper middle teeth. 'Thassit, right in the back there, right at the back of the shelf. Getting it all clean is how we earn a top Perfect Day Score. Lovely stuff.'

Jay kept scrubbing, reaching in further. Face screwed up due to the effort and the orange scent of the non-brand cleaning fluid. Behind him, the shop door *beep-boop*ed.

'Well done, well done, another punctual start to the day!'

Esther ran a tight shop: stock was always in, shelves clean, labels properly applied. But Jay didn't mind putting in this extra effort for the audit: he knew how important the Perfect Day 'mystery shopper' evaluations were for the store, and Esther was a good manager. Even if she did flirt with Noah, despite being married.

Jay gave his newly arrived colleague a nod, a smile and an 'alright' as he stood up and moved on to the next shelf. Noah caught Jay's eyes as they lingered a fraction too long on the

Trainee badge on Noah's chest. It wasn't straight: Jay could reach over to touch it up.

Jay turned away and kept scrubbing. Esther gave instructions to Noah about poster prices and watch batteries. She repeated to Jay's behind what she'd said about her confidence in him running the shop while she was out. There was a bit of heat, good heat, in his cheeks. He mumbled a thanks but allowed himself a smile while no one could see it.

There were a few minutes of quiet after she left. Then Jay felt the whack on his bent-over butt.

'Hey!' he protested as he shot up, and then 'Ow!' as he banged his head on the upper shelf. Noah was watching him with a cheeky grin, the offending *L1 Watch Training Manual* in his right hand. Jay, rubbing the back of his head, let Noah tease a grin out of him.

'Poster prices are under the till. Watch batteries are up there.' Jay gestured with his sponge. 'Weather will keep it a slow day, so that's good for us to get ahead on shop prep.'

'Yessir.' Noah did a fake salute, bopping himself on the head with his manual, and went over to behind the till. Lucky for him – he'd deserve it if Jay gave him a spank back.

One more shelf and they'd all be clean. When he was halfway through it, Jay plucked up the courage to ask, 'You're always on time. How do you do it?'

'It's nothing, buddy.' Noah didn't pause for long. 'I still feel my body is run on timetable. My brain has to wake up when it's time for alarm, eat when it's time for canteen, sleep when it's lights out.'

Over his shoulder, Jay could see Noah fiddling with the black plastic rings of the training manual's binder. A stubborn spot on the off-white shelf required his attention.

'It's like if I try to step off on my own path,' Noah

continued, 'I get this weird feeling. Like I'm going to get slapped down. You know what I mean?'

Jay laughed. 'You mean inside they don't prepare us any better for the outside?' He finished with the stubborn spot and turned. Noah had his eyes on him.

'What was it like, for you?' Jay asked.

'Inside?'

Jay nodded. Noah opened the training manual and flicked through a few pages.

'Pretty routine. How long did you do?'

Jay let his gaze run over Noah. Caught lusciously framed hazel eyes meeting his. 'Two years. At least the violent crime rate's lower on the outside.'

Noah laughed, and flicked through to the end of the manual, then rested it on the counter. 'Inside? I knew this guy. His mum made up all sorts of illnesses for attention. It had a name, Munching Zen, Biproxia, something like that.' Noah flicked back through a few pages.

'Wow, sounds weird. She would pretend she had like, what, a headache or something?'

'Nah, man, nah. Much more serious.' Noah shook his head and slapped the manual shut, beautiful eyes wide, grinning a young man's excited grin. 'Things like cancer. One time, this guy said, she even pretended her own mum was dying. That she was in hospital, with like a stroke or something. To get out of work, or get him out of school, things like that. Messed up, right?'

Jay laughed uncomfortably. Flicked at Noah's pecs with his cleaning cloth.

'He said—' Noah looked Jay right in the eyes and licked his lips – 'That she might even have poisoned her own mum, made her look sick, so she could get the attention.'

Shyly, Jay volunteered: 'There's a film with that in.'

'Yeah? Which film?' Noah's look seemed sincere.

Jay blushed but felt confident enough to go on: '*Sixth Sense*? It's about this kid who can see dead people. One of the dead people was killed accidentally by her mum 'cos of that condition. The kid ends up saving the sister.' Jay felt relieved that Noah didn't seem to be judging him for his interest in old films. He smiled. Noah smiled back.

It seemed as if they'd been sharing stories for only a few minutes when Esther discovered them. 'What's all this, then?' she asked; her disapproving, pushed-forward mouth showed she didn't intend to sound like a comedy police-woman. She rounded on Noah. 'You're not supposed to be doing your training now, I need you to sort out these prices.'

He blushed as he slid the training manual under the shelf, offered a clear and firm 'Sorry, boss, I just wanted to get ahead,' and got to work on the sorting. Esther looked at Jay. Back at Noah a moment longer. Then broke out into a toothy smile.

'All is forgiven, lads, all is forgiven. Make sure you move onto restocking that shelf, Jay.'

When she'd finished with the pep talk, she went into the back office and shut the door. Jay guessed she'd be checking blurry CCTV footage again to see if she could find a clear shot of who'd tried to force the shop's door last night. Lucky that the would-be thieves had been disturbed before they could check out the back of the store. And that the CCTV was so cheap, no one he knew would show up on it.

'*Level One Watches* is easy, you'll smash it no problem, mate,' Jay encouraged as he lifted boxes of polish back onto the shelves. When the door *beep-boop*ed to let in a customer out of the grey day, he shot to the till, standing close to Noah. His bare skin tingling against Noah's exposed muscles.

Noah stepped away slightly.

Jay kept the smile fixed on his face. 'How can I help you?'

After he'd cut the lady's two keys, and she'd paid, Jay went back to filling the shelves. She hadn't spoken English too well so the whole transaction had taken a little longer. Noah had complimented Jay on his patience. And his 'reassuring' voice.

But any colleague would do that, right?

Jay looked over at Noah, diligently sorting the watch batteries. It felt good to do something with his hands. Good to be given a chance. Good to be somewhere that offered opportunity and welcome to people on the edges.

Jay hadn't been paying attention to the voices outside the shop. But when the alarm of the door sounded urgently, letting in three customers at once, Jay realised who it was. He did turn to face them, but then quickly turned back to the shelf-stacking, in case their reason for being in the shop was genuine, and they would just be about their business and leave.

But then they started on him.

'Still doing your job, Ginige?' the eldest Lynas brother started with. His sporty deodorant squared up to Jay's nostrils.

'Where's that woman who normally gives you grief in here?' The middle brother ran a hand over his cropped blond hair.

'Maybe Ginige cleaned up after his new mate screwed her and all?' The youngest one laughed like a seagull.

Noah came out from behind the counter. Stood between Jay and the eldest brother, leader of the pack, and crossed his arms. 'That's enough, lads. Best be on your way.'

The eldest Lynas looked down at Noah. Slim but tall facing down short but muscley.

'Yeah? You and who?'

Noah paused for a beat. 'Me and the CCTV which goes straight to the police,' he said. He nodded at the small camera in the corner. It blinked red at them both.

The eldest Lynas's face twitched into a silent snarl. He chucked a tin of polish down on the ground, and led the other two away with a toss of his head. 'You've got no clue what he really did,' the youngest lobbed through the closing door. '*His* family don't want nothing to do with him.'

Jay and Noah stood motionless, facing each other. Inches apart. Breathing together.

'Thanks,' said Jay eventually, bending over to pick up the tin. He felt another whack on his butt, this time of a hand. 'Hey!' He shot up again.

Noah was grinning his cheeky grin up at him one more time. 'You deserve trouble if you wear trousers that tight.'

Jay let himself stand opposite Noah to return the grin for a few seconds.

Noah's grin faded. 'What did they mean? What you really did?'

Jay felt the joy drain out of his face. 'Nothing. It's just rumours. Don't believe everything you read online.'

Noah ran a hand through his curly hair. 'OK, buddy.' He tilted his head. 'I need to keep my nose clean as much as you do.' He went back to the counter as if nothing had happened. 'Better get these batteries done before madam tells me off again! Think I'm fifty per cent there.'

Fifty per cent.

Jay pushed the tin roughly onto the shelf, and rushed to the till, almost elbowing Noah in the process. The shorter man looked up at him. 'What's up?' Jay went through the receipts, afraid of what he might find.

Big problem. Jay had been so focused on his anxiety about

whether Noah minded him standing so close, he hadn't been concentrating when he'd cut the woman's two keys. He'd overcharged her.

But Noah had admitted his mistake about the training to Esther and she'd been OK with it.

Jay knocked on the door of the back office tentatively.

Esther opened it. 'Yeah?'

Jay shut the door behind him so Noah wouldn't overhear. His feet stared back at him, shuffling on the floor. He took a deep breath and dived in.

'I just charged a customer full price for two keys. Second one should have been half price. I'm really sorry, boss.'

Esther didn't say anything.

'I know she could complain and that might make you look bad, especially with the upcoming shop check. I'm really sorry.'

Esther pushed her lips out and sucked her teeth for a moment. Looking up at him, she shook her head. Then she shrugged and gave a small, sly, half-smile.

'Were we a bit distracted today?' She held her hand out. 'We all make mistakes, Jay. That the receipt?'

Jay handed her the incriminating white paper.

'I can process a refund back to her card. Keep an eye out on the store reviews for the next couple of days in case we need to respond to anything. And focus on getting them shelves stocked!' She laughed as she shooed him out.

Bathed in relief, Jay went via the kitchen area to get himself and Noah some water. 'Thanks, buddy,' gasped his friend after he'd glugged his down. Standing close to Noah was like a cool drink on a hot day, calming the unpleasant heat that had taken over his body. Jay looked at him down the glass as he slowly drained it. The urge to reach out and be held by Noah hungered inside. Noah smacked his lips again. His eyes were clear as his pupils dilated.

Could this be different from the last time he'd hoped for a connection with a guy?

46

Amelia

Maybe it was because of what she was going to get up to with Peter afterwards, but to Amelia the Probation Office felt like trouble brewing. A lone receptionist, keeping her head focused on her computer screen, was clearly latching on to any opportunity to earwig; and the workers visible in the back office were only communicating to each other with looks. Two people, presumably criminals, lolled dead-eyed in the waiting room with her. Everyone who occupied the stale space seemed ready to burst. It even smelled like a bloated corpse. The door to the Gents was propped open with a triangular yellow warning sign – some problem with the plumbing?

It was like when, back in Wales, she'd chanced upon an intact roadkill at the end of their drive. Making one quick check back at the accidentally open front door, knowing Mam would get mad if she saw her outside but would be busy with the newborn anyway so what did it matter, Amelia had stared at the ex-rabbit. Its eyes had been glazed, its fur matted but not revealing what wriggled inside, its movement forever halted. She didn't remember why four-year-old her had picked up the stick. Didn't know whether that little girl had just been curious about the dead bunny, or had known what would happen when she probed it.

Amelia drummed her fingers impatiently. This Olu guy had sounded nervous when she'd called that morning: apologising, going silent, asking her to repeat herself. Didn't even get her name right at the start of the call. She was basically doing his job for him by digging up dirt on Jay. Given how keen he'd been to see her after he'd verified her connection to the case, Amelia was confident he wanted to know what she knew, and would do something about it. That would make calling in sick today worthwhile.

A short South Asian woman, hair a mess, smart clothes bedraggled, collected an impeccably dressed, unimpressed-looking man from the lift. The woman had forgotten her swipe card, and had to ask the receptionist to let her in. A young Black man came out at the same time, and greeted the woman fawningly as he passed. Was this really Olu? Amelia rolled her eyes: she hated people who sucked up to the boss.

Amelia smiled as she stood up and held out her hand to greet him. His handshake was a bit limp. She wiped his sweat off onto her trousers. He led her into a side room. No windows, artificially lit. But it smelled less bad than the waiting room.

'So, Miss, ah, Amelia. You said you had some information to share with me?'

Amelia noted that he didn't appear to have brought anything to write on. He ought to pull himself together. She was business-like in telling him about her suspicions based on what Jay had told her, and the transcript.

'Why did he name Shaun? How did he know my— the body was in the freezer? Why did he accuse Shaun of planning to kill again?'

Olu gawped at her. When she didn't fill in the silence, he asked, 'So. What is it exactly you suspect him of?'

Fingers clenching, the skin at her temples stretching taut, Amelia took a deep breath and said patiently, like a mother explaining to a recalcitrant child: 'His story doesn't add up. He must have been involved in at least hiding the body, if not the manslaughter itself, i.e.' – jabbing the table for emphasis – 'not just letting Shaun cover it up because Jay believed him when he claimed it was an accident.'

Olu looked at her, then up at the clock on the wall.

'What—'

'*And* if he lied about that – how do we know it was even an accident?' Amelia grew hot as this buried idea took root in her.

'What's your evidence for these accusations?'

'These are transcripts from a nine nine nine call that didn't form part of the trial,' she said, producing the papers from her bag, handing them over triumphantly, tilting her head back a little as she stared him down.

He read them carefully, then handed them back, although paused in letting go. 'How did you get these? These should not be in the public domain.'

Amelia snatched at the sheets, tearing the corners a little before Olu could release them. She angrily stuffed them back into her bag.

'This is the kind of information you have to act on, right? Get him recalled, or reopen the investigation?'

Olu looked down at his empty hands, and sighed. 'You're right. We recall prisoners who have broken the conditions of their licence. And from what you're telling me—'

Olu turned his head as the impeccably dressed man walked past the interview room. In the resulting silence, Amelia made out the hushed pleas of the short South Asian woman through the door. 'Director … no idea … fully responsible … long service … checking on all the other POs …' Wow. It was certainly hitting the fan for somebody today. The man said something like 'I expect a full report before tomorrow,' as the lift doors clanged shut in the woman's face. She could be heard letting out all her breath, and then slowly dragged herself back past the interview room, not looking in. Olu stared through the glass viewing panel, swallowed, and turned back to Amelia.

'We don't reopen investigations. Sometimes I wish we could. I'm afraid I can't help you.'

He stood up. She couldn't believe he was showing her out like this.

'I thought probation officers were supposed to keep a close eye on their offenders?' snapped Amelia as the lift approached from the decayed building's innards.

'Miss Amelia,' said Olu primly, 'I appreciate you coming to see me. But you're not entitled to tell me how to do my job. Jay is very close to being discharged. We don't need any more trouble at this office. I wish I could do more, but I have a lot on.' He fingered the phone in his pocket. Slid it out. A message from a *Cathy*. Yeah. Clearly he was *real* busy.

The lift door ground open. Olu didn't say anything until she'd stepped inside.

'I understand it must be tough about your brother. But I would strongly advise you not to engage in any more illegal activity. Or to send more harassing communications to my service user.' Jay must have told on her about the WhatsApp messages.

Amelia stared at Olu from inside the lift. He stared back. The doors closed. She was still giving him the finger when the doors opened again. He looked bemused at her from the door into the office as, embarrassment burning her cheeks, she styled it out and pressed the Ground Floor button.

As she descended, she remembered how mad she'd felt when four-year-old her had been told off for poking that dead rabbit. Not like Mam and Dad had cared what she did anyway, once a usurping sibling had burst into her world. The baby, the child, the young adult had always been more important to them, even though she had been a good girl and worked hard. Their parents always going on about marriage and babies, when studying and career were what had been important to her. Steffan getting the opposite treatment.

It had only taken one delicate tap with the end of the stick to explode the whole thing. Bringing all those dead secrets into the light. Mam and Dad had been cross about the bunny, but the punishment hadn't been too bad. Amelia reckoned Olu's words were just as empty.

She messaged EmeraldSiren: she'd know a way for Amelia to keep poking until she'd proved she was right.

47

Shaun

'Come on now, Miss, sure you can make an exception for me.' Shaun used his silkiest voice as he tried to manipulate the prison officer. Leaned back in the chair, spreading his legs. He pulled the white, prison-approved T-shirt down against his abs, feeling his big nipples give the officer the eye through the cotton. He flashed a grin. She stared blankly at him from behind her desk in her office, then squinted at the screen.

'No, sorry, you can't go out two days in a row.'

She clicked the mouse. Not taking her eyes off the screen, she continued: 'Even if you've got compassionate early day release, this is a prison.'

'I know where I am, thanks,' Shaun snapped. Whenever he was thwarted, it was as if he were underground, packed tightly into the pitch-black soil. The muscles of his jaw, his eyes, his forehead tensed. Was that a self-satisfied smirk in her eyes? A slight upturning of one corner of her mouth? Did she despise him?

'Miss, please. I filled in a general app.' Shaun's voice became higher. Smaller. Weaker. How pitiful. Like when he'd begged Dad to take him with him. He brought his legs together and hunched over, hands clasped. 'My mum's in hospital, she's had a stroke, doctors say she'll die any day now.'

The officer didn't take her eyes off him as she jerked open a drawer. She pulled out a pad of forms, ripped one off, and pushed it, blank, across the desk. Her voice and face were unimpressed.

'I can consider letting you out again tomorrow.'

Pushing his resentment down, Shaun thanked her, and retreated to the prison library. Although this wasn't part of the Vulnerable Prisoner Unit, he felt safe enough here; the tiny room wasn't a popular spot. No surprise there, seeing as half the other inmates couldn't read or write. At least Ma had done something right for him on that front.

Checking no one was looking, he leafed through one of his favourite poetry collections. He'd rather die than reveal his soft spot for its world of monster-eating-monster, unwanted bastards, and pervading darkness.

Just like the real world.

The librarian hovered near her desk and then stepped away, locking her terminal. Approved computer use was the only way to get access to the outside world, unless you had an illegal mobile, or could survive the queue for phones on the wing.

He kept thinking about how it must look to Jay. In Jay's eyes, anyone he'd had contact with could be the note-sender. But if Shaun could speak to Jay again, he could tell him what he'd seen. That would make him take the threat of Amelia seriously.

Shaun looked up at the sound of the library door closing as the librarian stepped out for a moment. Would he have enough time while she was gone?

He had only just looked over at the computer when the

door opened again. He looked straight back at the sparsely populated shelves, casual like. Picked up a book and put it back. The librarian didn't say anything.

It was only when he turned round that he realised it hadn't been the librarian re-entering the library.

Three inmates had circled him. Their rows of shark teeth showing as his eyes darted from one to the other. No weapons in their hands. The gap between them not big enough to escape through. He didn't know if it was one of them who'd shanked him in the canteen before. That had happened much quicker. The dent of the scar felt hollow under his involuntary fingertips. They wouldn't dare knife him here.

Shaun retreated against the shelf, reaching behind him for a hardback.

The breath was short in his mouth as they grabbed him. Shaun could hear the librarian's voice, outside, insistent that she pass. His cry out was dry, stifled by a strong, sweaty hand clamped over his lips. Shaun's tongue could taste the finger that had slipped inside. His moans muffled, the muscular arm around his waist. He resented his body for how it reacted.

They sprang away, years of performative innocence clicking into place as they brushed back their hair, looked over some books, and sauntered past the librarian and the two prison officers at her side, cheerily swearing nothing was going on.

Back in his cell, Shaun banged his fist against the wall as the door was locked behind him. Gritting his teeth, he ran his hand over his short hair, keeping his mouth shut again.

Once before, they'd been able to go through with it ... He hadn't cried. He'd sworn that, staring straight into the therapist's eyes, daring her to disbelieve him. Daring her to judge him. As she'd adjusted her clipboard, she'd '*wondered*' whether Shaun knew that it was common for male survivors of – his glare, like the beam of an unrotating lighthouse, had stopped her using the next word – for male survivors to get an erection or even ejaculate during the experience.

'Our body can respond to touch, even when we don't want it to. This can be very confusing for the victim.'

He banged the wall again. Breathing through his nose, he sat down on his bed, squirming. With nothing better to do, he stared at the unclean floor through watery eyes. His mind disappearing into the past.

Ma had been crying in the kitchen on the day Dad left for good. Shaun had been fifteen. He didn't know why she needed to make such a big deal out of it. So what if Dad wasn't always around?

Shaun stood in the hallway, blocking the front door. Dad, still taller than him, but not by much those days, smiled at him as he held the small cardboard box with his remaining possessions. 'Come on, Shaun. I've got to get on.'

Shaun hesitated, only partly turning, and stopped short of placing his hand on the latch. A slight glower crossed Dad's face, but his voice was silky: 'Shaun, mate, don't worry, you'll see me again.'

Shaun wanted to believe it so much. To believe he wouldn't end up like his cast-aside, disintegrating mother. He pictured Dad proudly buying him his first legal pint. Clapping him on the shoulder, showing him off to his mates, giving Shaun a sixteenth-birthday card. Shaun would become a man. He'd call the shots.

He hugged Dad, the box between them, opened the door, letting the end of the bright day in, and clapped him on the shoulder as he passed by.

Outside, Dad turned. With the light behind him, his face was a hollow shadow.

'Listen, Shaun. We've had some fun times. But I've got my new family. Daniel's my son now. Be a man's man about it.' He clumsily waved a buzzing insect away with the box. Squashed it up against the wall. 'It's good we've had this little chat. Clear the air. You understand.'

The door of the council flat swung closed. As it did, the light was shut out, and Shaun was left staring at the dark. He slugged to the kitchen doorway. Emptily gazed in at Ma, who looked up from the table, surrounded by sodden tissues, her eyes red and her face wet. Arms bruised. The air thick with cigarette smoke.

'Shaun, love, it'll be alright, we—'

Shaun turned away, retreated to his room, and shut his door. Inside, he pulled off his T-shirt and trackies. He was still growing, but in the dirty, lopsided, unframed mirror he could see: he wasn't anyone's child anymore. He would never, ever end up like his mother. He knocked the undelivered Father's Day card he'd bought at the market into the bin.

Shaun looked away from the past, refocusing on his cell. Five years ago, he'd known that his girlfriend had meant it when she'd said, if she found out he'd cheated on her again, she'd leave and take their unborn baby with her. He was so stupid and careless, and needy. It had all come out anyway, so his chance to be a father and put things right had vanished along with her.

Shaun's gaze halted at the corner of his cell. There, where he tried to organise his few possessions, lay in wait his second, white note.

Everyone is going to know what you really are.

48

Amelia

'Ams. Sometimes you could just *not* win at all costs, you know?' Peter said, as their bus accelerated over a crossroads.

Amelia rolled her eyes. His friends had totally overreacted to her healthy competitiveness. It had just been a board games night. And she'd enjoyed the flavour of him after he'd had a cigarette, the feeling of his full lips on hers, the brushing of his beard against her face, the stroking of his kind hands on her shoulders and down her back.

Then EmeraldSiren's message had arrived.

She turned her head away from the memory, to look out at the dark Thames as their almost-empty bus crossed London Bridge. The river's surface, reflecting the city's lights, was still, concealing its drowning, polluted depths. Tower Bridge's spiky outline was illuminated in the distance. The pale grey dome of St Paul's peered out from between modern glassy buildings in the opposite direction. She had to focus on what was right.

Her phone alerted her to another notification.

'What are you doing now?' Peter asked quietly.

'It's just a message from my parents!'

Have you got the keys?

Amelia sighed. Of course, nothing about the wait for Dad's cancer treatment. She checked her bag. She'd definitely collected the keys from the tenant who had just vacated the flat.

Yes. And I've ticked off the inventory. The place is all clean for showings.
How is Dad?

Hopefully they'd find another tenant soon, so she didn't have to do too many viewings. On top of everything else she had to take care of.

The red of the traffic light kept its eye on her as the bus stopped short.

Amelia glanced sideways at Peter. Angled her phone away from him. Swiped back to the message EmeraldSiren had sent earlier that evening. Amelia couldn't escape her need for righteous closure. All the effort she'd put in, all the sacrifices she'd made: she couldn't give up on that when immediate gratification was only a few clicks away. Otherwise what would she have to face up to?

'I'm right about using these,' Amelia informed Peter again. The screenshots EmeraldSiren had sent had made her sober with delight at first. Their effect was beginning to wear off now. Peter's protests really weren't helping.

'*"You can't even prove that's Jay"*,' she mimicked back at him.

Peter rubbed his face, looking around tiredly. The bus's destination scrolled across the display screen in blurry orange on black. 'What if you make him out to be involved and it's not even him?'

Amelia brandished her phone in his face triumphantly.

'He sent a face pic early on in the message exchange. It's him for sure.'

Peter belched, failing to conceal it behind his fist, which he then used to knock his chest twice. 'So you've got some screenshots off Grindr which show him chatting ... Having a threesome doesn't make him a murderer!'

'A threesome that "didn't go so well". Come off it!'

They jerked to a halt at a packed bus stop. As the aisle next to them filled up with rowdy passengers, Amelia felt like she was being crushed. She couldn't move. She was airless. The crowd kept pushing in. Peter glanced at her. The bus kept filling up. Eventually, it pulled away.

Amelia pushed her attention away from the passengers hanging on the poles. She leaned towards Peter, and whispered at him, the body heat of the mob radiating over her.

'The transcripts show he knew where the body was. And he made a false accusation against Shaun. People can put two and two together.'

'You're acting like judge and jury. Is that even legal? Not just the nine nine nine stuff, the photos. Isn't that, like, doxing or something?' Peter whispered back.

'The call to the police should have been in the trial anyway. Then they'd be in the public domain. I don't have to say how I got them. I'm doing the probation officer's job for him.'

What had EmeraldSiren meant by ranting that Jay's probation officer *didn't have the resources to do the right thing, even if he had the written proof right in front of him?* And it was well out of order for her to imply Amelia had let her down. Not Amelia's fault Peter hadn't been able to hack into Jay's email.

Peter mumbled something about not being sure this would help and then was quiet. Head rolling forward, dark beard dribbling onto his chest. Unbelievable that he could be so laid-back when someone was noisily eating smelly takeaway only two seats away.

The weighed-down bus continued on its inexorable journey. Amelia didn't come to East Central that much. The winding, traffic-filled streets, and mix of old and glassy new buildings, lights still on, seemed much the same to her as any other part of the City. So different to where she'd come from. There, you could never build on a patch of flooded peat bog. Once it'd got you, sucked you down, surely that was it.

The bus spilled out a few passengers, and the air smelled cleaner. She didn't have to worry about feeling trapped.

Peter stirred. She doubtfully tried to tell him more: 'I mean, yeah, I don't know for sure what happened. Maybe Steffan caught him watching, and then, I don't know if Jay wanted to keep him quiet, or if it was an accident. But I'm sure he got Shaun to help him cover it up, not the other way round.'

Peter openly laughed at this. 'You have literally no proof of that. What are you trying to achieve here?'

She didn't mind the weight of his head as he rested it on her shoulder while the bus rocked.

'Do you really want to put someone who might be innocent through that?' He sounded a bit too coherent. 'Even if you don't accuse him of murder,' he murmured. 'You wouldn't want to out someone anyway. Not everyone is that accepting.' He closed his eyes.

Amelia stroked his hair and enjoyed the feeling of his beard as it nestled against her. 'I suppose ...'

'Maybe you should just try to move on?' he finished.

'I am moving on. I finally changed my address on the electoral register from my parents. Like you said.' She giggled. 'I used an envelope from the office. Don't tell Janice.'

As the bus pulled up to their stop – the cold of the night finally seeping into her; the relentless buzzing of the road burrowing into her brain – Amelia accepted that EmeraldSiren was right. After all the dead ends, the sacrifices, the times when oxygen itself had seemed to steal away from her lungs' grasp: Amelia's face flushed with the heat of being so close to vomiting her pain out onto Jay.

No point sending the screenshots to Olu: Amelia would put them to much better use.

49

Jay

Jay had never woken up in someone else's bed before. Noah's room was larger than his but crowded with a double bed, a wardrobe and a chest of drawers. Football kit, unrecycled free magazines and dirty laundry were spread liberally over the available surfaces. Jay hugged the sheets closer to himself, listening out for the unfamiliar sounds of housemates going about their business: front door shutting, a couple laughing from the room above, indistinct conversation from the kitchen below floating in through the open windows that overlooked the back garden. The sun calling to him through the partly open curtains, reminding him it was Thursday, he had to go to work.

Noah's place was between Woolwich and Eltham: part of a large, flat, suburban swathe of houses designed for families but now largely house-shares. From what Jay had seen when he'd crept up to Noah's room on arrival, and out to the bathroom when they'd finished the first time, the house was in decent enough condition: nothing obviously in disrepair, and the living room was still a living room, but plenty of spots that could do with a coat of paint.

Jay was surprised at how OK he was with being here.

The door opened, and Noah slipped in. They smiled at each other. Again. Noah's hands were cold when he pulled Jay's head onto his chest and kissed his forehead. 'Morning, champ,' he murmured into Jay's hair.

'Morning.'

Jay lazily stroked a circle into Noah's belly, his eyes focusing on one nipple through the just-right amount of dark chest hair. Noah moaned above him as his hand slid down Jay's smooth back.

After they'd finished for the third time, Jay took a shower while Noah made breakfast. He kept his phone off, telling himself it was close to dying and he wanted to save battery. Telling himself he didn't want to bother Noah for a charger, but knowing it was so he could keep the rest of the world on the other side of this bubble a little longer.

Not that things outside were bad: 93 per cent on the shop's Perfect Day score; Tony had stopped texting him; a week had gone by since the second Note; his final Probation appointment was two weeks away. And then the drinks (one each on Esther) last night at the Banker's Draft that had led to him and Noah getting off the bus several stops early.

Towelling himself back in the bedroom, Jay realised Noah had taken his own phone downstairs with him, so his charger was free. He plugged his phone in to get a little bit of juice, but left it on airplane mode to conserve energy (and keep it blissfully quiet). He went to *Apps*. Brought up the menu. Hesitated slightly.

Do you want to uninstall this app?

He wasn't pretending that what had happened with Noah was going to be some kind of 'happily ever after'. Grindr had provided him with a way to explore, under the covers, what

244

he guessed he'd finally accept was his sexual orientation. He laughed to himself and shook his head. Some of those chats! He didn't log in to see whether *Nameless 35yo* had messaged him about their supposed threesome. He needed to do this without thinking, without looking back. He tapped on *OK*, deleting Grindr, and then did the same with any text or WhatsApp messages he wasn't happy with.

Being around someone as comfortable with their sexuality as Noah helped. Shaking off the last dots of creeping dust that were holding him down: confusion, guilt, shame. Now he'd given himself permission. Freedom to be himself. What else could you be? Jay could laugh at himself about how obvious he'd been. Esther giving Jay and Noah a dirty laugh and a wink as they'd left the pub together.

Perhaps he should turn off airplane mode, just for a moment, in case Esther had contacted him about his shift later. Be amazing if she'd texted him saying he didn't need to come in, given Noah was off today. After breakfast, maybe they could go for a walk, or just stay in together all day.

An unknown number flashed up onto the screen.

Jay boldly pressed the green button. 'Yeah?'

'Jakey, where've you been? I've been calling all morning.'

The fresh air from the window was now cold on Jay's bare back.

'Shaun?'

'Listen, fella, I've managed to borrow a mobile. I can't talk long. Did you get it?'

'Get what?' Jay kept his voice low. There were some mistakes he didn't want Noah to know about yet.

'The second note.'

The cold crept all around Jay now. The blue light of the day like sirens whispering through the window, a faint mist telling him he would never escape, he could only ever come with them to the bottom of the sea. *Everyone is going to—*

'No, what Note?' Jay lied instead.

'I know, I … You haven't got one?'

Jay said nothing, listening to the silence as he waited for Shaun to continue. He still had a chance to live a normal life.

'I got another. Says pretty much the same thing as the first. I can show you when I'm next on day release. Listen, Jakey, I'm sure it's your one Amelia. Amelia Evans. The sister. You've got to do something about her, like.'

'Why do you think it's her?'

Pretending things weren't real hadn't worked out so well for him so far, but second Note or not, Amelia was no threat to today's happiness. Jay was confident of that.

He went on: 'You ain't got any reason to think that.'

The seed of a neglected idea began to take hold. A weed, sneaking up through the cracks of a neglected pavement.

'You know what, Shaun? I think it's you.'

Jay breathed in, enjoying the smell of the bacon and eggs Noah was preparing downstairs. It would be much easier if it were Shaun.

'Those Notes never showed up until you got out of prison, you know what I'm saying? And now you're stalking me at Magda's, smuggling phones into prison to call me. Why you even out of prison early anyway, mate?'

Jay breathed a little, waiting for an answer, demanding one. Shaun was the sender, his happiness was safe. There was no way Shaun would expose him, given how it had favoured him to go along with Jay before. Shaun had just sent him those Notes to get revenge.

Jay imagined Noah's look of disapproval if he found out about Shaun. Jay wouldn't let the Irishman in anymore, wouldn't allow him to jeopardise the life Jay was determined to make for himself.

He tightened his grip on his phone as Shaun answered:

'Me ma is … she's in hospital. Ma's dying, Jay.'

Jay looked at the phone as if the number of minutes spent on the call could confirm what he'd just heard. He thought about his own mum. He didn't know where to start. He put the phone back to the side of his head.

'I'm sorry.'

'She had a stroke.' Shaun was breaking up slightly. 'She's in Queen Elizabeth. That's why I've been in Woolwich. Why they let me out on day release unaccompanied so early. I saw who Amelia was speaking to. And it's not safe—'

Jay was startled by Noah opening the door. He kept the phone hidden under his hands.

'Breakfast's ready.'

'Cool, I'll be right down.'

Noah shut the door. Jay leaned forward and brought the phone up carefully to his face. 'Listen, Shaun, I'm really sorry. I've got to go. Don't worry about Amelia. If she's sending those Notes, she's got nothing. I've spoken to her. We can forget about her.'

'But Jay, she's—'

Throwing his phone on the bed, pulling yesterday's Timpson uniform on, Jay made his way downstairs. He savoured the smell of the fry-up. Peering uncertainly through the doorway, not sure if any of Noah's housemates were still in, he came into the kitchen and smiled at the sight of Noah dishing up. The counter was scattered with cereal; unwashed plates, knives and forks lazed in the sink; and the bin was overflowing. But this smell and sight were just what Jay wanted right now.

One thing puzzled him, though.

'That's odd,' he said, pointing. Frowning.

'What?' asked Noah, not turning from pouring baked beans out of the microwaved bowl onto the plates on the side.

'I thought those were nocturnal— night-time creatures. That they didn't like to come out into the light.'

Noah turned. He screamed when he saw the large house-spider making its way across the linoleum.

'Get it! Get it! Get rid of it!'

'Are you serious?' Jay laughed. 'Mate, big man like you, scared of a little bug like that?' Jay kept laughing as he clapped Noah on the shoulder, scooped up the spider in both hands, and threw it, oop, oop, was he going to throw it at Noah, nah just kidding, he threw it out the window.

Jay was still laughing as he sat down at the small breakfast table Noah indicated. Noah looked pale but was focusing on bringing the plates to the table, not making eye contact with Jay. Jay smothered his smile and gave Noah a gentle kick under the table.

'Sorry, I know people have all sorts of phobias. I had an aunty, hated pigeons, couldn't stand the sight of them. There was this time—'

'Inside? I knew this guy.' A bit of colour had returned to Noah's face as he squirted ketchup across his rashers. 'Everything in his cell had to be lined up just like ...' Noah rapidly slid his knife on the table parallel to his plate, and then mock-agonised over the final three millimetres. 'Proper OCD.'

Jay laughed uncomfortably but then got stuck in to the meal. He realised how much refuelling he needed. He gasped with satisfaction after downing half a glass of apple juice.

'You know ... I'm a bit like that. It's not OCD, I mean I do have thoughts that bother me, but I just like things to be like ...' Jay arranged his cutlery parallel to his plate.

Noah winked. 'I'd noticed. What's that about, buddy?'

'Dunno. Makes me feel a bit safer, I guess. Like I have control over something. You know what I'm saying?'

'Yeah, I know what you mean. I guess I'm like that with my routine.' Noah kept shovelling in eggs.

They smiled at each other.

Jay enjoyed the salty, meaty pork; the sweet, tomatoey beans; the smiling yellow eyes of the eggs looking up at him from a plain round face. Sitting down at a table to eat a cooked breakfast. He smiled again at Noah, letting the savour of the night and the morning sink in and rustle through his bones. He enjoyed Noah's curiosity about the richness of his background: yes, Jay had relished full Englishes growing up, and also lentils, curry, *pol sambol*. And yes, they celebrated Christmas, while Amma had also taught them about the Buddha's enlightenment.

At the front door, Noah gave him a fond kiss. 'The routine isn't all bad though, is it? Like Timpson's? Keeps us out of trouble.'

It was only after Noah had gone back, after Jay had reached the bus stop, after he'd seen his phone was still in the red, and realised he must have accidentally unplugged it from the charger when he was on the phone to Shaun, that a connection lit up in Jay's mind. A memory of another inmate Noah had told him an anecdote about. He checked the time on his phone and then switched it off. Looking both ways, he crossed the road to catch the bus going the opposite direction. He could make a detour back to Woolwich, to the hospital, and still get to work without being late.

If his idea was true, he could put all fears of losing his new life out of his mind.

50

Jay

As Shaun's ma awaited her son's final visit, the machines bleeped and wheezed around her. Jay gazed at the nails protruding from her skinny fingers, the paper-thin hospital tags chaining her wrists, the alien lung that was not hers clamped over her mouth. The crowd of white coats around the end of her bed shuffled away. Ghosts of the life she could have had, drifting out of reach of her translucent hands.

'Another stroke,' the consultant summarised to his medical students. 'An inevitable complication of Long Covid, given her history of smoking.'

Jay looked down at the chart at the end of her bed. Froze at the sight of a white envelope stuck behind it.

Addressed to ... *Shaun*.

Checking no nurses were watching, Jay tipped the contents of the envelope into his hand, and sat down on the chair at the side of the bed.

I think of a time.
  The man from number 45 had come to the door angry.
The two boys who hadn't been able to run away fast
enough cowered behind him, more afraid of you than the

*old man whose window they'd kicked a ball through. The
boys' parents could pay for the damage. Another trip to the
pawn shop for me.*

*I was so grateful when one of their mums next spoke
to me. When she told me what had happened to the boys,
I couldn't understand why anyone would think that of
them. Did children that age even understand what 'gay'
meant?*

*I told you it was a rumour, a thing people said that was
untrue. Yes, like a lie. Bad boys had spread the rumour,
and the two boys had ended up getting hurt.*

*You were looking through one of my magazines.
Topless, oiled, muscular Ricky Whittle. You slowly turned
your head to me. A smile crept across your face, and you
told me you was old enough to know the power of a
rumour.*

I shall not open my eyes anymore.

Jay looked up at the dying old woman. He wiped the tears
from his eyes with the back of his hand, got up, and slid the
note she'd scrawled for her son back into its envelope, and
put that behind her medical chart. He rubbed a hand up and
down one arm, and got out his phone. So Shaun had been
telling the truth. Jay texted him on the borrowed number
he'd called from, in case the message could be passed on.

> I'm sorry about your mum, mate. Maybe we should
> chat about what to do about the sister, Amelia

Looking over at the poster on the wall by the bed, he ac-
cessed the free hospital Wi-Fi.

As soon as he'd connected, his phone blew up with
notifications.

Tagged. Tag after tag. He'd been tagged on every social media account he had. *Ping ping ping ping ping.*

Jay stared at the screen, wide-eyed. He collapsed back into the hard chair next to the bed. His heart felt like it was going to die. He looked around, wildly. He was an animal about to be put down.

> Can't believe Police Watch championed this guy. Cancelling my donation.

> Not kink-shaming, but that's disgusting.

> So it WAS murder? AND he was in on it? Not trying to be funny, but that was obvious from the beginning. Don't know how the police missed it.

At least his brother had unblocked him:

> *Jay, what have you done? Amma is in bits.*

Jay chased the thread of posts and notifications back to the source.

A video, only posted late last night, embedded in a comment on a local news website article about Shaun's imminent release. Seventy thousand views and shooting up. Reactions going viral on every platform.

Welsh accent. On loop.

'These are screenshots of a Grindr conversation.'

Silence.

'These are transcripts from a nine nine nine call.'

Silence.

'These clearly show Jay Ginige knew about my brother's

death all along. That he was there for, for … It went wrong and … Maybe Jay even killed him.'

Amelia's face grew redder, her forehead crunching up as she raised her voice for her final demand to the camera:

'Shaun Flanagan's in prison for manslaughter. Jay Ginige should be in there for life.'

Silence.

'For murder.'

51

Then

Steffan

Such wonderful people in the charity shop. All doing their bit, either buying, volunteering, or donating potential gifts.

Shaun is more of an outdoorsy person. I'm sure of it, from how he asked about my work. And from how he felt. My fingers digging into, running over those muscular shoulders, a back built for carrying a body like mine ... It was tremendous. He was so hungry: he wanted me to want him too. His short, lingering stays in the sunlight on my bed, before he 'has to get back to the chippy's', growing that little bit longer each time.

I decide the small trophy is the thing. At first, I think it is an Egyptian scarab, symbol of rebirth and protection. But then I realise it's a metal moth. Empty screw holes stare back at me from the front of the black, oblong base, tantalising me with the suggestion of the plaque that had once adorned it.

I let another customer pass, and that's when I see the photo frame. It's at the same time faded and robust, distressed wood with a subtle emerald-green spray-painting. Tej often wears green. Given how much she has done for me, how much she has been there for me, I want to get her something too.

I'm not sure what to get Jay, or whether to get him anything. We're just neighbours, after all.

Back at the flat, I linger over the threshold as I slowly close the front door behind me. The soft click of the lock as I stroke the hard latch into place. The metal cold under my hand, contrasting with the warmth of the air.

I leave Tej's photo frame in my bag: I will give it to her soon. I didn't need to get anything for myself: I have enough. I pop the trophy temporarily onto the shelf above the bed; free of the clutter of the shop, it seems exposed, with nothing to blend in against. I imagine how small it will seem in Shaun's hands. I smile at the thought of being held by him again.

The flat opposite is unlit. I feel mean: when Shaun was last here, I joked with him about my messages to the shy neighbour opposite who never went outside. I wonder if Jay has been lured out into the world by the light, or still lurks in the dark, like a creature burying its bone in the shadowy woods.

I glance at the 'get well' card Tej gave me, imagining the sound of the buzzing bees on the cover pressing into my head. I close my eyes. Take a deep breath. Reset, and open them again to message Tej about what's been getting at me.

Amelia's emailed me. I don't know what to do

Nothing from Shaun; yet more messages from Jay. I reply:

That's really sweet of you. I'm not sure a Tamagotchi is quite a substitute for looking after real animals Let's not get carried away 😊

His response startles me with its speed, lunging at me across the ether:

Don't act surprised, I know you like it
I'm just trying to be nice

52
Now

Amelia

As the shoppers ahead of her took their sweet time at the self-service machines, Amelia checked her phone. Still blowing up with the fallout for Jay, as the spores released by her post continued to spread across social media. Twitter outrage, TikTok speculation, Facebook comments-section experts, Instagram ... At first, she'd been relieved when she'd shared the one-minute video. But yet again things weren't working out as she'd wanted. She smiled grimly at another post of hate for Jay:

> I know someone who saw him leaving work early. You reckon this means he was fired??!! Hope so!!!

Flicked through every app.

> Keep your eyes out, lads, he lives in Woolwich.

She uncomfortably turned a blind eye to the less palatable views some of her new allies shared: when would she find out that her sacrifice had jeopardised his probation?

Jay's accounts were dead. A few messages of support for him annoyed her.

Amelia grew silent, and closed the app, at the filtered images of a Beautiful Soul, taken too soon. RIP Steffan. Shared by people who'd never even known her brother.

She wished her texts, messages and emails were silent. Unbelievably bad day at work. Probation Review brought forward because of her exposé. Confirmation of the outcome now in her inbox.

That was it, then. Unemployed again. The police had been in touch, but weren't doing anything yet. Amelia ignored the panicked messages from Wanda about not mentioning she'd got the transcripts from the Witness Care Unit. She logged in, but EmeraldSiren had deleted her forum account: Amelia guessed bitterly that she'd got what she wanted from her.

Finally, a self-service checkout became vacant. She hurried over to it, dumping her basket onto the metal tray. She hit the screen, and swiped one item after another into her bag.

All those Christmases, birthdays, Mother's Days, Father's Days – never forgotten, never missed, never enjoyed. And look what she had to show for it. She could have been 'the happy daughter'. Their only daughter.

Sometimes she didn't understand herself.

The unscanned second Pot Noodle in her bag made her feel happy. Her chin jutting up, heat puffing up her body, her lips curling into a smirk. Knowing it was all hers now: she wouldn't have to share. She wouldn't even have to pay for it. She glanced up at the screen above the till, with its continuous flashing red sign cautioning shoppers they were being monitored. She was confident the fat security guard wasn't watching the feed from his post by the door. Didn't she deserve a little something for herself after the day she'd had? And Tesco was a big corporation: it could afford the loss.

The real reason she'd been fired was obviously Janice's blonde friend. Eyeing up Amelia's job. Well, she was welcome to it: at least she wouldn't have to see Peter anymore, who'd moped back up the stairs to his floor, avoiding making eye contact, even though he was the one who'd dumped her. So much for her parents' hopes for marriage and grand-children.

'Excuse me, Madam, can I have a look in your bag?'

The straw-haired security guard's middle-class accent surprised Amelia. Her automatic smile faded when she realised he was serious. She looked over her shoulder.

'Is this really necessary?'

The man raised an eyebrow. She'd said the wrong thing.

'I mean, sorry, I'm in a hurry. I have to get back to work.'

Amelia tried a smile again. She pulled her bag closer to her, folding over the top in her hands so the contents were concealed.

The security guard frowned. Another man, behind Amelia, said 'Excuse me,' as he stepped round them and out of the entrance, the grey sentries of the security scanners not making an alarm call as he passed through.

'I just want to look inside, Madam.' He gestured at the bag. Amelia looked over his shoulder at the security terminal. She saw the live feeds of the till cameras on there.

Her mouth dried. Were they just live or did they also keep records?

People were starting to look and talk now. Amelia saw them out of the corner of her eyes, heard them at the tills to her right, felt them watching and judging behind her. A man at one of the tills laughed to his girlfriend. An old Black lady shook her head to herself as she made sure to scan a larger item and struggled to put it into her bag.

Maybe he wouldn't be able to tell one Pot Noodle from another.

'Sure.'

Amelia placed the bag slowly onto the ground in front of him.

He crouched down and started rummaging. He laughed when he held up the 1L Bacardi. 'This just for you, is it?'

Amelia laughed back nervously, twisting and crushing the receipt concealed in her pocket. Good thing she hadn't dumped it into the bag like she normally did.

She swallowed when he put the rum bottle on the floor next to the bag, making it easier for him to get a good look inside. She felt the sweat congregating on her forehead. Everything in her body speeding and heating up to tell her she was in danger, her brain knowing it was her own fault. Maybe the chocolate trifle was the issue? Maybe the discount code hadn't scanned right? Everyone deserved to be let off once, didn't they?

'I'm a regular here ...'

Now he held a Pot Noodle in each hand. He looked between them both, and then into the bag again. 'You don't happen to have the receipt, do you, madam?' He looked up at her, eyes deceptively wide, mouth hard.

Please, Amelia thought above the pounding of her heart, the husk of her mouth. *Please let me off. I'll hold up my hands.*

Don't kick me when I'm down. No boyfriend, no job. No hope if I get a criminal record. If you let me off this time, I'll make it right.

'Sorry, I didn't print one off.' Get rid of the evidence in her pocket. Choke it so it won't tell the truth about her to anyone. She wouldn't even acknowledge that truth to herself.

'She definitely paid for that alcohol,' said the self-service supervisor, coming alongside Amelia. 'I had to approve her age and everything.' Amelia tearfully mouthed 'thank you' at her, from the pit of her stomach.

The security guard weighed up the two Pot Noodles. Took another peek at the rum. Dropped everything back into Amelia's bag and handed it to her.

'OK, well you take care this time.'

The air outside the oppressively hot supermarket seemed especially fresh as she got away from her latest mistake. It was like spring light breaking into a sealed-up room through years of accumulated dust. Digging deep into the mud had infected every area of her life with the smell and taste of decayed soil. Would she or Jay be the one who was buried by the video she'd published? Would it be worth it? Amelia gripped the handles of her bag and stepped forward into the fading day.

53

Cathy

Another Thursday evening at Group. Martha, Louise the organiser, two other women, and Cathy. Although she hadn't found out nothing when she went to the Probation Office, Cathy had thought she'd turned a corner.

'Thought I'd forget about these meetings, thanks to therapy,' she claimed awkwardly.

She hadn't spoke to Jay since she'd seen the Instagram images of him earlier that day. *#TallDarkAndDeadly #TakeMYBreathAway*. The women who fancied these blokes were almost as scary as the bastards themselves. What if Jay had been planning to do to her what he and Shaun had done to his neighbour?

She'd spent the day in her room, shivering. Burning scented candles to calm down. Checking the locks on the door. Spying out the window. Deleting all *them* apps off her phone. She regretted having messaged Olu after she'd stormed out of the Probation Office when she couldn't get him to herself. Thought she'd been so clever to exchange a few flirty texts. She'd felt some sympathy when he mentioned his housing situation, how he was having to look for somewhere new. And he seemed frustrated by the system not letting him handle his offenders properly. She'd thought he was one of the good ones! But could any man be trusted?

A whole day spent being circled by fear. Jumping, gripping onto her chair, every time footsteps came close.

But when she was sure Jay wasn't around, she'd crept down to the office. She'd taken as many other residents with her as she could.

'OK. Management has agreed to a residents meeting,' Tejinder had eventually responded, hanging up the office phone after the call Cathy had forced her to make. 'To listen to your concerns.'

They better do more than just bloody listen. Needed to kick him out. If he weren't down the nick already. Something to get rid of him. To keep Cathy safe.

Alice had been focused on whether Cathy was in immediate danger. *Was Jay unemployed?* Cathy didn't know if he'd be fired over the video's accusations. *Had he ever used a weapon?* No, he'd never used anything against her. *Had he ever forced her to have sex?* No, turned out he was gay, despite what he'd claimed before. *Did he use illegal drugs?* Cathy had to laugh at the thought of all the camomile tea. *Did he spy on her or leave threatening messages?* No, Jay wasn't the one spying. *Did he control her daily activities?* No, well, he'd walked her to Group sometimes.

The women got their cardboard cups of water for the start of the session. Things were heating up, so no tea. As they sweated, the posh woman from a few weeks ago leaned towards a newcomer. Showed her her phone. An influencer's voice sounded tinnily from it: 'I'm not saying he's a murderer, but … OK, I'm totally saying he's a murderer.'

Louise began her session gently.

'Do you want to tell us about Jay, Cathy?'

One woman were open-mouthed. Another tilted her

head to one side. Martha and Louise looked at Cathy with warm eyes and smiles, like the good Christian and group organiser they were.

Cathy's muscles tensed. She put her hands in her pockets, and didn't make eye contact. She explained to the group what Louise already knew.

'I live in a hostel with Jay. Jay Ginige. He helps me come to Group. On bad days.'

'Oh my goodness, so you do know that degenerate?' interrupted the middle-class woman, nose screwed up. Martha clutched her cross. The new girl adjusted her uncomfortable-looking clothes.

Cathy swung round.

'Yeah, I've seen it first-hand, trust me. That cycle of trauma – apparently it affects men the most.'

Louise gently enquired, 'Does everyone feel like that?' She looked from face to face in turn, not getting any eye contact back, but Martha spoke up.

'The man, the man I told you about before? At church?' She paused to smile. A broad, honest smile. 'He is a good man. A modest man. A kind man.' She let her cross hang loosely on its wooden beads against her dark blue blouse. 'Some men are good, some are bad.'

'Some are both!' The posh woman was the only one who laughed at her own joke, although Louise gave her a smile.

'What do you think, Cathy? Is Jay bad, or good?' Louise asked.

'Or both!' the posh lady insisted.

Cathy didn't know how to see things not in black and white. She took another gulp of water, emptying her plastic cup. The heat in the room was getting to her.

'I need the toilet.'

Cathy slipped out as the newcomer gossiped:

'Was the woman who made the video out of order? I heard she's been arrested, too.'

She made her way upstairs, and down the deserted corridor to the women's toilets.

While she was washing her hands at the sink, one of the three cubicle doors opened behind her. Cathy was startled, and shot a look into the mirror, but it was a woman coming out. A familiar, casually dressed, tall, Asian woman. At first, Cathy let the taps continue to run. Didn't take her eyes off the mirror as Tejinder washed her hands and then applied lip balm. Tejinder put it down at the side of the sink. A blue and white stick of Vaseline SPF 15. She smiled at herself awkwardly as she smoothed her hair.

'You got time to be running a group? Shouldn't you be getting Jay out of the hostel?' Cathy's voice was cold on the tiles.

Tejinder glanced back at Cathy in the mirror. 'Not my group – I just attend.' She turned her focus back to tidying up her hair.

'You know what I mean. I don't want to be living with him no more.'

Tejinder offered her response to the mirror: 'Don't blame us for the system, love. Everyone needs somewhere to lay their head.' She stepped over to the exit. 'Whatever he did, I doubt he's a real threat to you.' She swept out, like a warrior princess, leaving her lip balm on the sink, and Cathy alone in the toilet.

Cathy sighed. Examined the lip balm. Played with the lid. It was fun to twist it and make it come out, like a Push Pop. She'd always been a bit of a moth to a flame for sweets. The dentist had scolded her at her infrequent visits as a child. The Vaseline was a plain beige colour. Cathy didn't wear much actual make-up anymore. She looked at herself in the mirror, raising the waxy stick towards her mouth.

Behind her, she realised the second cubicle door was still shut. Embarrassing. Someone had been in there the whole time, listening to her losing her rag. Being out of order. She knew it wasn't fair to take her stress out on someone else who had problems too. She just wanted to feel understood. To feel safe.

Cathy hurriedly twisted the stick of lip balm back into its place. Dropped it onto the side of the sink.

She was too slow.

The cubicle door opened.

She had almost made it out of the toilet without making eye contact when Ant grabbed her from behind, one hand over her mouth, the other around her wriggling torso and pinned-in arms. The ex she thought she could outrun.

'Make a sound, and I will break your bleeding neck,' he breathed into her ear.

She nodded. Wild-eyed, no choice going along with it. If only this were all happening in the world the other side of the mirror. But when he let go of her, blocking her escape, and she faced him head on, he was still there. She'd been so sure she could make a safe life before he was released.

He was as tall as she remembered. Flat, silken red shorts showing off his footballers' legs. The tattoos of the crescent moon and a burning flame on the back of his hands were new. The dark, hollow look in his eyes was the same. So was his silky voice.

'Alright, babes. So you in therapy now? Thought you'd have a laugh sending letters to my family? Putting me down ... I've missed you.'

Cathy breathed carefully. Maybe one of the other women would need the toilet. The massive amounts of tea always ran straight through them. But they were on water today. And most of them had gone during the break after the first half of the session. Ant reached across to turn off the running taps. Perched on the edge of the sink. Lanky leg sticking out, ready to trip her up if she tried to run for it.

'I said, I've missed you.'

'I've missed you too,' Cathy quickly blurted back.

Although it was still light outside, the toilets seemed dark. Ant smiled at her answer, uncrossing his arms.

'Good girl.' He patted the sink next to him. Cathy edged over reluctantly. Taking her time to turn and sit, not right next to him. Feeling the Vaseline underneath her.

'Come on, babes, don't be shy!' Ant put his arm round her and pulled her right up to him. Hand on the side of her head, pulling it into his chest, keeping his hand in her hair. She could smell the sweat and beer raging off him.

'So, why'd you run away? Why'd you take the kid?' Ant's question was soft. 'Filth didn't have me banged up that long.' His grip was hard.

'I, I'm sorry, I just, I couldn't handle it anymore,' Cathy whimpered.

'Handle what? The Ant-Machine?' Ant's laugh was painful. His right-hand fingers dug into her temple. Cathy couldn't see his face.

'All of the, all of the problems we had, Ant. Things weren't working out for us. I thought we both needed a fresh start. You were very unhappy,' Cathy pleaded.

'Unhappy? We were having a great time, babes. Remember the trip to Brighton?'

She focused on his silken shorts. Red for danger.

'Ant, please, let me go.'

'Let you go? Let you go? You make me come all this way and then go off with one of your man friends?' His hand was around the back of her throat now, pressing her into his chest.

'Please, Ant,' Cathy choked out hoarsely. 'You're fine, you've nothing to be ashamed of.'

Ant shoved her across the room. She cried out as her head struck the tiles.

'Ashamed? Who says I'm ashamed? You're the one who can't be trusted. Cheating on me all the time. Stealing my son from me. Where is he?!'

Cathy kept her eyes closed. Striking the floor had cut her forehead. Pain, fear and anger drugging her. 'They took him! Social Services took him!'

She cried out again, from the floor. A sharp, pent-up keen. A loss she'd been running from more than she'd been running from him. 'They took my son away.'

She kept her eyes closed. Rocked herself. Whispered: 'They took him because of you.'

Ant crouched down. His hand stroked her hair, smearing the blood from the gash over her forehead. 'Was it you who grassed me up to the police? Was it?'

Cathy trembled: 'You know it wasn't, babe. They picked you up right after the fight. Still outside the pub. First thing I knew was when they came round.'

'I should never have got done for that.'

His bloody hand kept stroking her hair as she shook her head in agreement.

'I'm sorry, babe, I got scared. I got confused. That's why I ran away. I should have been there for you when you got out,' she pleaded.

Cathy dared to open her eyes.

Ant was looking right at her. 'It's alright, I'm here now. I'm sorry, I just love you so much. I've been working hard, trying to save up for you and our boy. We'll get him back. Come on, let's get you cleaned up,' he said kindly.

He pulled her up from the hard tiled floor. Cathy kept her face slightly turned away from him and his polyester shorts as she scooped up some water and splashed it on the cut. The blood just ran down her face, splattering pink and wet onto the white porcelain.

'Can you get me some tissue, babe?'

'Sure, babes, whatever you need.' Ant went round her to the blue paper towel dispenser. Leaving the door unguarded. When he had some towel in both hands, Cathy made a dash for it, leaving the taps running, the sound draining away behind her.

His hand was gripping her hair.

He pulled her backwards, throwing her down to the floor.

'You think you're too good for me, d'ya? You can't treat me like this.' He stood by the end cubicle, banging its door against the wall over and over. Face contorted, spittle flecking his mouth.

The door to the toilets opened. Ant stopped slamming the cubicle and looked over.

'Think you've got the wrong bathroom, mate,' he said nastily.

Cathy twisted her terrified face so she could see Tej.

'Help me.' Every word Cathy managed to push out was punctuated by a sob. 'Please.'

Ant moved to stand in between her and Tej. Looking down at her, he said softly, 'Of course I'll help you, babes.' Ant turned to face the newcomer. 'Nothing to see here, mate. Just a man and his woman. She's had a bit of an accident. Mind giving us some privacy?'

'I came in here for my lip balm,' said Tej. She carefully stepped over to the sink, flat shoes not making any noise.

Picked up the SPF 15 from where it lay, unnoticed and undisturbed by Ant. Popped off the lid and twisted it out. Applied a little bit in the mirror. Kissed her lips. Three times. The smacking the only sound in the toilets.

Tej twisted the stick back in to the white holder.

Popped the blue lid on.

Closed. No more Push Pop for today.

She turned, her back to the sink, standing up straight, facing Ant head on.

'I just came in here for my lip balm, but if you think I'm leaving her on the floor with you obviously up to no good – no way. Get out of here!'

Cathy scrambled away and up. Ant's eyes flicked to the door. Cathy prayed Tej's loud voice had been heard. Lucky she was so tall and strong. Ant had never liked picking on people his own size. He looked defiantly at them both. His red face was paling. Tej's phone was in her hand. Were those concerned voices in the corridor? He swaggered out, slamming the door behind him.

The external door banged shut. Tej exhaled, and fanned herself with her other hand as she pulled Cathy up. 'You alright? No offence, but you're a mess. That was pretty scary.'

'I need to get back to my group,' Cathy said, not knowing where she was. Not really understanding what had happened, that it had been real. It was not so different from all them times before. But there hadn't been anyone to help her before.

'We should call the police,' Tej was saying. 'I'll be your witness.'

'I have a number I can call. It's in my bag, in my group room. Can you take me there? Please?'

Cathy sank into her chair as Martha dabbed at her forehead. Louise was on the phone to the police. The new member held the posh lady back from going out to look for Ant. Cathy and Tej agreed they'd walk back to the hostel together. Tej went back to her group up the corridor.

Cathy was exhausted and confused. But the one thing that was crystal clear? Tej had shown her what was right. When she got back to the hostel, she'd make it up to Jay.

Hopefully it weren't too late to stop him being kicked out.

54

Amelia

Ugh. When had Thursday night become Friday lunchtime? Amelia turned her drool-covered face to the side, taking in the half-empty bottle of Bacardi, then looked down at herself, still fully clothed, lying on her bed. She squinted at the uncurtained window. The sour, evaporated smell of her attempts to drown out her worries, her past, herself filled the room.

She dragged herself into a seated position, like a hungover yogi. What was this pose? Lotus? Half Lotus? Half Mast?

Salivating over the cardboard in her mouth, Amelia trundled her arm over her duvet to where her phone had collapsed out of her vacant hand at some point in the night. It woozily pushed her a text telling her she had nine voicemails. Embarrassed, it showed its records of outgoing calls to Peter, Janice, and her parents around 2 a.m.. Retched up an Instagram notification about some popular girl from school.

With a 'meh', she ineffectually swatted at her phone to make it stop. The phone fell onto the floor, taking with it the notifications, but replacing them with voices. Voices from a distant … radio phone-in?

Amelia crawled to the edge of her bed and peered over.

Her phone was spreadeagled on its back on the dusty

carpet. A link Peter had sent her had opened unintention-ally. Out of the speaker came an unwanted wakeup call from the show's host:

'So, the cause of death may not have been strangulation – but that seems to be just speculation on YouTube. And here are some more of the reactions on Twitter:

"It's terrible that she's outing him."

"He's scum, death penalty is too good."

"The Court of Public Opinion is no replacement for Courts of Law."

"Why are we talking about this as a gay issue. Stop por-traying gay men as deviants!"'

Jabbing into her brain through her ears as she stared down at the out-of-reach phone.

'Let's go to Margaret, who says she knows Jay. Margaret, are you there?'

'Hi, yeah, I've met Jay, can you hear me?'

'Yes Margaret, we can hear you. Tell us about your rela-tionship with Jay.'

'I've met him a couple of times. I'm a CPN, Community Psychiatric Nurse.'

'Oh wow, sounds like a rewarding line of work. What was it like treating Jay?'

'Oh, no, he wasn't my patient. I just meet him on the bus. And at the duck pond.'

Amelia laughed at the old bat. The radio presenter's face said it all as he tried to get her off air.

'OK, well—'

'He's had a hard life, but I don't know how much he takes responsibility.'

'Do you think a viral video like this, helps?'

'You've got to be strict with people, otherwise they don't change. Someone has to take the blame.'

'Is there a difference between blame and responsibility?'

'Oh, you sound like my psychologist colleagues.'

'Seriously though, doesn't this kind of "doxxing" make the victim as bad as the persecutor? Two wrongs don't make a right.'

Had the video frozen? No, the presenter was still looking thoughtful as Margaret took a moment to respond.

'To be honest, I wish I could have done more for Jay's mum.'

Amelia pulled up the duvet, covering her mouth with it, so only her eyes were spying on the phone. No one would know she was considering the implications of every word for herself. She could digest the message safely in secret.

'OK, we've got Cathy on the line, who actually knows Jay.'

'I don't believe a word of it. Yes, Jay is gay—'

'So you do believe some of it?'

'Don't be a smart-arse. He's gay, but not gonna lie, this story about him is totally out of order.'

This is why she didn't watch videos like this: they made her head hurt. She glanced over at the open bottle of Bacardi. She envied this 'Cathy' for not taking any bull.

'I understand you live with Jay, at a hostel in Woolwich?'

*'******* hell mate—'*

'You're live on air, Cathy, could you watch your language?'

'You've literally just told everyone where we live. You know people like me and him have people who want to hurt us?'

Amelia shifted uncomfortably on the bed. Her fear and relief at escaping the security guard for shoplifting intruded into her mind and body. Her anger at her housemates calling a house meeting because of the video joined in.

'But let me tell you something. Jay did lie to me, yeah. But he's no killer—'

274

'My producer would like me to stress we are not saying he is.'

Well it bloody feels like it. He's a good person, he helped me. We're all kicking a dog when it's down. Me too. And I'm sorry.'

'What—'

I never thought I would say this, right, but all this stuff about Jay? Who knows what he saw, what he did. I was brought up, you don't tar birds of a feather with the same brush.'

'So do you think he's innocent?'

'Listen, mate, all I know is, we've all got to stick together. We've all gone places. Done things we're not proud of. I ain't in no position to throw stones.'

Sheep dip swirled in Amelia's stomach. More background callers came and went. She wasn't looking at the phone as she cried. Allowing her tears to drip onto the stained carpet. Everything she'd lost because of her obsession: friends, her job, volunteering. Peter. Nothing would change what she needed to say to Steffan, to her brother.

Her tears stopped for the moment. She risked moving, reaching down towards the phone to shut it up, shutting out these people who had someone to talk to—

'We've got him on the line, we've got him on the line. A lot of people have been claiming he's been sent back to prison, but he's here. Jay Ginige, what would you like to say to our listeners?'

So the social media storm had flushed him out. Amelia shuffled sideways on the bed to get a better angle on the video, recorded only an hour earlier.

I'm sorry. You try to make an example of people, and I may be a coward. Ashamed. But I believe in being kind, and justice. I've already had to meet with my probation officer. We all make mistakes. I want to make it right, and get on with my life. Amelia doing this won't bring her brother back but if I could meet her I'd—'

Amelia swung at her phone but hit the rum bottle. The pungency of the white spirit hit her in the face, knocking her back onto the bed. It splashed out over the floor, its first assault missing her phone but, as the bottle lay on its side, vomiting its remnants onto the sorry carpet, the spreading stain threatened to overwhelm her device.

'No!'

She rescued her phone, falling as she did so. Panting, she rolled onto her back on the floor, aching. The video hadn't been live, so it was too late to call in and tell them …

A message. From her parents. Heart palpitations joined the party with her other symptoms. With a groan, she moped into her half-mast pose again. Pushed her greasy hair away from her sweaty face.

Please contact this friendly young man. He has seen the advert for the flat and would like an urgent viewing.

Not trying to be funny, but given the condition she was in, any potential tenant was going to have to wait until Sunday at the earliest.

Amelia stared limply at her 'wardrobe'. She needed to change. Her head felt lighter after the tears, but now her heart was pounding. It was scary to gaze into the sheer amount of hurt and loss wedged inside her. Like peering over the edge of a dark quarry. Letting all that out would overwhelm her.

Her gaze rolled onto her desk. She could titrate her feelings. Accepting reality one particle at a time. That sounded like a fair deal. Slowly breathing in and out. The air diluting her toxic breath. She struggled to the window to let more O_2 in.

'Ow!'

She looked down at the second-hand hardback book she'd stubbed her toe on. She'd never got far into *The ACT Approach to Unresolved Grief*. Never even started it. Just hoped that, by osmosis, acceptance would pass into her. She didn't want to have to do the hard work of reading and digesting. Choking on feelings.

Feelings could be worse than facts: she couldn't control feelings.

But abrasive, vindictive facts were what had pushed her down here.

Sitting, she pulled the book up onto her bed, and brushed dust off its cover. Her eyes drifted over to her hockey stick, abandoned down the side of her bed. She pulled that out onto the bed too, smiling wistfully as she stroked the wood and fabric, smoothing off the years of neglect. She wiped at her eyes, the dust on her fingers got into them, and in the confusion she started crying again. The parental affection she hadn't had. The brother she'd lost. The mistakes she'd made.

Through the fresh tears, she looked around her, taking in the whole room.

She opened the book.

55

Jay

Saturday. As for all remaining high street shops, the busiest day of the week for Timpson. Even on a rainy summer day. Maybe that was why Esther had only encouraged Jay to take Friday off sick.

He stood in front of the red shop, the windows of the pale flat above it examining him.

He'd been spaced out on Thursday after seeing Amelia's video, and then looking up to see Shaun's mum. The only sounds he'd been able to focus on had been the crashing in his ears as he'd watched Amelia destroy his life on repeat, and the pinging of notifications as speculators across different social media sites tracked down his personal accounts.

He hadn't consciously heard the desperate, drowning shrieking of the machines, hadn't fully felt the elbows and hands of the emergency medical team shoving him out of the way, hadn't even realised she was dead until after he'd left the hospital. As he'd stumbled out of the ward in a fog, he'd looked back at the crowd around her bed, the body convulsing periodically as they shouted '*clear!*', but it was only on the bus to work, when he'd noticed a dead fox by the side of the road, that he realised he'd been with Shaun's mother at the moment she'd died. And he'd been so focused on himself he hadn't even had the decency to realise.

The cold, light rain was starting to seep through his hoodie.

His last shift, straight after the hospital, had been disturbing. He'd regressed to being furtive with customers, hypervigilantly fixed on them as they entered the shop and came up to the counter. Men and women looking from the shoe polish over to him, then back again. But never saying anything. In the end, Esther cracked. *'You can go early.'* Unable to bear the tension, Jay guessed, even though she'd said it was because he'd been summoned to answer to his probation officer. *'Don't come back until Saturday.'*

Jay pulled his hood back. Let the rain wash over his face. He held on to the sound of Olu's voice from their emergency appointment the day before yesterday, the familiar tones propping him up.

The details of the exact words Olu had uttered had been hard to follow, like reaching for the light above the surface of a drowning bath. The walls of the interview room, one he'd never been in before, had seemed especially secure and hushed: it had been the one furthest away from the lifts and the waiting room, with only a small window in the door, not even a fan to stir up the air; but the artificial light had been the same, screwing itself down into his mind, screwing him up.

'I've received some information to support an application for recall to prison.'

Who could have anonymously alerted Olu to Amelia's social media accusation?

'I need to fill in this incident form, Jay. Check it out with my superiors.'

Setting him up to go down with the balls of paper in the black bin in the corner.

'I have to warn you that you could be recalled if anything more serious, like physical evidence, or a confession, comes to light.'

Whatever.

Jay still had Olu's number in his phone, like an invisible line tying him back to (what he hoped was) the lifeboat. He held on to the phone in his pocket as he pushed open the shop door. Esther and Noah looked up at him from behind the counter, a training manual held between them like an unconscious body. Esther lowered it carefully onto the counter, then checked again, and hid it underneath. Noah looked down and fiddled with the till. Jay stood in the doorway.

Silence from in front of him.

The soft patter of the summer shower behind.

He wanted Esther to pull one of her dirty faces, and make a joke about not having expected him to be the one to have had a threesome, to be a dark horse, anything. For her to laugh one of her throaty laughs, and head off into the office, leaving them to it. So he could blush, and from the grin Noah would give him, he would be able to tell that things were alright between them. That things were going to be alright.

Esther's face didn't change. She came out from behind the counter.

'Good morning.' She opened her office door and stepped inside.

Jay followed, Noah avoiding his eyes. He grasped his phone with one hand.

Esther shut the door behind him. They both took a seat. She ran her tongue over her teeth, pushing her lips out and making a noise like something going down the drain. She removed the lid from a pen. Replaced it.

'What about yesterday?'

What could Jay say? He'd spent Friday in his room at Magda's. Sneaking out for Pot Noodles from the kitchen. Showering over and over. Even Tejinder wouldn't look him in the eye. The flaky, painted walls of his room rocking him to sleep. Not keeping anything out, barely holding him together. But he couldn't be contained forever. And he needed to make good on his radio phone-in promise; he was glad Cathy had ventured out of her room to tell him to call in.

He looked over his shoulder automatically, as if he'd catch sight of that Ant guy lurking. Lucky Tej had been there for Cathy. Jay needed to ask Cathy for a photo of her ex, in case he could spot him hanging around anywhere she might be vulnerable.

'They had a residents meeting at the hostel, but I didn't go. Don't know what the outcome was. Maybe I'll get to stay on there.'

Esther checked something on her computer, and exhaled a lot before speaking again.

'Jay. Head office were very concerned about that video. Very concerned. It's one thing to give people like us a second chance. But if you did something worse than you were convicted for' – her hand wouldn't take any interruption from him – 'then that's another kettle of fish.' She exhaled a lot again at this point.

Jay dug his nails into his palms, but couldn't stop his eyes from tearing over.

'I've done my best. Put in a good word for you. And your remorse on that radio show yesterday seemed to go down well.' She nodded at an email on her monitor. 'Just have to see what they decide. If a society don't forgive, if we ain't innocent until found guilty, then what do we get?'

Jay's eyes flooded over. Through his bowed smile, he forced out: 'Thank you, thank you, thank you. I know I've done wrong, I know I need to do better, but I can be a different person. I want to build a new life. I will.'

When he looked up, Esther was smiling a little. Not a lot: her mouth was off to one side, and she was spinning a black biro and tapping it on the desk, but it was still a smile.

'You don't have to be a different person, Jay. Just the best person you can be.'

At this, she threw the pen down, made a scornful sound – a spitty 'ch' chucked over her lips – shook her head, and laughed.

'"The best person you can be"? Oh my days, you've got me at it now! Come on, them customers aren't going to serve themselves!'

Jay hesitated at the office door, hand on the doorknob. Tension running down the right side of his neck and into his shoulder. He dared to let some of his concern out:

'What about Noah?'

Esther sucked her teeth. Swung in her chair, looking back at the computer screen. Picking up the biro and tapping it on the desk a few times. Her face slowly relaxing as it came to rest on him again.

'Maybe you can sort that old stock and recycling from the Perfect Day clear-out. It's stopped raining.'

Out the back, Jay slipped in his earphones, and listened again to the section of the true crime podcast that was sympathetic to him. He felt lukewarm relief. His muscles and breathing languidly lengthening and slowing. As he flattened empty boxes, folding them in his hands so they were as close to invisible as possible, as easy to dispose of as a guilty secret, he thought of Noah in the shop, the other side of two faded red walls. He'd ignored all Jay's calls and messages since the morning of the fry-up and the hospital visit. Had that been a Grindr notification coming from his phone in the shop earlier? Jay bitterly looked up and down the shared space that ran along the back of the shops. The wall around it was not much taller than him. The recycling store at Magda's was more secure. But there were no prying eyes here.

The light in the sky was grey.

Jay slotted the cardboard slips into the blue bin. Some of the packaging was awkward to get through the hole, so he had to lift up the lid with one arm and drop it in. Then he remembered the first time he'd spoken to Steffan in person. By the bin store. Out of Flat 401. He dropped the rest of the recycling into the bin silently, and let the lid shut with a slam. He replayed the podcast's reassuring words, '*Social media is inadmissible, but—*'. Pulled his earphones out of his ears.

Jay turned around. Tony was watching him, from eyes dark and hollow.

'What you doing here?'

Tony smirked, holding up a padlock, and tossing it in one hand a few times. 'Security round the back of your workplace is not too good, Jay. Not too good at all.'

Jay looked past Tony to the gate onto the street. 'How did you? Why are you here?'

Tony stepped forward, wiped rainwater off one of the green bins, and swung himself up onto it. Lanky legs hanging off the side. Putting the padlock down beside him, he got out a cigarette. Offered it to Jay with a gesture and his eyes, then lit it and took a drag. After blowing out, he answered: 'I'm thinking I ain't got time to wait for an inside man.' He looked round at the isolated store-yard, the nearest residential area a street away. 'Take-your-mate-to-work day!' Tony's eyes narrowed wickedly. He crossed his arms, and raised his chin. His thin lips sneered around his cigarette.

The moon and flame tattoos on the backs of his hands stared at Jay intimidatingly.

Jay strode over and put his face right up in Tony's.

'Now you listen to me, mate. You leave this place alone. Leave all these shops alone. I even see you here again, I'll call the police. You get me?'

Tony sniffed. Blew the smoke away from Jay but kept his eyes on him. Their lips only six inches apart, the drifting smoke making Jay blink and cough.

'And what would you tell them? Haven't you had enough of your fifteen minutes of fame yet?'

Jay took a step back. No doubt the guys for Tony's 'jobs' knew guys still in prison. What if one of them had found out something from Shaun?

Tony swung himself down off the bin.

'This is the life you cut out for yourself. Mate.' He stubbed out the cigarette under his shoe, no damns to give about the fire risk. 'Told you before. What's the point in trying to go straight? You're gonna die trying.' Tony provoked Jay with his narrow, contemptuous smile. Teeth ready. 'They'll never have you, after what you've done. Would of thought you'd've learned by now. After everything that's come your way.

'And why you wanna be normal, anyway?' he continued, leaving the padlock where it lay, and opening the gate. 'Microchipped, obedient. Like a dog. Screw that. Go out in a blaze of glory. You and Cathy already had your fifteen minutes. Where's mine?'

Jay's mouth went dry with suspicion.

'How do you know Cathy?'

Tony – Jay now had the feeling 'Tony' might not be Tony's full name – closed his eyes and shook his head. Laughing at himself as if he'd made a careless mistake. Opening his eyes, he looked almost forgivingly at Jay.

'I never lied to you about having an ex, son. I just never said she lived in the same hostel as you.'

Jay tensed his muscles. Drew himself up to his full height. The mask fell away from Tony's face. The tired face of a man halfway through his life who, when he feels vulnerable, hurts someone else to make himself feel strong again.

'So brave and open of you,' Ant said softly, closing the black gate, and planting himself in front of it. Tattooed fists clenched, long legs ready to spring.

'I won't let you hurt her again.' Jay readied himself.

Ant laughed. 'You forget about the bad behaviour clause or something?'

Jay hesitated.

'You let me down, Jay. I was stupid to think helping you out would get me anywhere. But you're going to get yours.'

Jay brought his fists up in front of his torso. The fighting stance from prison surging into his muscle memory.

Ant's face twisted. 'You know what happens to grasses?' he shouted.

The two men rushed at each other. Two strides, and they were face-to-face. Eyes locked. Ant's face straining on his neck like a dog on a leash. Jay's eyes widened, and he drew his fist back.

'Jay, stop!'

Jay didn't let himself be distracted by Esther's voice from behind him.

But Ant was pausing, looking over Jay's shoulder. He looked back at Jay. The lines on his face told a sad story. But yes, there was a witness now.

He feinted at Jay. 'Alright, killer?'

Jay feinted back, growling.

'Jay!' Esther's voice was firm, not frightened.

Jay held his ground.

Ant looked around again. Backed away. Reached behind him, opened the gate, and slipped out, shutting and padlocking the black metal after him.

'You know what happens to grasses.' Footsteps ran away from the shop.

Jay turned, breathing steadily.

Esther nodded. 'You did the right thing.'

Jay kept the office door open so Noah could overhear him and Esther agreeing what to do next. He wouldn't let the risk of Tony – Ant – telling what he knew about Jay stop him from doing what was right. Even though Tony knew only a partial truth. Esther made the call to the police. As he left for the day, Jay knew what she meant when she said, 'You take care now.' They both knew what happened to grasses.

Standing apart from Noah at the bus stop was awkward. Looking while trying not to look. When the bus arrived and they'd boarded, Jay stepped onto the stairs going to the upper deck. He gripped onto his phone, picturing the speech he'd drafted on it about what had really happened in Flat 401, willing Noah to understand there was something he wanted to tell him.

Noah didn't join him, but said, 'Buddy. I'll … I'll text you.'

56
Then

Steffan

Tej doesn't look at me as she continues unloading her shopping bag of supplies for our girly girls' night in. 'Be careful if he's like that. Envy can be destructive. "If I can't have you, no-one can", kind of thing,' she says, concluding her latest well-meant sermon on my love life. She gets out two wine glasses and a bottle of rosé. 'Have you decided which of your two men is most trustworthy, then?' she asks, innocently focusing on unscrewing the bottle's lid.

Opposing memories force their way in front of my mind's eye.

*

Shaun ensures his flies are definitely done up, and that there are no stains on the outside of his jeans. Checks himself out in the mirror.

Getting up from the bed, I say, 'It's been fun, but if you need to get back to work, that's what you've got to do.'

'And you're discreet, like?'

I laugh, and shake my head. *Of course.* Of course, I never tell anyone when he's coming over. Doing stuff with guys who are in denial, or in the closet, helps me keep anything serious – and the threatening feelings that provokes – at bay, but I've read this one before.

... I see sex with men as more exciting ...
... Women are such high maintenance ...
... I'm straight as they come ...

Oops. Either shaking my head, or what we just got up to, brings on a wave of dizziness. I sit down sharply.

'You alright?' he asks, scrutinising me in the mirror.

'It's nothing,' I say. 'The anaemia can give me low blood pressure. I'm still waiting to be well enough to return to the animal sanctuary – they don't want me fainting out in the fields!' Which is why it actually suits me for him to come here.

He flashes me a smile. It's silly, but it scares me: it makes me feel like he's pleased to hear I have a vulnerability.

'Cheers for the release, anyway,' he says.

I struggle to understand why he isn't leaving.

I get up quickly and open the door. Shaun makes some more small talk.

'And don't worry, I won't tell anyone about this. Promise,' I say, faking cheerfulness as I hold the door open. He heads out past me. He turns silent as soon as he is in the corridor and waiting for the lift, even though my studio is the only flat on this floor.

I close the door behind him, ensure it's locked, and check my phone. Reply to Jay's latest message. I feel bad flirting with him while hooking up with Shaun, especially as I might like him more after all. Maybe if I tease him enough, he'll overcome his issues with being gay? I feel sorry for how much prejudice he's absorbed: one message anxiously asked whether it was true that all gay men were into poppers.

I saw those talented actors putting on another matinee again

lol sounds like a show worth watching

Yeah although the audio can be a bit hard to make out

Maybe you should go over and give them a critique?

As Jay types his reply, I wonder what he's thinking, given how long he's taking. Is it cruel of me to joke about him being nothing more than an audience member? Will that make him feel shut-out and inferior? I don't feel that way about him!

Fine. Maybe I will

'Have you decided which of your two men is most trust-worthy, then?' Tej asks, innocently focusing on unscrewing the bottle's lid.

Not for the last time, I wonder: are there some mistakes so wrong, we cannot forgive them or make them right?

I don't answer.

57
Now

Cathy

There was never a time of day when the two-floor TK Maxx was empty. This Sunday afternoon was no exception, even though it had pissed it down in the morning. Cathy didn't mind. Her body was even moving a little to the music. She watched out for heat rising in her neck, cheeks and forehead, but no one was looking at her. No men, no women neither. Jay was within shouting distance, if anything happened.

She went back to browsing the racks. Sliding the cool metal hangers along the bar. Taking her time to run her eyes over the sizes and the price tags. She mentally compared them to the balance she'd checked at the ATM.

This dress was nice. Not sure about the back though. It had been such a long time, she didn't even know what her colour was anymore. She liked the look of this pale one. Patterned but not camouflage. She pictured it fluttering in the evening air. Smiled at herself in the mirror. She would show it to Tej later. She'd get her help to buy something smarter, whenever she got the chance to testify against Ant in court. The stitches in her forehead throbbed at the idea. The police would pick him up. And he wouldn't lurk around here with them and Jay on the lookout for him.

She clenched her hand around the hanger as she hurried to the queue.

Alice's final messages were about *how to learn to trust and take risks again.* Cathy would do her best to hold on to Alice's focus on *doing what works*, and *moving on with life.*

Her eye fell on a neon purple box. The cover decorated with massive images of glass jars full of coloured stripes. *Candle Making Kit.* Cathy didn't have to justify her spending to Ant now. She reached out for the box. It was heavier than she expected. Turning it over in her hands, she felt light. She smiled, thinking of old times she could enjoy again.

After she'd paid, Jay was waiting for her by the exit. He was looking at a crate of strange green and black sticks with a clear plastic cage on the end. They looked like them grabber toys. He looked funny. Probably embarrassed to be caught buying himself a kid's thing.

'Still think it's pretty bold of you to be coming here. Nice one!' he said.

'Yeah. Well. Got to crap or get off the pot, haven't you?' Cathy snuck a quick check of the men around. 'What's that?' she asked, gesturing at the plastic toys.

'Oh, well, Noah ... is afraid of spiders.'

Spider catcher was written on the side, she could see now.

'That's a great idea!' she said, pulling one out of the crate.

'No!' he shouted, knocking it out of her hand, back into the crate. 'I mean, no,' he said softly. 'I don't want to go over the top. It might not be good for him.'

Cathy laughed. To be fair, dating was a total minefield.

They walked in a comfortable silence round the corner back to the hostel. She was just about to ask Jay if he'd had a reply to that text she'd sent for him earlier, when they both slowed down. *Like seeing fins circling an inflatable in a pool ...*

Tej was on the steps of the hostel, arguing with three

clearly related lads Cathy recognised from somewhere. They all had cans in their hands. Two were staggering. The one who wasn't jeering or laughing was slurring.

Jay was hanging back.

'Come on, then!' urged Cathy. Jay kept his eyes on the men, and shook his head, but still followed a step behind her.

The youths turned as she approached. 'Oi oi. Uncle Anthony was right,' said the one at the front. The muggy summer air, hazy with pollution, pressed down on Cathy. Ant's nephews? Had they come for her?

The man stepped past, ignoring her, and stabbed his finger into Jay's chest. Jay backed off. One of the other animals leaped up the steps and grabbed Tej before she could get inside. Tej struggled with him until the third helped hold her still.

The side-street was quiet. There was no one watching from the hostel's windows. Cathy took refuge behind Jay.

'You've become a celeb, Ginige. Not just a sex pest: a proper grass!'

One of the two holding Tej thrust his hips and made howling noises. The other laughed. The leader looked back at them, grinning.

'Tony's your uncle? But his surname isn't Ly—'

The young men cackled like hyenas. The tallest one moved towards Cathy and Jay. Jay kept Cathy behind him.

'On *Mum's* side, idiot.' He pushed Jay in the chest. Another bad man who was tall like Ant.

Laugh it up, lads, laugh it up. You're gonna go the same way as your uncle. Cathy held her shopping bag in front of her face like she was scared. She couldn't make out what Jay was saying to them over her quick, whispered 999 call. Something about how he was going to make all this go away.

There was a knife in the front man's fist. Jay held up his hands and backed away, drawing him away from Cathy.

The man kept going. 'Filth like you don't belong in Woolwich.' He spat to the side.

The lad wasn't distracted by Cathy dropping her candle-making kit box. But he noticed alright when she held up one of the glass jars against his neck from behind.

'I will bleeding bottle you mate if you don't drop the knife.'

He looked over his shoulder. Nothing gave away how she felt inside. But if she had to rate it on one of Alice's mood scales, this would be a ten for Absolutely Bricking It.

The tall, shaven-headed youth looked down at her un-broken glass which couldn't cut butter. He smiled. Twisted slightly to bring his leering, smirking face nearer to hers. 'Hi, Aunty Cathy.' Blew her a kiss. But then he looked past her, and the smile faded into clenched lips. Jerking the knife away from Jay, he ran down the street.

'Come on, lads!'

The two holding Tej looked behind them, pushed her onto the steps and joined in the running.

Cathy heard the sirens now. The police car sped past. Jay ran over to help Tej up. Cathy was trembling. Another police car cut the runners off at the end of the road. The one ray of afternoon sun, pushing through the sheet of clouds covering the sky, caught their hostel's windows and bricks. It was like a movie.

Cathy felt like she'd swum a winning race. Her lungs swelling with deep, satisfied breaths. She couldn't believe what she'd done. She'd stood up for herself, for someone else who needed help. She'd showed a man. A man who actually deserved it. She turned back to Jay and Tej, grinning.

Bloody brilliant. Jay grinned back. Tej looked a bit pale but waved to show she was alright really.

The three of them saw off the men being handcuffed and pushed into the cars. Cathy and Jay helped Tej up into the office. Jay made her a cup of tea, and together they waited for the police to come and take statements. Cathy kept her eye out for Ant.

58

Amelia

On the other side of the road, the tall buildings at the river-side cut the sky like a Stanley knife: mostly smooth, but with jagged edges where the cutter had slipped and revealed slits of grey sky. A lanky man slipped in-between the towers still under construction, heading out of sight towards where Amelia knew flat 401 lay. Maybe he was the prospective tenant her parents had asked her to do a viewing for later?

Amelia turned her gaze away from the Woolwich river-side, and back to the gravestone in front of her. Having ended his days in the concrete jungle, her younger brother would rest forever here, at the collision between nature and newness. She couldn't escape that anymore. And she couldn't deny the final email to Steffan she'd sent before he died: Don't blame me if you die in that flat.

She gripped the phone in her pocket. The very same one she'd used to send that email. This morning, she'd received a message from a journalist who wanted to interview her about Jay. They wanted to stir things up for him, just as they were beginning to quiet down.

Amelia focused on the gravestone, ignoring the burial taking place on the far side of the graveyard.

'I'm sorry. I never got to tell you ...'

She lifted up the damp bunch of poppies out of the black vase which rested on top of the grave. Checking for witnesses, she slipped the silver ring on a chain out of her pocket and into the bottom of the vase. She checked again that no one had seen her conceal the thirtieth birthday present with the sweet- and earthy-smelling flowers. The untended grass rustled slightly. The blades like raised eyebrows of watching eyes, inviting her to say more.

Amelia felt her heart giving way.

'I've spent so much time trying to find someone to blame,' she said to the gravestone. Untended red lichen ran down the side of it like a bloody tear. 'It was easier to get angry at you, at anyone, than to accept ...'

A faint scratching sound, like someone trying to escape their coffin, came from the funeral as the mourners each took their turn to cast dirt onto it.

'If I'd just been there for you.' The blood-red lichen blurred in the clear grey light of day.

'Remember when you were four years old and you banged your head on the low wall in the garden? No, you wouldn't remember, you were too small. You had this tiny cut but it was bleeding and I was so worried. I thought you might die. I only wanted to be a good older sister.' She let the tears flow down her cheeks. 'I'm sorry I couldn't protect you.'

The stone was silent.

'Revenge was never going to solve how I felt. I understand that now.'

The stone was taking it all in.

'I never did get a response to my last email. I guess I was too late to make it right.'

The poppies nodded, as if they were communicating on Steffan's behalf: *We all make mistakes. I know everything you've done, and why. You're still my sister: I still love you. I know you've tried your best. There are ways to make it right. And be good enough as you are.*

Wiping her face, Amelia laughed. 'And at least you're not totally messing things up. No job, no boyfriend, no life. Might even go to prison myself! Had a massive row with Mam and Dad on the phone yesterday. It's not looking good for him.'

The funeral group was moving on now. A straggler at the back caught Amelia watching, and she bowed her head again.

'Maybe working hard and being right aren't the only things in life.' She kicked the gravestone playfully. 'What do you think I should say to Peter? And do I go back to teaching?'

She checked the time on her phone. 'I've got to head off. I'll be back, maybe on the way home, but if not, another time. I've got to do a viewing for our parents' – for your – for the flat. Sorry. This is going to be the last time. Anyway, I'll see you again.'

She ran her hand over the gravestone, the wet lichen coming off, mixing with her tears so it looked like she was bleeding.

Even though flat 401 was only on the fourth floor, going up in the lift made Amelia feel like she was heading somewhere important. She knew it had been somewhere fatal; she didn't want it to be final anymore. Didn't want her life to have ended with her brother's.

She finished what she'd started on the train: she deleted her news website video, her forum account and correspondence with EmeraldSiren, and Wanda's messages and Witness Care Unit number. She also deleted the journalist's message from that morning, unanswered. Jay could get on with his life: it would only drag them both down if she pursued him further.

The living-room window had the best view, although she could swear that even more jagged towers had pierced the skyline since her last visit, slicing at the dimming blue that struggled to make its way through the grey clouds.

Through the window by the bed, she checked whether anyone was watching from the flat opposite.

She pulled the curtains shut.

A sign in the foyer had said the buzzers weren't working, and that delivery men should phone their customers to gain entry. So, she wasn't surprised when the knock on the door came without warning.

She opened it without looking through the eyehole.

'You?!'

It was too late: the intruder had already shoved their way into flat 401 with her.

And locked the door behind them.

59

Jay

As he looked out of his window onto the summer evening light, Jay felt relieved to see the sparrows still enjoying their freedom with each other. He reread the text Noah had sent him that morning:

Up for a drink after work?

His smile stretched his face. The hope fluttering behind Noah's words gave him the same electric thrill as it had all day.

Cathy had laughed when she'd caught him making camomile tea in the kitchen after he'd first got it. He'd been deliberating how to reply for at least two hours when she snatched his phone off him.

Yes

She'd laughed again after pressing *Send*, as she handed his phone back to him. They hadn't talked much, but it had been nice to hear she was meeting someone for a drink that evening, even if *'just as friends'*.

It was lucky he'd accompanied her to TK Maxx afterwards. He might check Tejinder had recovered OK in the office on his way out. It had been good of her to tell him that he was going to be allowed to stay on at Magda's. *You have a home here, Jay. It would take more than a viral video to take that from you.'*

He spotted Cathy leaving. She was cautiously looking at who else was out there, but didn't look back at Magda's, didn't wave. Tony wouldn't be out there, with the police having just taken his nephews into custody. Cathy's pale, salt-and-pepper dress fluttered as she disappeared into the distance and around the corner. He turned to look at his own selection of date clothes lying on his bed. Basically the same as his normal clothes.

He hadn't been able to eat much all day, his stomach protectively curling up so it wouldn't have to take the anticipated blow of rejection. But Noah had suggested meeting – that had to be a good sign, right? Maybe he should have bought that plastic spider-catcher – not all gifts were harmful.

Another text. Jay grabbed his phone.

Timpson House have given you the all-clear, matey

The smile across his face was tearing it up. Everything was coming together for him. He guessed Esther had put in a good word for him with Noah as well as with HQ.

The Lynases, uncle and nephews, hadn't got far when they'd tried to outrun their failure. He wouldn't be going down that route. Maybe grassing up Tony would go in his favour, mean they could all forget about Amelia's crazy video? Pretend like it had never been recorded. Never been uploaded. Never threatened to sink what remained of his life.

He didn't even care about leaving Woolwich or changing his name now. The past few days, he hadn't searched on SpareRoom or the Deed Poll website once. Living here wasn't so bad. He could make a new life for himself. It was more or less out in the open, and it had gone alright, no? Either way, he was due to burrow his way out of Probation in less than two weeks.

Sitting on the bed, pulling jeans over his muscular thighs, Jay looked up and saw a sparrow outside the window, gazing in at him, its head tipping from side to side curiously. Its eye wasn't entirely black, as he'd thought from a distance: the pupil watched him from a centre of warm brown, surrounded by black plumage, away from which trailed feathers of white. Jay stared back. Was it normal for a bird not to blink?

It flew off to rejoin its friends.

Fishes definitely couldn't close their eyes. They were also supposed to be able to forget really easily. Imagine that: you couldn't stop seeing things, but you could get them out of your mind as soon as you wanted – sooner, probably.

Jay was the opposite. He could close his eyes all he liked. Avoid reminders: the place, men who looked like him, things that smelled like that time; white envelopes and little brown bottles were harder to escape. So he couldn't forget. Something unwanted always came creeping in. He could push them down all he liked, into the depths, the dark, but the memories always came for him. Crawling, surfacing, exploding out of a bag that he never wanted to be carrying with him, that he didn't even have time to pack properly, bursting all over the street as he ran for the Megabus, making him late, making all the passers-by stare at him.

Making him know what he'd done.

What he could never undo.

Fish couldn't close their eyes; Jay couldn't forget. He had

to look. Five years ago, other eyes had stared back at him. Two eyes had been green: brilliant, charming, inescapable; the others had been brown: accusing, begging, lifeless.

His phone buzzed. Another text. Jay pulled on his T-shirt before he dared look. *Please don't be Noah cancelling.* He stood there, hands at his side, breathing slowly, keeping his eyes on the darkening screen. Finally he dashed forward and grabbed it.

An unknown number. Jay let out his breath, smiled, and rubbed the back of his head. It wasn't Noah cancelling.

Want to know what I really did?

Jay's face set hard. Cracked concrete paving over ringing ears and knife-like vision. Heart and lungs going like crazy. So this is what it all came down to. The last five years, the last three weeks, the last three days. This whole moment. Mad.

His phone buzzed again. He opened the picture message.

Amelia Evans. Lying on a settee, hands behind her back, a cloth tied across her mouth. Staring at the camera.

Tears started at Jay's eyes. She must be so afraid. It was like back then. This was it.

It could only be from the person who had sent the Notes to him and Shaun.

Bastard. Who are you?

His phone buzzed again. A one-line address. No building number, no street name, no town, no postcode. Not needed. It was where everything had ended for Jay. And for Steffan. Of course, it had to be there. It was always going to be there. He could never get away from it.

Jay, crying, screaming out with rage, threw the phone down onto his bed. Face down.

Clenched his fists. Paced and up down, three times.

Stopped.

Gathered and released big breaths, getting ready for the final innings. Stared the phone down before picking it up again.

What do you want?

Jay sat next to the phone. Squeezing his hands. Looking down at it again and again. Picking it up, checking. Finally it buzzed, and he leaped on the reply.

Another photo; a familiar face. One he would never forget.

Dread pulling him down. Futile to think it could have been anyone other than— A single-word message.

Now.

He had been so dumb to think it could have been anyone else, that anyone could be trusted, that anyone could let him go. He reread the messages over and over, desperate to understand them in a different way, desperate to make them mean anything other than that he had been well and truly fooled by someone who intended to take their revenge for what really happened that day.

He banged the window shut. The cheerful cheeping chattering of the sparrows crowded in on him, making it hard to think. The grey early evening light was too bright, his room was unacceptably full of a muffled buzzing, and his flesh was cold.

Of course. It was the same unknown number he'd been called on from before. Jay thought pointlessly of how easy it was for prisoners to get access to forbidden technology. Where had he hidden it? Inside the TV in his cell? What had he had to do to get it? What was he willing to do?

Jay looked at the photo of Shaun's wolflike, grinning face, the green eyes burning with a frightening fire. Had Jay been so unforgivably wrong?

What the hell are you suggesting, mate?

Your one Amelia knows, Jay. We need to keep her quiet, like

So Shaun was still claiming Amelia was a threat. Jay sat, sweating into the bed. You couldn't put a fire out with petrol. Jay sank back against the wall at the head of his bed. Stared out the window. Laughed an unconvincing laugh. Told himself Shaun was fooling.

His phone buzzed for him again.

You've as good as done it with me before. Let's go all the way this time

The hollow smile disappeared from Jay's face. Tears pricked his eyes again and then were dismissed. His teeth gritted. All his senses slowed down.

He banged on the window to frighten off another watching sparrow.

Three of them in Flat 401 again. He could do this.

He let Shaun know he was coming, and then texted Noah

to say he was sorry, he couldn't meet after all, even though he really wanted to. Something had come up.

Shaun's final text and attached photo were unsubtle.

Just like before fella – don't tell anyone else you're coming over 😒

Jay hadn't needed Shaun to zoom in on the arm of the settee by Amelia's head. He'd already spotted the yellow and black Stanley knife, triangular blade exposed.

He had no choice.

The light at the end of the day cast his shadow across the blank wall of his room. He wrote out a note, which he concealed in his pocket: he hoped it would do him justice. Going over to the basin, he plucked the Isle of Wight postcard from the mirror. Gazed at the dreams of a new life it represented. Reread the writing on the back.

Tossed it into the bin.

As he walked away from Magda's, he looked back. He raised a hand in an awkward salute at Tejinder, who was watching him through the office window on the ground floor, pale, gripping the edge of the desk with the printer on it.

The old red-brick building leaned towards him, open, softly making eye contact. His muscles were heavy and tight from hiding from the truth. Magda's had housed and looked after him for so long: she understood his emotional pain.

He was slowing down when he passed the bench in the square where he'd sat with Tony. He kept an eye out for people around him, and sped up.

Magda's had the strength and wisdom to know what path he should take. He hoped she could forgive him. He needed to do this to be able to live.

Given what he'd really done.

60

Shaun

He hadn't expected to see Jay sitting with Ma. Was he proving to himself that, sur-*sodding*-prise, Shaun's mum really was in hospital? Shaun hadn't made that up. He had better things to do.

He lurked at the door to the ward, salivating over what was about to happen to Jay. Being out of prison was like good sex: the more you got, the more you wanted. So many things were like that for Shaun. They held the promise of satisfying him, but either grew rank, filling up his mouth with disgust for what had been sweet, or were empty to begin with, a hollow piece of fun that made the hunger pains worse. But still he kept tracing the same pattern, deeper and deeper, until there was only one way to go.

He'd laughed at the prison therapist who'd asked him that question about his childhood. The attractive unnatural blonde trying to make herself look intelligent with those stupidly thick glasses, laying on the '*I can imagine that must have been very painful for you*' thick over her scientific bollocks from books and lectures and training courses. As if he were some kind of 2D stereotype. No, he hadn't pulled the legs off beetles and watched them wriggle. What was the point of tormenting a bug? Bugs didn't even register underfoot.

It was the people, the people who looked down on him, who trampled him, who stole away love who needed to be shown they were mistaken. To make him right. To let him live the life he deserved.

Shaun moved aside, spying through the window, to let the consultant and his gaggle of medical students pass, as the handsome doctor banged on about 'stroke', 'Long Covid', and 'smoking'. Sure, now Ma was dying physically, but she had died as a person a long time ago, when she let herself be walked over by his bastard of a father. He could never respect that. What's the point in living if you can't be special?

He could never be special, now. Not specially good, at any rate.

If Jay'd just kept away from Steffan ... Two exotic spices desperate for a taste of each other.

Shaun crushed the empty plastic cup, and discarded it.

He wanted to think that he'd planned his endgame all along. He didn't want to admit that it had occurred to him when things were already in motion. That at the start he'd just been planning to spite.

Fingernails were digging into his palms. He was this close to banging on the window, barging into the ward and showing Jay the video himself, he was.

Whatever he tried to soothe himself with, it wasn't enough, wasn't what he needed. Same as with his plan. He'd intended to expose what Jay really did, that had felt good, sure. But then he'd thought – so what? And – wouldn't that go badly for him?

The media coverage and the court experience had been humiliating. Everyone knowing what Shaun had done. But prison ... Not being able to twist people round his little finger. Having to get on his knees before lifers or bent prison officers. Bent over.

Shaun felt the tea pressing against his bladder, but he didn't want to step away from the ward until he was sure Jay had seen Amelia's video, and the whole world's reaction to it. Why hadn't he checked his phone yet?

He didn't want to admit that finding the sister on that internet forum had been luck. He pretended to himself that the seed for looking for someone else who might want to tear Jay down had been there all along, someone who could do their bit in making him not just humiliated but worthless. Shaun had felt so powerless when he'd been held, stomach down, into the slimy prison shower room tiles, naked cheek pressed against the rough floor, soapy water stinging his eyes, scum that didn't drain properly fingering its way into his mouth.

He wasn't confused. He was straight. And he wasn't a victim. Shaun checked out one of the female nurses to prove his point.

Yes. This was it. Jay was pulling out his phone. Looking at the free Wi-Fi details stuck on the wall. Now he'd find out something else Shaun had learned from Dad. It had been fun to team up and bully Ma. Like the time she'd cleaned Shaun's room without asking, and thrown some of his men's magazines away. It had been soothing, a high, to hide her cigarettes, and watch while the cravings drove her mad.

He watched, at a distance, the light come on for Jay, who compulsively repeated the video only to get the same answer. Shaun lapped up the desperate, animated attempt to escape. Couldn't get enough of seeing him get what he deserved for treating Shaun that way.

Shaun also watched the lights switching off for his poor, harmless, hopeless mother.

Shaun thought of a time. A mad trip to Beachy Head she'd taken him on, not long after Dad left. She borrowed a car for their late-night outing. Past the lights of the chaplaincy, under the anxiously watching stars, up to the lighthouse. She stood at the edge for a long time. He'd never seen a lighthouse in operation before. He imagined himself at the top of the tower, gazing out kindly at the lost, desperate ships as they yearned for a place they could come to rest safely, his scheming lamp guiding them to their destination for the night. Moths to a flame. He pictured killing the light, and feeling a smile heat his face as all the lost souls crashed on the dark rocks beneath him. In the end, he'd put his hand into hers, and said, 'Come on, Ma,' ready to take her, silent, back to their rank, hollow home.

Jay deserved what was he going to get: he was the one who'd ruined everything with Steffan.

61

Then

Steffan

As I follow Tej's instructions to forgive and make things right, I read the start of my email to Amelia again.

> Hi! Lovely to hear from you! I mean, I could have done without the reminder of my imminent old age 😔

I type in a reference to *Mum and Dad*, then delete the first three lines. Tejinder acts like the email in my inbox is a gift. But I remember an evil gift can be harmful.

Nothing new on WhatsApp. Read, still no response. Have I messed things up with him? I should have heeded Tej's warning. *'You demand too much from men, and they scorn you'*; it was ridiculous to think he might be ready to come out, or have feelings for me. And if he had, what I told him about his 'rival' would no doubt have obliterated them.

I pace over to the bed, and pick up the trophy I'd bought as a gift for Shaun. Charity. I tearfully put it back, never to be gifted. Useless piece of chintz no one wants, so sad on the shelf. I stretch my neck, my hand palpating the tender flesh. I'd let myself linger on Shaun's green eyes, his curly brown hair, the feel of his muscles, so full in the warm weather. Full of love, I'd thought.

I've got so much more to live for. I replay today's voice-mail: *'Hi, Steffan, we're so looking forward to having you back at the animal sanctuary when you're all better!'*

And Amelia is trying her best. I delete everything I've written.

It's nice to hear from you. Really nice. I know it can be hard, the way our parents treat us differently. But what you said really hurt me.

I am blood – I deserve better than her lack of direct contact, and indirect snipes whenever we're at our parents together, culminating in joining in with them to blame me for things not working out with my ex, and the illness I got as a result. I know it was foolish of me to have gone along with him and slept together in that long grass – I don't need reminding.

But then there were times like when I'd banged my head on the wall in the garden. Amelia looking after me then is one of the few memories I have from Wales. I look over at her first birthday gift to me: stuck to the wall with Blu Tack, her childish attempts at representing the Welsh dragon and my Chinese (Year of the) Horse in one painting. She would only have been four or five.

Of course I would like to meet up again! Not just to get the birthday present you mention 😊

When I think she might be ready to make amends ... I need to get this right.

My phone sounds.

I grab it, and breathe easy. The whole day seems bright.

The city beyond the window of my flat buzzes with life.

He still wants to come over. To a body made for loving, for him.

I save my email of *rapprochement* to Amelia for later. As I say, I want to make sure I get it right.

I tidy up the flat. I have let it go over the past few days: the throw is hanging off the sofa, exposing the holes; washing-up is piled in the sink; stinking ready-meal containers are bursting out of the bin. When I've made the place more presentable, I let Tejinder know I'll be having a visitor, and that, yes, I've taken my blood pressure and, yes, it's a bit low – but that's to be expected.

He's coming round ASAP. I put my phone down, and light the vanilla candles (for ambience, not illumination). I'm glad I shall have the opportunity to make sure things are right between us. Tej leaves me a quick voicemail: *'Hey, Steffan, hope you have a nice time with him today.'* I was so excited, did I even name him?

I shake off my doubts about my ability to make the right choice, still lingering thanks to my ex. For what I hope is the last time, I wonder: are there some mistakes so wrong, we cannot forgive or make them right?

62

Then

Jay

In the lift up to the top of the tower that houses Flat 401, I feel proud of myself. I don't have to hide myself away: I can afford to take this risk. To live instead of just surviving.

I keep telling myself this even as my mouth continues to dry out and my heart continues to pound.

As the lift doors open, I breathe. I focus on the white envelope I'm clutching – I didn't have any wrapping paper – addressed to *Mr S. Evans*.

When I was growing up, everyone knew everyone back on the Burrage estate; but after I moved here, before I'd doubled down on working from home, I'd return to nothing but a row of faceless doors. What would be worse? Everyone knowing my business, or no one?

I'm facing Steffan's door; I hope I'm not disturbing him with anyone. I lift up his letterbox carefully, using my right hand. Lifting the letterbox to slip in the envelope exposes the sounds. As I listen, I give myself three pieces of reassurance: *his is the only flat on this floor. No one can be watching. I'm totally invisible.*

My mouth dries. My heart thuds. My crotch stirs. I slowly lower the letterbox. My face burns with the frustrated wish that Steffan could be with me, only me. 'Happily ever after'.

But I don't belong. I'm not a part of this. I can't be one of them.

I shuffle over to the lift, and press the button to escape. The inside of my head is starting to feel dirty. I'll be honest: some of the sounds disturbed me. I'll feel safer back in my flat; it suits me to watch from over there. No one can see what I'm up to, and I can still live through the people I see beyond my window. This is the closest I've ever come to being a part of what I desire, and it feels too much.

The lift doors open, and the empty, mirrored cube stares back at me. My own eyes dare me. *You cannot be a part of it, but you want to taste through others' lips, feel through others' fingers, live through others' lives. Lives that are better than yours: brighter, glittering, free.*

Free.

The only thing worth being.

Don't you want that? Don't you want to be free? To be held? To be loved?

I'm still holding the envelope. The lift doors, tired of waiting, close me out, and seal me in to my choice. I creep back to Steffan's door. It dares me; I am a useless child drunk on fearful excitement.

I push.

Unlocked, it reveals an overwhelming wave of vanilla, a mirror layout of my flat, and the sounds.

They beckon me onwards.

I edge along the outside wall of the bathroom. Just to find somewhere to put down the envelope which conceals my gift. Sneaking a peek round the corner to where I know the bed must bounce. I tell myself I won't go too far.

I knew it: he didn't really want me, anyway. My rival is even more amazing close up. His strong arms pin Steffan onto the bed: one hand over both Steffan's hands, over his head, and the other gently around his throat. His handsome face twisted with the effort. He looks up, spit and sweat dripping. He has seen me. My throat tightens. Steffan wants this, he has always wanted it through the window, but does this guy? I offer him the smile I saved up for the bullies at school: a pathetic, appeasing currency, buying their approval with my pulled-back lips, exposed teeth, and submission. Gulls, drawn by the Thames and the rubbish, wheel outside the window and laugh coldly in the warm daylight.

The man Steffan has told me is called Shaun smirks back at me. His long, angular face is made lopsided by his mouth; his curly, dark hair begs to be tousled in secret; his green, disturbed eyes let me know my place.

It's just the three of us here. Shaun is slowing down, still looking at me. We are watched by a small trophy on the shelf above Steffan's bed. A metal moth on a black coffin. A sombre figure alongside the cheery bees on the card next to it.

My mouth has deserted me. The mocking gulls outside the window won't stop laughing.

I want to believe this means nothing about me. But Steffan's acceptance was going to make me better than I am.

Pausing for breath, Shaun reaches over to a white paper bag on the side, takes a jelly sweet for himself, then offers me one. My right hand reaches over, trembling. I deserve to burn in my shame.

The sour green candy is also sweet.

Shaun is offering Steffan a small brown bottle.

'Trust me. Try them,' he says.

Steffan looks unsure, looks at me. I hate him for making me get involved. I hate him for making my urges mean something. I hate him for wanting Shaun not me.

I snatch the bottle from Shaun. Force it under Steffan's nose. The solvent smell of the poppers stretches its tendrils up towards me.

'Trust me. Try them,' I say. Shaun smiles at me, then down at Steffan, resting his hand on his lover's head. My neighbour has no choice but to comply. I count to nine as he inhales. Steffan looks up at Shaun, pupils dilating despite the sunlight streaming in through the window.

This isn't even what I really want. I retreat round the corner, leaning against the wall, the sound of all of our breathing buzzing in my ears. A groan, and then all our breathing reverberates and slows down throughout the flat's oppressive air. I dare myself to look round the wall, at the couple on the bed.

I turn a blind eye to my neighbour's airless, sightless cry for help, help, help me. His empty, grasping hand has fallen away from him, and hangs over the end of the bed.

Shaun pants. Looks out to my empty window opposite. Discards a satisfied smile at me. He checks on the unmoving figure on the bed.

'Oh my God. What's happened? I can't be here,' I cry out.

Shaun's face is a dark thing now. I've come too far to go back; I'm afraid for myself.

'Call an ambulance!' I whisper.

He looks concerned. Checks Steffan's pulse. Then he smiles at me, baring his fangs; I think he is going to kiss me.

'Your man's just passed out. Happens sometimes with poppers.'

I look down at the envelope that I'd brought for my neighbour, that I'd used to carry something he could care for.

'I think he'll be alright, but maybe we should call an ambulance. I think he had a condition.' Shaun gestures to where my phone hides in my pocket.

I knew he had a condition.

I shake my head. Shake the purple Tamagotchi out from the envelope, onto the shelf. Leave the instructions inside. As if bringing the gift out into the open could make up for what I've done. It was supposed to be something he could care for. He was such a caring person.

'Sure, I'll stay here and take care of him, like,' Shaun calls through the door as I run away.

I've barely got back to my flat when Shaun comes over to tell me that S—, that S. Evans never came to. He looks hollow, but says we'll need to cover up what happened – for both our sakes. And even though the poppers were an accident, Shaun says I'd be the one to go to prison for longer – seeing as how I was the one who gave them to him, and wouldn't call an ambulance. If I just keep quiet, he'll make it all go away. Neither of us wants people to know.

It's pathetic that I'm more concerned about what I have to lose than what I've just done. Than what we're going to do to his family.

But no one can know what I really did: in that moment, I hated him – and he died.

63

Now

Shaun

Shaun stood by the sofa, knife in gloved hand. The unlatched door tentatively swung open towards him.

'Just like our first date,' he teased.

Jay shut the door behind him carefully, looking round the studio flat, eyes widening at Amelia's head, which was straining up from the sofa by Shaun's left thigh. He swallowed.

'Now lock it,' Shaun commanded. Jay complied, but stayed furtively by the door.

Shaun smiled widely. Spread his arms.

'Jakey! Come on in! I'm not going to bite. We're in this together, remember?'

Jay edged, slowly, into the room. Not touching anything. Switching his eyes between Shaun and Amelia. Shaun felt himself grow hot. Irritation grinding his teeth behind his smile.

'Still stinks, doesn't it?' Shaun gestured with the business end of the Stanley over to the bed. He enjoyed how on edge Jay looked. He gestured at the fridge. At the bathroom door. Jay jumped each time. Shaun laughed like a drunk uncle at a wake.

'Come on, Jakey, don't be scared. Come over and say hello

to our little friend. Are you still shy about touching?' Amelia flinched, turning her face away, smothering it in the side of the sofa, whimpering through the gag Shaun had fashioned out of a left-behind tea-towel.

He brought the knife inches from her cheek.

'What's this about, mate? This isn't what we discussed.' Jay wasn't behaving how Shaun wanted.

'What do you mean, mate?' Shaun couldn't believe he had to piss again. Cheap cider went right through you. Pity he hadn't been able to get anything stronger for this last party. 'You wanted us to get on with our lives, didn't you? She needs to be out of the picture for that.' Another menacing gesture towards the captive woman for emphasis. 'Grand, right?'

'Nah, she doesn't know anything, Shaun. You could have just let her live, you know what I'm saying?'

Of course the stupid bitch didn't know anything. But Shaun knew the power of a rumour. Many times over. Five years ago, it had been so easy to lie to the police about Jay's involvement, in return for time off his sentence. This year, it had been so easy to hack his phone's location, and trick Jay into having a dodgy chat online: people will give away anything on those apps.

The transcripts Amelia had got by herself were a bonus. That would definitely make it look like Jay had reason to go after her. Especially after his text about needing to '*do something about Amelia*'.

'She's dangerous, Jakey. You saw the video! She wants to take you down, take *us* down.' Shaun remembered to adjust himself, and pulled his T-shirt a little tighter. *That's it, Jay, you like what you see, don't you? Take the bait. Bite me.*

'This is nuts. You had to go and bring her here. I could have got on with my life. Forgotten about … it.'

'And you can forget about it,' Shaun said smoothly, turning up the Irish accent. 'Soon. No one else knows she's here.' He omitted the word 'yet'.

'You can silence her nice and clean like.' Shaun chuckled at his own neck-slicing motion. He narrowed his eyes at Jay when he saw the other man wasn't rushing over to cut her up. He circled around the sofa, keeping it and Amelia between him and Jay. Jay mirrored him, circling round to his left, further away from the front door. Shaun paused when Jay was nearer Amelia, diagonally behind her head.

'When you hate something about yourself, you have to destroy the evidence,' Shaun said reasonably. 'Olu has the envelope,' he added.

Jay drew out a phone from his pocket, and looked at the screen, frowning.

'Throw that over there!' Shaun shouted, cutting the air. Jay hurriedly complied, the phone disappearing behind the TV stand with a thud. Shaun breathed in and let it out.

'You know, the one from that day.' He couldn't believe Jay's probation officer hadn't done anything about the Tamagotchi instructions Ma had kept in a sealed sandwich bag to avoid contamination. She'd been so happy to promise that the police would never get hold of something he'd said could incriminate him but he couldn't risk throwing away.

The fear rolling off Jay was intoxicating.

Blood pumping, muscles tingling, he smiled down at his captive.

'As far as anyone outside this room knows, Jakey,' he continued without taking his eyes off the frightened woman, who was clearly desperate for someone to save her from the mess she'd dug herself into, 'you didn't even see her sibling die through the window. You were never here. It's just this little troublemaker you need to keep quiet.'

Shaun didn't like to say Amelia's sibling's name, because that would be admitting …

Shaun took another drink of stale cider to wash the taste out of his mouth. The thought of other people knowing the truth about you could be terrifying.

Amelia mumbled something. Muffled moans probably begging for release, or that she would never tell, or something.

'Shut up!' Shaun shouted. He wiped the spit off his cheek with his forearm.

'Shaun, please.' Jay made eye contact with him. 'This isn't like with Tejinder. She was on to us. But you've done your time. We both have. You know what I'm saying? It's over.'

'Over!' screamed Shaun, lunging across the room, backing Jay right up against the wall, jabbing at his face with the knife, raging inches away from the other man's face which was turning away from him. 'Look at me! Look at me!'

The heat rose between them. Their firm bodies pressed up against each other. He wanted to cut Jay open, get deep into him, make him feel the sharp pain of the metal in his neck. Cold like prison shower-room tiles.

'You think you can get off scot-free after what you did! You're done! Done!'

Jay was mumbling now, stammering, eyes turned away again as Shaun penetrated him with his gaze. Another memory of that stupid prison therapist interfered with him: *'We can never get enough of what we don't need.'*

'Forgiveness? Forgiveness!' Shaun shrieked. He saw his own spit marking Jay now, the white flecks of his bodily fluid on the caramel skin. He pushed away the want to lick them off. Memory of an awkward almost-kiss with another boy at fifteen. He never got to kiss Steffan, did he?

Shaun pushed away from Jay and strode over to Amelia.

Crouching by the sofa, looking at Jay, he yanked down her gag, letting her gasp and cry. The knife hand pointing at Jay, he put the other around half her throat and shouted in her face.

'Tell him! Tell him, Amelia! Tell him you forgive him! Tell him you forgive him for letting your brother die right here. Your whore brother who invited him over! When he already had me!' He threw her head back onto the sofa. Her face was red, she just sobbed, struggling to breathe. Pathetic.

His arm was trembling as he kept it pointing at Jay, the triangular threat of the metal slice of death keeping the grass pinned against the wall. He saw the vein pumping in the side of Amelia's throat. Calling to him.

Jay's voice floated in to him from a few feet away: 'I'd do anything to have a normal life.'

Shaun smiled a shark's smile to himself. Swung his head round to stare Jay down.

He was violated by the urge to say, *You think you can push me down into the dirt while you trample my back, letting the others all spit on me. You're wrong.*

You'll kill her, to save your own skin, and then I'll call the police to tell them about what you've done. You'll go to prison for robbing me of what I deserved, and then you'll know what it's like. You'll be exposed for what you really are: worthless, unlovable, both your ma and dad despising you, running off without you, leaving you alone in the world with nothing. Everyone who has brought me to this, must be brought down with me. Otherwise, the only way to be special is in death.

But Amelia's interruption prevented him from verbalising the words which were more than just words: now his desire for revenge had festered for so long, they were more like a part of his being.

'Hate to sound like a *Scooby-Doo* character, but you'll never get away with this,' she choked out.

Shaun turned back to her. Frowned at the interruption but then smiled another shark's smile as he looked down on her.

Laughed.

Took a final swig of his cider, and then laughed again. Laughed like Dad laughing at Ma.

'Why not? I've gotten away with murder here before, haven't I, darlin?'

Amelia's face was draining from red to white. The wet from her eyes was smeared all over her. She breathed through her nose like a dying dog. She made as if to leap up at him from her imprisoned position. Pinned down on the sofa, she opened her mouth and assaulted him with a scream that choked into a sob.

Laughing, always laughing, Shaun covered her mouth. His hand felt so big; bigger than around the can of cider. He didn't want the neighbours on the floor below to hear. Yet.

Jay's voice whined, pleaded, begged at him.

'You? But that … that was an accident. That was my fault.'

Jay slumped against the wall.

'Wasn't it?'

His head fell back, eyes glazed.

'Shaun?'

64

Then

Shaun

No need to worry: I won't breathe a word.

Don't pretend you and that Jay fella never got up to something. He seemed pretty friendly when he left a few minutes ago! But now it's just you and me.

Shame you had to come to. Defies the whole point of me bringing those poppers. Thought I'd managed to get your little friend to do my dirty work for me.

I don't want a 'relationship' with you. And now that Jay guy won't be able to have one either.

The thing is, 'Mr' Evans': I've got a reputation to maintain. An image. That's all I am. One of the lads, man's man, normal guy. Better than normal.

This isn't normal! You think the world will let me hear the end of it if it finds out? You want me to be squashed like an insect up against a wall? You want me to be the one who is discarded. You want me to be nothing but the rotten, worthless, hollow darkness at the bottom of a human heart. You want to mean something about me, but you don't mean anything. You don't.

You don't even want me.

What a joke.

Honestly.

Don't beg now.

It's good we've had this little chat. Clear the air. One last time together. Unexpectedly naked before my rival showed up, but that's on you. Your hair and lips pulling me in, forcing me to need to be with you again.

You understand why I have to end it like this. I need to be sure. It hasn't gone exactly as planned, but the truth? It would have destroyed me.

You can't breathe?

No need to worry: *no one* will breathe a word.

65

Now

Amelia

The sky had cleared a path between the clouds for the bloodied sun. The sun was watching Amelia, bound and gagged on the sofa in flat 401. The sun was setting, burning hot, but Amelia was frozen. Frozen with fear, frozen with rage, frozen with the reignition of her endless capacity for the desire for vengeance. She pictured herself as *Battlestar*'s President Laura Roslin, ready to end Shaun with every last weapon she had. She would be Nemesis, she would be Death, she would strike him down and he would not even imagine rising again. She would strip the very flesh from his body, his meagre bones on display for any passing bird to peck at, defecating him out all over the city. His worthless, meaningless, disgusting life splattered like so much wet dust.

He was the one responsible for all this.

She looked down at his ungloved hand, which had slid off her mouth and was resting on the top of her chest. Sweaty, pawing, crawling hand of a—

'Murderer,' she denounced. Insidious tears slunk down her cheeks. Shaun looked down at her again, pulled his hand away and wiped the offending liquid off, as if she were the malignancy. Her hands, bound underneath her, hungered to rip his eyes out.

Shaun hadn't tied her tight enough for them to go numb, but she wriggled to relieve her discomfort. He stood up and switched the knife from his right to his left hand, pointing it at her as he warned, 'Stay down.'

She froze again.

He took a few steps back, nearer the front door.

'You've kind of made it difficult for me to go anywhere,' she dared to retort. Was Jay here to rescue her? He was more muscular than she'd expected, but he didn't seem to have brought any kind of weapon, and he'd thrown his phone out of reach when Shaun had asked him.

Was he really going to do what Shaun wanted?

Straining her head to the left, failing to escape the decaying sofa smell, she didn't think Jay had known what Shaun had planned. Five years ago, or now. He was slumped against the wall by the window, head back, dark eyes on Shaun.

The sun was setting in between other buildings; modern, cladded towers obscured the view of the river that curved away. *Red sky at night* ... She couldn't see any people. If only she hadn't shut the curtains by the bed, then maybe the person in the flat opposite would see what was going on. Would call the police, or rush over themselves. Break the door down, wrestle the knife from Shaun, save the day. He'd be even handsomer and an even better kisser than Peter too.

She burbled out a laugh. A little one, at first. She clamped her mouth shut, trying to squash it. Jay looked at her. Then it grew louder and larger, filling up the stifling space around her.

'What's so funny?' Shaun sounded angry.

The laughter burst out of her, echoing off the undecorated walls of this would-be home, shaking her whole body where she lay, pushing more tears out of her eyes. Here she was, ready to board the starship, hurl the villain into space, wreak revenge for her brother – and she couldn't even scratch the itch on her own fanny. What a load of twaddle.

'Maybe I should just, should just beg for my life?' she managed to squeeze out in between hard-to-breathe laughs.

'Beg all you like, it won't do any good.'

'*Oh please*,' she continued through the trembles, '*please spare me! I promise I won't tell anyone about your naughty little secret*.' She laughed even more when she remembered how she'd used the office post to apply to get on the electoral register at her current address. Imagine thinking that was risky behaviour!

Reflected in Shaun's eyes, Amelia could see her words meant death. But the hoarse, dirty roll of Jay's laugh made them both look over. 'How'd you know?' he asked her, winking, holding up his right hand and crooking his little finger, wiggling it like a worm on a fishing hook.

Amelia paused, bamboozled. Stared at him, then burst out laughing some more when she realised what he meant.

'Really?' she gasped, hot tears blurring her vision.

'Yeah!' Jay's smile was massive as he nodded.

'Shut up!' Shaun swung the knife at both of them. 'Stop talking!'

'Can I see?' Amelia teased. 'Untie me and I'll get it out for you.' The fear giggling through her veins.

'Nah nah nah, mate,' Jay was shaking with laughter too now as he shook his head. 'You're not his type. You know he likes—'

'Shut up!' hissed Shaun. 'I told you to stop talking!' he shouted. 'Shut up!' he shrieked, plunging over to Jay, dragging him to his feet, banging him back against the window, and holding the knife up to his throat.

Amelia couldn't see the knife itself, only the angle of Shaun's arm. And the exposed, throbbing, swallowing half of Jay's neck. The sun forcing her eyes to narrow after her and Jay's laughter both cut out.

Leaving them with nothing but the waiting silence.

Shaun spoke after ragged breaths: 'You're gonna kill this bitch. And then you're gonna be done.'

Jay's eyes locked on Shaun's.

'You shouldn't use that kind of language, mate,' Jay murmured firmly.

Shaun threw him down and to the side. Amelia heard the whack.

She strained round the corner of the sofa, risking falling off. Jay was propping himself up on the TV stand. Touching his forehead. Looking weakly at the blood on his hand from the cut on his head. His handprint making a stain on the carpet. Blood was so hard to get rid of. And it smelled. Amelia remembered Steffan's accident with the wall as a child. It was the iron in the haemoglobin, rusting as it combined with the outside oxygen.

'You think you're so smart, so much better than me, don't you! You're pathetic.' Shaun's face was disfigured by spit and rage. He loomed over Jay, his body seeming to expand, a black shadow against the window, the light from the setting sun struggling to make its way round him.

Jay spoke weakly from the floor: 'She doesn't know anything, Shaun. Those notes were just an empty threat.'

Side-on, Shaun's face sneered.

'It was so easy to drop those off at your hostel.' He looked down his nose at Jay's face as it sank further into defeat. 'Your *mate* Anthony soon learned that people he knew, I knew. Finding where you lived? It's like life – everyone in prison had their price.'

Amelia didn't know what notes they were talking about, but she knew she didn't want to die:

'Please, you don't need to do this. You've been in prison, you don't want to go back, this isn't going to help.'

He turned towards her slowly, panting like a hunting dog over a carcass.

'You've got no idea. What it was like inside. What my life has become. After this – I can start over. Be a man's man.'

His movements towards her seemed slow. A hostile snake flickering its tongue, gliding over the surface of a dark, bottomless Amazon. Inescapable, penetrating eyes locked on to its immobile prey. She squeezed her lids shut. She imagined the police banging at the door, shouting, breaking it down, grabbing him, and a kindly WPC telling her it was all over.

The knock at the door was real.

She only opened her eyes when it came again.

Shaun was frozen right above her. He was staring at the door. Behind him, under the window, Jay was staring at it too. Amelia made eye contact with him and nodded, imperceptible at the periphery of Shaun's vision. She hoped.

She coughed. Cleared her throat. 'Don't you think you should see who that is?'

Shaun looked down at her, back at the door, then down at her again. Out of the corner of her eye, she saw her chance to live, in Jay sneaking along the floor on all fours. She looked up at Shaun, right in the eyes.

'Probably a concerned neighbour. They might call the police because of all the banging and stuff.'

Jay, pressing against the wall right behind Shaun, slowly struggled to his feet. Shaun frowned as he focused on the door, flicking the Stanley knife closed and open, the weapon's jagged, clicking, schlicking sound making Amelia flinch. She kept her eyes on him.

'Perhaps you could persuade them everything is fine and to go away without making a fuss?' she added helpfully.

As Shaun leaned down, spitting in her face that he wasn't stupid, Jay lunged for the door and grabbed onto the lock. Roaring, Shaun leaped past the sofa and clamped one hand on the injured man, pulling him away and hurling him back down to the floor. The door swung open in Shaun's face, knocking him back but not down. He still had control of the knife, and held it up at the woman in a ghostly dress who'd stumbled into this. The newcomer cried out, and held up her hands in surrender, face blank.

Not the police. A neighbour about to go out on a date?

Swiping sideways, Shaun motioned for the woman to go further into the flat, to pass behind the sofa, and end up behind Amelia. Out of her line of sight. Shaun, still pointing the knife at the would-be hero, backed towards the door. Reached behind him. Fumbled for the lock. Twisted it shut.

Jay, clutching his head from the floor, looked up and over Amelia. 'Cathy?' he asked weakly. 'What are you doing here?'

'Tejinder told me what you'd told her.' Amelia heard this Cathy woman puffing herself up, uncertainly. 'I wasn't going to let you face this bastard alone.' Amelia rolled her eyes: she appreciated the bravery, but they were screwed. Still at the door, Shaun snorted, knife by his side, surveying the chaos.

Jay looked over Amelia's head as he continued to address Cathy. 'I could have taken care of this. I needed to.' His eyes, one half-closed, dropped back down to the ground. Blood was congealing on his face. 'A man died here. I did nothing to stop it. I could do the same again this time. Walk away, end my probation, get on with my life. Free.' He murmured, 'Buddha said – *No one saves us but ourselves. We ourselves must walk the path.*' The four of them observed a worn-out silence.

Shaun scratched the side of his head with the handle of the knife.

'I deserve to die. I want to do what's right. But I don't want to pay the price,' Jay resumed. He looked up at Shaun. 'Let her go. I'll confess whatever you want. You're right: I'm good for nothing but hiding.' Breaking down into a sob, he concealed his face with one hand. 'Every night covering my eyes because I can't bear to see the helplessness on a man's face. And after all these years – it was your fault all along.'

Jay's wretched sobbing punctured the shared resignation.

Cathy was the first to speak again. 'Jay …' Amelia heard her move sideways behind her, coming into her line of vision by the window.

'No fucking farther,' snarled Shaun, whipping up the blade at Cathy.

She put her hands up again. 'I'm already going to send one tall, sporty bloke back to prison. You want to join him?'

Shaun spat out a laugh, backed into his corner. 'Why would I go back to prison again? Jay's gonna take the rap for this.' He reached for the black and yellow can he'd left by the door when he'd opened it for Jay. Took a long dreg. Amelia imagined it must be stale and lukewarm by now. Like roadkill on a summer day.

Cathy's hands slowly lowered halfway down. Clenched into fists. 'The parole board is not gonna look kindly on this. You're looking at serving your full tariff. Maybe longer.'

Where was she getting all this from? She spoke so authoritatively. Shaun looked like a robot that was shutting down. Draining of power.

'You don't want that to happen. Believe me, mate. You've got a chance here. You don't need to make things worse for yourself.'

Shaun popped out the end of the knife a final time. Deadened, he slouched round the back of the sofa again. Amelia sensed his hand resting to the right of her head. Her body, already adrenaline-soaked, responded. Her heart beat faster again, her mouth dried up, her muscles burned.

Shaun's voice dully degraded the air she was determined to breathe. 'What's to stop me from killing the three of you and walking away? I can take you all.'

Cathy unclenched her hands, palms up. 'I'm sure you wanted this to turn out different.'

Jay was still woozy in the corner. Amelia imagined she could hear sirens as Cathy continued:

'I know men like you.'

Amelia prayed she could see flickering, flashing lights of blue finding their way up from the street below.

'We'll never let you win.' Cathy looked over her left shoulder, out the window. Speaking to Jay, she added: 'Olu's downstairs. He's going to tell them what's going on.'

Jay laughed to himself, shaking his head. 'Olu? Mate, you dog!'

Amelia thought she could see a faint shade of red creeping into Cathy's face. *Olu? The probation officer? What was he doing here?* Jay was reaching round behind himself with one hand, awkwardly pulling a white envelope from his back pocket, staining the paper red. He held it out towards Cathy. Amelia tensed. She couldn't feel any movement from Shaun behind her.

'What's that?' Cathy, keeping her eyes on the knifeman, reached out and took the sticky envelope. She opened it, and took out the note that lay in wait inside. Read it, frowning. Her expression had changed when she looked down at Jay again.

'Give it to him,' Jay said, not making eye contact. Silent,

Cathy handed the note across Amelia, who saw one of Shaun's hulking hands, straining at its glove, snatch it.

'It's a photocopy. Tejinder made it for me before I left Magda's to come here. She was going to give the original to Olu for me. She understood why she couldn't call the police straight away,' Jay said to Cathy. Amelia couldn't hear anything from Shaun behind her. 'So it's all out in the open now. Whatever happens here. Everyone will know. And now I reckon that will mean they can work out what you really did, too.'

Amelia looked at Jay and Cathy. They were motionless. Her eyes darted over to the door, squinting at the latch. It was still locked. She heard a destructive rustling sound from Shaun behind her. The screwed-up note flew and landed between Cathy and Jay.

'You two. You're going to be the ones who move on? After all this ...'

Amelia wasn't sure if she could hear footsteps tramping in the hallway outside.

In the glooming of the ending light, she could make out moths at the window. Fluttering their wings at her, calling to her to come away with them. To the moon. Clouds lingered in the distance, the promise of rain to wash away and start a new day.

This was her chance. She would pick herself up. Tomorrow, she would start applying for jobs. Tomorrow, she would text Peter, say she was sorry, her obsession was over. Tomorrow, she'd tell her parents they could sell this place or let her live here, she wasn't being their second-best child anymore. She would live her own life, be her own person. She'd been through enough, they all had, and it was over now. She deserved to reclaim and rebuild her life.

She was so sure she would.

Behind her, close now, Shaun laughed. The laugh of a man who is seeing his home burn down in front of his eyes. The merciless flames licking and dancing. The sound starting off low, bubbling up through his chest, screaming out of his throat.

Not long now.

The tramp of heavy feet outside. A bang at the door. Amelia mentally calculated whether Cathy could reach the door before Shaun reached her. As Shaun bent over Amelia, drawn knife in both hands, she was reminded of Sephiroth slaughtering Aeris in *Final Fantasy VII*. Jay staggered to his feet and stumbled towards them.

Cathy rushed to the door. She fumbled with the latch, unlocking it. The door burst open, banging against the side. Shaun's can spilled onto the floor. Why couldn't she see Shaun anymore?

Uniforms flooded into the room. Olu, dressed awkwardly in smart casual clothes, was shouting and being kept back in the hallway. Why couldn't she see Cathy anymore?

Jay was shouting too.

Amelia imagined a popular girl from school, the one she'd recently got an Instagram notification about, living in one of the neighbouring flats. She'd be taking photos of the ambulance waiting for Shaun downstairs. Sharing it to the residents' Facebook group, or to the WhatsApp chat with her hockey club friends. Amelia hadn't played hockey for twenty-four years.

Shaun was keeping the officers at bay.

Why couldn't she see Jay anymore?

Shaun still had the knife.

He was coming for her.

He—

'Not her as well.' Jay planted himself in between her and

335

Shaun. Shaun held out the knife at him. Jay held out his bloodied palms, and shook his head. 'You'll have to take me instead.'

Shaun lunged. Jay grabbed him. The two grappled. The blade was coming towards her. Jay twisted it away; Shaun twisted it back.

'You'll have to take me instead!' shouted Jay.

Which of them was stronger? Which of them would win?

Despite the ringing of her own terror, she managed to make out Shaun saying, 'I will never be ... just the darkness at the bottom of a human heart.'

The stench of Shaun's blood was like rust, as the result of his suicidal slash dripped down the side of the sofa.

Still alive, Amelia hid her eyes from the red sight of death. A black uniform manhandled her out of her bindings, freeing her blood and feelings to flow around her body again. She struggled to sit up, as Jay's attempts at life-saving blurred to her left.

As she took in the first breaths of her new life, her gaze took refuge on his screwed-up, white confession. Despite the blood smeared on the page, she could still make out the handwriting:

In the lift up to the top of the tower which houses Flat 401, I feel proud of myself ... I can afford to take this risk. To live instead of just surviving.

66

Jay

At least in the shabby, three-by-five cell, only a single slit in the door was staring at Jay, unlike in the court above. All those eyes bearing down on him. He'd looked them in the face, but the effort had taken the life out of him.

He rolled onto his side and stared at the cold, dirty tiles of the holding cell.

A life sentence was mandatory in cases of joint enterprise for murder. But whatever term he was going to be sentenced for the next day, Jay was sure he'd get a discount on the minimum tariff because of his guilty plea. Would the judge also take into account: *(a) showing genuine remorse, (b) readily cooperating with the police,* and *(c) presenting a low risk of reoffending*?

If he was sentenced to more time inside: what courses would he do in prison, to help him get an Approved Job when he was out again? And what would his Approved Address end up being?

The jangle of the custody officer's keys echoed up and down the corridor outside as other defendants were escorted out to their waiting transport.

The ghostly look of hollow triumph on Shaun's face after

he'd tried to take his own life in Flat 401 taunted him; he remembered the murmurings from the gallery as his lawyer had shared with the court how Jay had blocked Shaun from Amelia, and how Shaun had then, when he'd been thwarted ... Jay couldn't have imagined a human body could leak out that amount of blood through such small, precise cuts.

His brother had been right at the back of the public gallery. Jay hadn't been able to make out his expression.

No Margaret. No Tejinder.

Noah hadn't come either. Jay would have told him (what he'd thought had been) the truth if Shaun's drama in Flat 401 hadn't made it too late, and changed everyone's understanding. At least Esther had been there today, supported by her husband. She'd smiled tearfully at Jay as he'd entered his guilty plea, nodding.

Maybe he wouldn't be sentenced to more time inside?

The air of the cell was stale. But he wouldn't stay here for much longer: soon he'd be joining the others in the white Serco van. Police Watch protestors primed to bang on its side as he was driven through their crowd.

It was a bit freaky, not gonna lie: the same prison. Same walls, same food, probably plenty of the same inmates. But he'd be better prepared this time: he'd got his phone numbers written down, his kit bag with cash, books, and cheap tracksuits in. He'd got his plan. He knew the rules, the lingo; when to keep his head down, when to speak up; how to stay clean, not to expect to get clean. He'd have a routine; he'd speak in a firm, clear voice; he wouldn't let them intimidate him. He'd get through the next however-many years, of TV, courses, and lock-up, in no time. Just dig himself in, burrow down, and he'd be ready to fly again. The Isle of Wight would still be there. Safe.

He probably wouldn't be sentenced to more time inside, anyway.

The slit in the cell door slid open. Olu. Some of the tension sank down. His former probation officer murmured something, before the custody officer's steps and keys faded away up the corridor.

Olu turned back to Jay. 'What's going on, man?' he asked through the door.

Jay got up. 'You good, mate?'

'Yeah, I'm good man, I'm good. Still doing the old Probation gig, trying to make a difference, trying to represent, you know how it goes. Doing the right thing.'

Jay nodded a few times through the hole in the door, his lips pursed. 'Maybe you'll be my probation officer when I get out again,' he joked.

'Ha ha, not sure about that,' Olu said, half-smiling. 'Thanks for being honest and not making it any more difficult for me.'

'Sure, mate, no problem, no problem. And, just telling it straight, I'm probably going to be on licence for the rest of my life now, you know what I'm saying? So you never know!'

Olu laughed. 'Get out of here, man.' They paused over the unfortunate choice of words, then laughed it off. Olu looked to his side, down the corridor. 'Listen, Jay, I've got to go. Meeting Kerry after her craft fair, you get me?'

'Kerry?'

Olu smiled at Jay but dropped his eyes to the floor, rubbing the back of his head.

'You mean ...?'

Olu nodded.

She'd probably always be 'Cathy' to Jay, but it was good to hear she was back using her real name. After everything

339

she'd been through, and the courage she'd showed – she deserved to reclaim and rebuild her life.

'How is she?' he asked, feigning casualness but knowing.

Olu fiddled with his sleeve. 'She's good, man. Much better now Ant is in prison. And her kid's pretty cute.'

Jay smiled, tears warming his eyes.

'She let me use a contact to get in to see you off. She appreciates you taking on Shaun …' The rest of the truth hung in the air like cold fog.

'No news on whether he's gonna wake up from the coma?' Jay asked.

Olu stayed quiet.

Jay turned the conversation away. 'Cathy— Kerry, eh! Told you I knew why you made that home visit!' He forced a laugh.

Olu joined in. Their laughter became real after a few chuckles. Then the return of the jangling keys meant Olu really had to go. He slipped a faded Isle of Wight postcard through the slit in the door. *Maybe we could study moths together sometime? Sx*

'You'll make a new life for yourself, Jay. With God, all things are possible.'

The trip inside the white van wasn't as frightening as his first time. He knew that the other men, caged up with him in individual, seatbeltless holding boxes, peering out at each other or through the darkened window, were just like him: moths burned by the flame of their own wrongdoing. He understood himself a bit better now; maybe one day, more people would have the strength and wisdom to do the same.

He knew not to make too much eye contact.

He'd done what he'd done. So had the others. They didn't need to hurt each other to get through it. Jay's heartbeat was steady. He closed his eyes, tipped his head back. In that moment, he felt weightless. One last day on remand: tomorrow he'd know whether the Court thought he could be forgiven.

The van halted. Its door unlocked with a clang, like a bell sounding deep underwater. The light at the end of the late spring day blinded him as he stepped out. The prison's barred eyes staring at him. Its solid bricks ready to hold him.

Everyone finally knew what he'd really done.

Epilogue

The light on my gravestone seemed queer. The late-rising sun shone through a break between the towers of brick, glass and steel sprouting around St Magdalene's churchyard. The churchyard would be green again, one day. Spring always comes.

Jay waited to speak, getting his voice under control.

Spring always comes. But the modern buildings cast long, cold shadows. They were like twisted trees surrounding a glade suffocating under stone and damp grass. Beyond them, out-of-sight traffic buzzed like flies.

'You must think it's weird, me just standing here,' he said, laughing shyly. 'I wanted to come, soon as I could. Had to swing by the hospital.'

He stood tall, watching. Ran a hand over his torso, which was wrapped up in a jacket that hugged his muscles.

'Minimum term as long as I'd already served! So that's me on Probation again. For good.' He touched his face, clean-shaven again. 'Up to you to decide what I deserved.' His expression maintained a fragile peace. 'I want to make sure I've told you.' His full lips trembled. 'I regret everything. Coming over. Not staying. Not calling an ambulance. Not owning up sooner.' He bowed his head as he cried. The tears tangling in his thick black lashes. 'I know it doesn't make a difference that it wasn't me who killed you.'

This was a place for ends and beginnings. The end of

regret is the beginning provided by making peace with our own mistakes.

'I wish ...'

Raising his head, he dried his eyes, and leaned down towards my gravestone. Smiling fondly, he placed the battered purple Tamagotchi inside the black urn, on top of Amelia's silver ring on its chain. It seemed right that his final gift to me ended up next to what my sister had recently left: a small plastic tube, containing a tick (of all things!). The disease-ridden insect was slowly dying now it had been removed from its host.

Next to them, a newspaper clipping and a blank note lay in wait.

Jay pulled the clipping out from the urn. Scanned it, and looked around. The grass and trees whispered; sirens beckoned in the distance. A spring breeze washed over him.

... unprecedented decision to change Shaun Flanagan's conviction to Murder. After the verdict, Ms Evans, who herself previously escaped prosecution for obtaining a 999 transcript, made a statement outside the court: 'My brother and family were denied justice for years. Nothing will bring Steffan back to us. At least now his reputation has been cleared.' Her mother added: 'I cannot say I'm happy, only relieved, that Amelia and Steffan's father is still alive to see this day.'

Jay returned the clipping, and took out the blank note. Wrote on it with the moth-themed pen that Amelia had left for him.

There are some mistakes so wrong, we cannot forgive or make them right. But at least Shaun can't hurt anyone ever again.

343

After folding up the note, and leaving it behind in the urn, Jay flew away.

As the ferry approached the Isle of Wight, Jay wondered at the open sea around the island. Bright, sandy beaches; quaint, winding roads; and friendly, welcoming people. Just as he'd dreamed of. The air would be fresh, the noise pollution would be non-existent, and he would live free, out in the—

His phone buzzed. A final WhatsApp message from Amelia.

Jay cracked his knuckles, looked to the side, and unlocked his screen.

He'd deserved to reclaim and rebuild his life.

He'd been so sure that he would.

No one can know what I really did.

After reading and archiving the message, he stroked his arm, and confirmed the directions to his new 'Approved Address' again. He didn't push away the memory of Amelia attaching infectious ticks to Shaun's comatose body as Jay distractingly chatted up the nurse on duty; he welcomed recalling her careful explanation as to how the parasites the ticks carried would do the same to Shaun as he'd done to her brother.

The sun lit up a white gull as it flew ahead. The waves cleansed the air as the boat ploughed through them. The spray of the sea on his fingers told Jay he was almost at the next stage of his journey.

He would never emerge from Probation; he wouldn't let anything stop him from keeping his freedom alive.

* * *

If you loved *Flat 401* and want to be first to know when Kingsley Pearson's next book is out, then sign up to his newsletter.

Sign up now!
https://www.klpearson.net/newsletter

Acknowledgements

Writing a novel and getting published, while a rewarding experience, can be a long and tough road. I have many people to thank – apologies if I miss anyone out.

Early tutors and authors, whose encouragement and positive feedback at the start helped me continue when times got tougher: Alison MacLeod, David Mark, Imran Mahmood, Russ Thomas, Vaseem Khan, Jon Barton.

Other Clinical Psychologists who are authors, who paved the way and generously shared how to follow them: Drs Philippa East, Steph Carty, Chris Merritt.

Organisers, tutors and mentors of the Harper Collins Author Academy, for providing me with knowledge and networking, as well as yet more positive feedback and encouragement: Rose Sandy, Gale Winskill, Phoebe Morgan, Kathryn Colwell, Saara El-Arifi, Sadé Omeje.

Early readers, for their invaluable insights: Alex, Ellie, Ria, Holly, Tom, Leah Hocking, Carolyn Nakulski. Your encouragement and challenge helped me stay focused on making the book the best version of itself, staying true to my vision while also keeping in mind the mind of the reader.

My local critique group, Greenwich Writers, whose camaraderie and candour helped me keep going while making the book better; especially George, Katie, Hannah Brennan, Liv Johannesson, Natalie Moss, Nick, and William Armstrong.

Sensitivity readers who provided paid consultation

pre-querying. Although the text is quite different now, and the characters you read for do not feature so heavily post-edits (or in some cases, at all), you helped enrich both the development of the book and my understanding of some minorities with experiences different from my own: Alyssa Harder, Rachel, Samiat A. Bakare. My friend Manveer also contributed generously with consultation on Tejinder.

Any other writing friends I've made along the way, including but not limited to Tania Tay, Chris Bridges, and everyone I met through the Mo Siewcharran Prize: Chandani Thapa, Faaiza Munir, FQ Yeoh, Foday Mannah, Anu Pohani, Dayal Kindy. It's been great to be part of each other's journeys.

Paul Engles for taking me aside to whisper encouragement at the Mo Siewcharran Prize ceremony; the Mo Siewcharran Prize committee for shortlisting me, and the Penguin Michael Joseph Undiscovered Writers committee for longlisting; Ed Wood for providing generous feedback after a successful pitch at Harrogate. The Cheshire Novel Prize likewise gave useful feedback which positively shaped my querying journey. Elane and Sarah at I Am In Print facilitated my learning and development, as well as being encouraging and lovely people.

My agent, Silé Edwards, for taking a chance on me, seeing the potential in the book, and believing in me the whole way through. Your support and strategy have got me to where I am now. Can't wait to see what else we achieve together!

My editor at Orion, Leodora Darlington: thank you for also seeing the potential in me and the book. It has been great working with you to get it into its best shape and into the hands of readers.

My partner, friends, family and colleagues for taking an interest in what can be quite a temporally and mentally consuming activity! And not failing to be supportive, encouraging and celebratory.

And, of course, last but not least – you, the reader: the thought of this story reaching you keeps me writing.

Author Letter

I enjoyed creative writing at school, but only took it up as an adult in the second half of 2020. I'd (psychologically as well as physically) survived the first part of the pandemic by shutting down and shutting myself indoors – exercising, watching *Vera* and *Shetland*, and playing computer games to pass the time. (I was lucky to have a job that quickly and easily switched to working fully remotely.) But when the lockdowns returned after a break over the summer, and the company I was working for had a change in management which meant redoing work with no signs of moving forward – I needed a creative outlet. Needed to generate something new, not just survive the same day over and over.

As I learned more about the craft of writing and how the publishing industry operated, I realised it would be years before my book hit the shelves (if ever). As a Clinical Psychologist, I wondered: what state of mind would readers be in at that point? What would they need and want, given the challenging situation we were all going through?

Without wishing to downplay the experience of those actually incarcerated, I imagined that we would feel like we had been released from prison. Thus, the seed for *Flat 401* was born: an idea for a story featuring a protagonist who was kept inside for a crime he didn't commit. This seed grew when watered by following the principle of 'write what you know'. During the pandemic, what I knew was looking out of the window of my London flat: that gave me the idea (like in Agatha Christie's *4.50 from Paddington*) of a murder witnessed through a window.

These ideas combined with others into a story I wanted to tell. I wanted to write a book like the ones I most enjoy reading: compelling, dark, unpredictable, well-characterised, with stakes that are high but human, that hits you in the feels, a bit tragic. Given my personal background (as a gay, mixed-race man), and that I lived in London, I also wanted it to be 'diverse', and have something to say, without being preachy.

As a Clinical Psychologist, I also wanted readers to be able to take something away from the novel. At some point, like Jay, Amelia and Cathy, I think we all have to make difficult choices in our lives. I hoped to communicate the idea that, if we use our courage and conscience, we can do the right thing, and enable ourselves and others to live our best lives with whatever abilities and chances we have been given.

Only you can judge whether I succeeded in my aims. Thank you for reading. I hope, however you found the book, you are able to make the best of whatever freedom and life you have.

Book Club Questions

1. Some of the author's favourite scenes include the Prologue; when Jay receives the Note; the appearance of Shaun at the hostel; when Ant attacks Cathy in the toilet; when Jay confronts Anthony at Timpson; and the climax in Flat 401. What scene in the book is your favourite, and why?

2. The characters are often motivated by a strong psychological trait or state. For example: Jay – shame; Amelia – avoidance of her own feelings; Cathy – fear; Shaun – revenge. Which character's motivation do you find the hardest to relate to? Which character, overall, do you relate to or like the most?

3. There is deliberately repeated moth imagery throughout the book, which includes the idea that moths are drawn to a flame. Similarly, Jay experiences that *'The sour green candy was also sweet'*. In what ways were different characters drawn to things which seemed good for them but turned out bad?

4. How would you apportion blame for what really happened in Flat 401?

5. What do you think each character deserved? Who did you most want to get a different outcome?

6. *'Are there some mistakes so wrong, we cannot forgive or make them right?'* The novel illustrates different positions on forgiveness: which do you agree with the most? Can everything be forgiven? What does a person need to do to achieve forgiveness? Can we expect victims to enact the same level of forgiveness as society as a whole?

7. One of the author's early readers described this as, 'A book about how its characters want to live – about what it means to "live", to have a life worth living, to be free, to be oneself. About what people are prepared to do to enable living.' What did you think about the characters' choices in this regard?

8. *'We've got him on the line, we've got him on the line. A lot of people have been claiming he's been sent back to prison, but he's here. Jay Ginige, what would you like to say to our listeners?'* How possible do you think it is to engage in constructive dialogue with people who have radically different views from you on social issues?

9. *'How we are brought up can set the stage for how we relate to others as adults.'* Most of the characters experienced things which contributed to why they thought, felt and acted as they did. What did you learn about the cycle of trauma? What were your responses to how characters were affected by their past and present experiences, and how they did or didn't move on from these?

10. Jay, by facing up to what he's been through, is able to move on to what's important to him in life. What do you think you might take away from this novel about reclaiming or building a life that's full of what's important to you?

11. Picture yourself recommending this book to someone. Who is it, and what are you saying to them?

Credits

Kingsley Pearson and Orion Fiction would like to thank everyone at Orion who worked on the publication of *Flat 401* in the UK.

Editorial
Leodora Darlington
Snigdha Koirala

Copy editor
Sally Partington

Proof reader
Marian Reid

Audio
Paul Stark
Louise Richardson

Contracts
Dan Herron
Ellie Bowker
Oliver Chacón

Design
Chevonne Elbourne

Editorial Management
Charlie Panayiotou
Jane Hughes
Bartley Shaw
Lucy Bilton

Finance
Jasdip Nandra
Nick Gibson
Sue Baker

Marketing
Ellie Nightingale

Publicity
Emily Cary-Elwes

Production
Ruth Sharvell

Sales
David Murphy
Esther Waters
Victoria Laws

Rachael Hum
Ellie Kyrke-Smith
Frances Doyle
Georgina Cutler

Operations
Jo Jacobs